GATES OF CHAOS

KEEPERS OF THE GRAIL 2

TAMAR SLOAN

Cover by Laercio Messias
https://laerciomessias.com.br

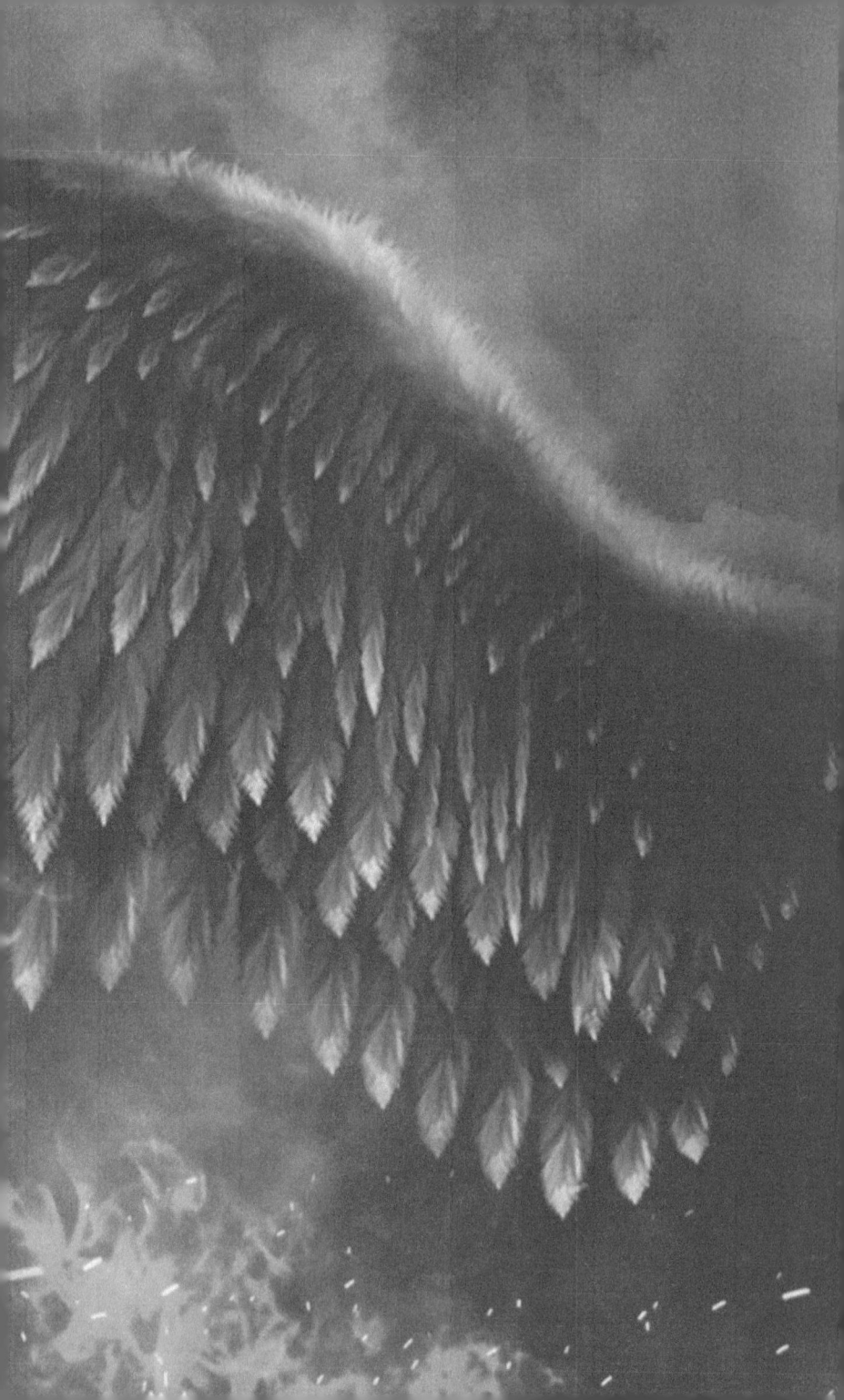

PROLOGUE

Xeven stands beside the obelisk. The forest around him is silent in a way it's never been before. No birds call. No night animals move. Each and every insect has been blanketed with the weight of this moment.

The tall man opens his palm and stares at the vial resting there. The slow moving, luminous matter inside is a stark contrast to the dark smear of blood that coats the glass.

"The Grace of an Innocent," he murmurs.

The pearl-colored contents are suffused with the power of the Heavens.

His hand clenches around the vial in a gesture that's far too involuntary. He hesitates for the briefest of seconds before his mind shutters closed. This is his role. This is what needs to happen. He's been told enough times—it's the only way.

Gritting his teeth, he contracts every muscle. With a single, sharp movement, he throws the vial against the obelisk. The glass smashes and the luminous liquid splatters over the stone monument.

The effect is instant. The rune symbols flare to life, turning a flaming red. The first crack appears at the center of where the Grace hit, fracturing outward. It splits over and over as arteries become veins and veins become capillaries. A lightning network of fractures spear through the obelisk, the fires of Hell blazing brightly as they're fed by fresh air.

First one clawed finger appears, then two. They wriggle and the crack widens. A second hand appears and more fingers scrape through. Xeven takes a step back, knowing what's coming next.

Demonic hands pry open the obelisk. With a crack as loud as thunder, the stone monument splits and shatters. It tumbles like it was little more than a house of cards rather than an ancient guard that has withstood millennia.

Shadows spill out, tumbling over each other in their haste to escape. The demons streak for the sky then remain there, hovering. Waiting.

They know they were just the prelude.

The sinuous body that slithers out is both beautiful and terrifying. The woman who walks up the stairs rising from Hell itself is all voluptuous curves and luscious waves. She pats her flame-colored hair as her body moves in undulating, sensual ripples.

She stands among the rubble and destruction, drawing in a deep breath. Then, she throws her head back and screams. The trees around them shake and tremble as the age-old cry of newfound freedom ravages their branches. The forest that was still and frozen a minute ago becomes a thrashing, flailing storm. It's battered by a taste of what's to come.

Xeven drops his head as the demon sashays past, her eyes glowing with the fires of possibility. He should be rejoicing. They've succeeded.

But there's a small voice, one that can barely be heard but

refuses to be silenced, screaming deep in the recesses of his mind. And it's scared. No, terrified. Xeven shakes his head. It's too late.

Lust is now free to wreak her chaos on Earth.

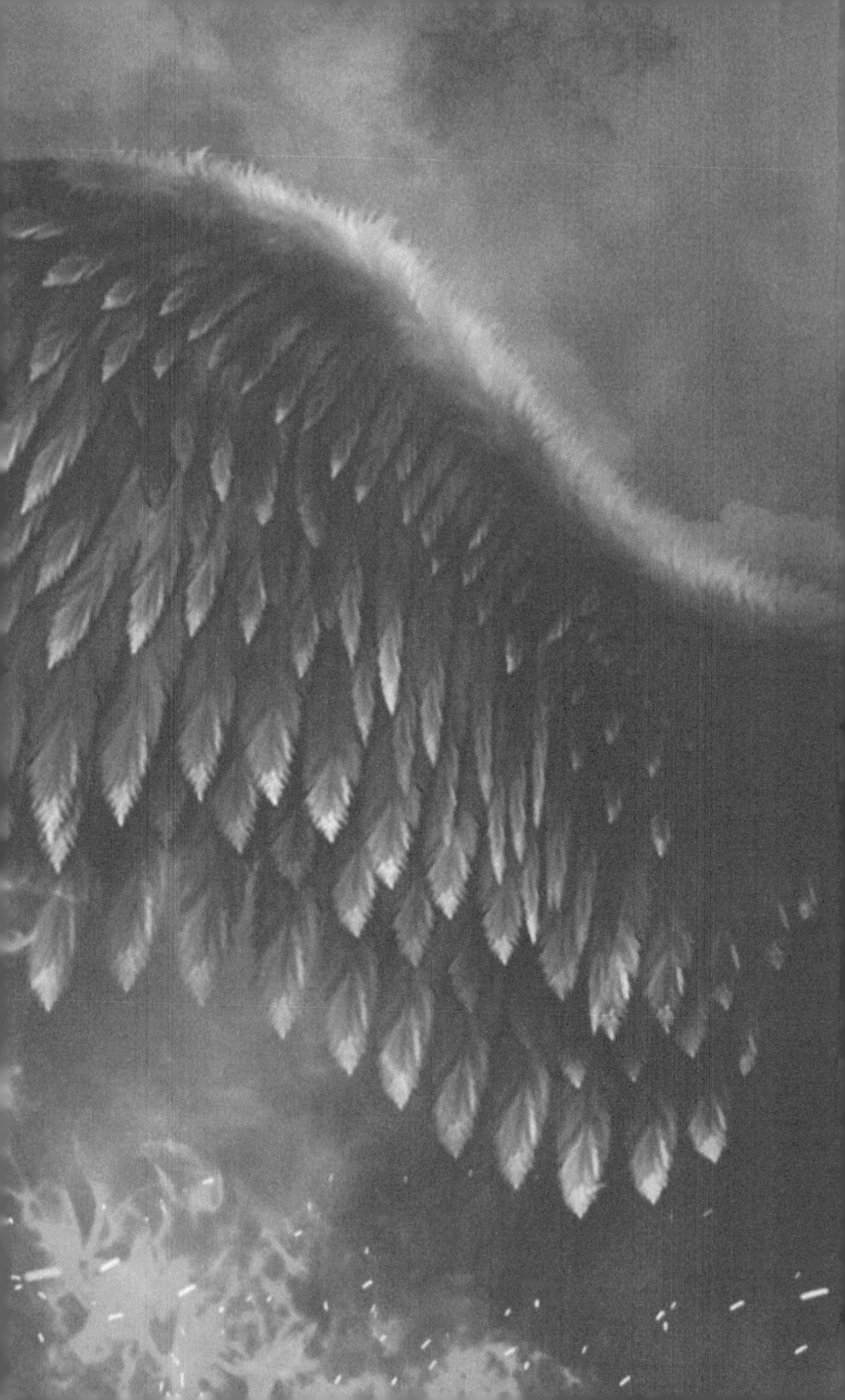

CHAPTER 1
ARIELLE

"It was a beautiful service," Arielle's mom murmurs.

Arielle nods, rubbing her upper arms. Despite all her tears, her cheeks feel tight and dry. Shell's funeral was as beautiful as she was. Loving words and sweet memories and wracking sobs had filled the air as they'd stood around the grave site.

Gabby had spoken about the mother who had loved without condition. Arielle's mom had spoken about the sister who was also her best friend. And Arielle had talked about the aunt who had been as generous with her encouragement as she was with her smiles.

Throwing the handful of dirt and hearing it hit the coffin had almost broken Arielle. It was Reign subtly moving a little closer that had kept her upright. His calm, silent presence had been her strength, whether he meant it to be or not.

Footsteps come down the staircase and she looks up, seeing Colt descend. He shakes his head, his red locks flicking over his brow. "She just wants to be alone."

Gabby had taken herself to the room she's staying in at Arielle's house the moment they returned from the cemetery, quietly closing the door behind her. The fact she doesn't even want Colt with her is telling.

Losing her mother has changed her and her world forever.

"I'd better go see to the guests," says Arielle's mom, sounding like that's the last thing she feels like doing.

Shell was well loved, meaning dozens of people have attended the wake, wanting to pay their respects to the woman who touched their lives.

Each one of them believing she was tragically murdered along with six others in some strange ritual sacrifice.

Arielle's hands clamp around her arms almost painfully. Only a handful of people know the truth, that Shell was killed because no one realized she was an Innocent.

And her death isn't just a loss in the fabric of all their lives. Her death has opened one of the Gates of Hell.

Her mom exits the kitchen, carrying a platter of cheese and crackers, her face drawn as Reign steps aside to let her pass. He studies Arielle closely.

"How are you doing?"

Arielle chews her lip, not sure how to answer that. Especially to the guy who she once assumed was a total douchebag, and now she knows that's a galaxy away from the truth. But what does that mean for her? She mentally shakes herself. Her heart is too full of grief right now to be answering questions like that.

For now, she's just glad he's hanging around, being attentive in a way she doesn't understand.

She sighs, realizing whatever she says will be an understatement. "It's tough."

His lips twist as he jams his hands in his pockets. "One of the advantages of not having anyone is never having to lose them."

"You have Mac," she points out. She's about to add herself to that list when Mac herself enters the kitchen.

"Who has me?" she asks, placing a handful of glasses on the sink. "Man, people can drink at one of these things."

"If only we understood trying to numb the pain by ingesting a substance to alter our physiological state," says Reign wryly.

"True." She presses a hand to her forehead. "Do you think anyone would mind if I have a glass of the red stuff myself?"

Arielle reaches into a cupboard, getting fresh glasses out. "Great idea. Let's have two."

The thought of taking the edge off the grief clawing away at her chest sounds quite appealing.

"Whoa." Reign leaps forward, holding his hand over the top of the wine glasses even though there's not a drop of alcohol about to be poured. "You don't want to do that."

She looks at him, his handsome face so close she can see the concern in his jungle green eyes. "If it's good enough for some..."

Reign has never hidden the fact he's used his own 'substances'.

But he shakes his head. "It's a slippery slope you don't want to go down. Believe me."

She takes a step back, the need gone even quicker than it arose. She has Gabby to support. And her mother.

And something to prove to both of them.

"Just joking," she says. "I should go out there and help Mom."

Looking relieved, Reign nods. "I'll come with you."

Mac clangs the wine glasses she'd just picked up against another one. "As in, go out there and like, talk to people?"

Reign frowns at her. "Yes. Thank you for outlining what's involved."

Arielle feels a flutter of warmth at their familiar banter. It reminds her that some semblance of normality is waiting for her.

She turns, taking two steps toward the door, steeling herself for the endless condolences.

Another one is in danger.

Arielle freezes as Trinity's voice floats through her mind.

"Ari?" asks Reign. "Is everything okay?"

She's about to tell him she's as fine as she can be, considering, when the kitchen fades away. She's no longer standing in a room her mom painted yellow.

An obelisk is standing before her, soaring high into a dark pink sky. It cracks, just like she knew it would, blood-colored light pouring from the fractures.

No...

She takes an involuntary step back, finding that something holds her in place. Her eyes widen with horror when she sees she's not alone. Naked bodies, so many naked bodies, are littered around on the ground.

"Ari."

She blinks, finding Reign standing right in front of her, gripping her arms. Mac is behind him, looking worried.

"What happened?" he asks. "What did you just see?"

She opens her mouth, unsure how to describe the horrible scene. The people were so vulnerable, stripped of any dignity in their final moments. She gasps, realizing what the vision meant.

The consequences of Cain's actions have begun.

Mac moves in a little closer. "Ari, maybe we can help."

But before Arielle can speak, the doorbell rings. They glance at each other, wondering who else could be here. As far as she knows, everyone from the funeral arrived almost an hour ago.

"I'll explain in a sec," Arielle says, heading to the door. Her mom is busy with the guests, and Gabby's still upstairs. The least she can do right now is answer the door.

The doorbell peals again as she grips the knob, making her frown. The person isn't particularly patient. She pulls the door open, her frown only deepening when she sees who's on the other side.

The man is tall and broad, wearing a white shirt and tan slacks. Thick waves of golden blond hair brush his shoulders, framing a flawless face. He's arresting, every feature symmetrical and refined. And not anyone Arielle knows.

"Sorry, this is a private affair."

She goes to close the door, but the man steps forward, blocking it with his shoulder. "I've come to pay respects to the woman I love."

Arielle blinks in surprise. Shell didn't have anyone in her life like that. She never did.

Which means this guy is lying. She tightens her hand on the knob, hoping he'll go quietly if she insists.

"It's okay," comes a voice from the top of the stairs.

Arielle turns, seeing Gabby standing there. She descends slowly, as if she's aged in the time she's been in her room.

She stops at the bottom, her gaze meeting the man's. "He's my father."

CHAPTER 2

REIGN

The dude's too perfect, which instantly puts Reign on the defensive. His face looks like it was painstakingly carved from marble, and his hair looks like it belongs on a poster in a hairdresser's. What's even more interesting is that Colt takes a subtle step back as he crosses his arms.

The man—Gabby's father—enters, his gaze scanning the welcoming committee of five as the door closes behind him. Penetrating gray eyes, so luminous they're almost silver, land on Reign. They narrow slightly and a strange burning sensation sears his chest.

Reign crosses his arms, too. He's reserving judgment about whether he likes this guy.

Gabby's father's gaze flickers over Arielle, practically dismisses Colt, then settles on Mac. His eyes narrow and his lips thin.

Yep. He just went down a few notches on the like-o-meter.

The guy looks back to his daughter. "I'm sorry, Gabrielle. I would've come sooner, but there were matters to attend to."

Mac leans in close, whispering. "Where's the nearest exit?"

So she's sensed it, too. "I'll admit, he looks like he's part of the Douche Club," he whispers back. "But he's Gabby's dad." And she's an angel. "That should make him one of the good guys."

Reign makes sure he puts emphasis on the word *should*. He's spent his life trusting his gut, and he's alive because of it. And right now, his gut was just singed after one look from the guy.

"You sound as convinced as I feel," she mutters back.

"Let's wait and see what he has to say."

And why he's here.

And whether Reign needs to protect Arielle.

Gabby nods, her face drawn in lines of grief. "I appreciate you coming."

The man's shoulders—broad, muscled-topped shoulders—sag. "I had to be there for the reapers as they brought Shell's soul to Heaven."

Gabby's lashes flicker as she processes the news. Reign suspects it would be bittersweet. Her mother's soul is now in heaven, but it further reinforces that she's gone.

"Thank you," she says softly.

Her father straightens, his massive chest inflating a little. "We need to talk, Gabrielle." He glances around the room at the audience he obviously doesn't want.

But Gabby shakes her head. "These are my family and friends. I trust them with my life. Whatever you need to say, it can be said in their presence."

Arielle's gaze flies to Gabby, seeming surprised at this statement. Reign watches as she quickly schools her features, wondering what that was about.

"Very well," says Gabby's father. "We'll talk later."

Reign's arms tighten into pretzels. The guy's already carrying secrets.

The motion seems to attract his attention because Gabby's

father turns to him. "Choose your path wisely, young man. And I'd advise you to embrace the fate that awaits."

"I'm not much of a hugger," Reign retorts, unsuccessfully keeping the annoyance out of his voice.

The man looks away, ignoring the response. His gaze falls on Mac. "And you," he says, his tone hardening. "You have very little time left in this world, so use it wisely. If it were up to me, I'd smite you here and now."

Mac has gone totally still in a way Reign hasn't seen before. His best friend is a fighter. One who usually doesn't wait and gets in first. She's grown up in a world of kill or be killed. But she's totally immobile. Terrified now that she knows who she truly is.

And that just pisses Reign off.

He leaps in front of Mac. "Or, you could be grateful that she helped your daughter fight off Cain," he grinds through gritted teeth.

Gabby's father's face turns hard and cold, his silver eyes blazing. He looks like he's about to change his mind, and a whole lot of smiting is about to happen.

Bring. It. On.

Gabby clears her throat, stepping into her father's line of vision. "Dad, this isn't really a great way to make a good impression."

But her father doesn't back down. "I don't care what a demon thinks of me."

So he knows. And it's why he looks ready to rumble.

Colt snorts in disgust, then promptly disappears. Reign blinks. He had no idea Colt could do that.

Gabby turns to Reign and Mac. "I'm so sorry. Maybe it's best if you leave."

Reign glances at Arielle, whose flame blue eyes flicker with anguish. It reminds him they're at a wake. They're here to honor Shell's memory, not contaminate it with anger and hostility. Gabby, Arielle and Sierra deserve better than that.

He takes a step back, grasping Mac's hand. "Sure," he says. To be honest, he's used to getting kicked out of places. They both are. "Keep us posted."

Gabby nods. "I promise."

Reign enjoys seeing the flicker of annoyance in her father's eyes. He steps around him, taking a silent Mac with him. Arielle mouths two words as they pass.

"I'm sorry."

He shrugs, wanting to tell her it's not her fault. In fact, it's probably a timely reminder that they come from opposite sides of the track. Something he keeps conveniently forgetting.

He and Mac exit, shutting the door behind them, cutting them off from whatever is going to be said inside. They both sit down on the first step, a silent understanding that neither of them are going anywhere.

Reign angles his head. "Can you hear them?"

Mac's freakishly good hearing was always a mystery...until they learned she's a demon.

But she shakes her head. "They've moved into the kitchen."

Leaning back on his elbows, he sighs. He's not even sure why he's here... Arielle's grief has kept him here. As does the knowledge that shit is far from over. But what exactly does he think he can do? What's his role in this?

Reign scans their surroundings as if this quiet suburban street has the answers, only to startle as he finds Joseph of freaking Arimathea sitting on his other side. He clamps down on the curse word that slams up his throat. Not because he's pretending he has any level of class, but because he doesn't want to alert Mac.

"He's here, isn't he?" she asks, proving she's far more astute than he'd like her to be.

"Yeah," he growls through a gritted jaw.

"Hey, Joseph. Welcome to the party."

Joseph shakes his head. "This is no time to celebrate," he says somberly. "Too much is at stake."

Great. Of all the apparitions to get, Reign had to get one without a sense of humor.

Joseph plants his hands on his knees, his long robes flowing onto the steps. "Are you ready to accept your fate, Grail Keeper?"

Reign resists frowning. From the moment Shell was killed, he knew. As the threatening pink faded from the sky, he had no choice but accept it.

Joseph isn't a drug induced hallucination.

"Have you decided to start listening to him?" Mac asks archly.

Reign pushes the heels of his hands into his eye sockets. If Joseph's speaking the truth, it means Reign is tasked with protecting an artifact no one has seen in centuries. It means he's tied to this whole battle of good versus evil, when he's not entirely sure which side of the fence he was born on.

He's not even sure what being a freaking Keeper of the Grail involves.

"I think he and I might need to have a chat," he says finally. Grudgingly.

"Good," Joseph says, obviously relieved. "Because you're the only one who can save the world from total destruction."

Reign surges to his feet. What the fuck?

"What?" Mac leaps to her feet, too. "What did he say?"

Reign slices his hand through the air as if he can stop any of this. Joseph disappears, his bearded face looking disappointed all over again.

Mac plants her hands on her hips, her gaze scanning over Reign's shoulder. "What did you say, Joseph?"

"Save your breath. He's gone," he huffs. "And whatever he said, it's nothing worth repeating."

Only that Joseph's setting himself up for one hell of a disappointment.

If Reign's the only one standing between humanity's salvation or annihilation, then the world's screwed.

CHAPTER 3

ARIELLE

Arielle watches as Gabby and the others turn and head to the kitchen, realizing she's angry. The way Gabby's father treated Mac and Reign wasn't okay. She was just about to move when Gabby did, stepping between them.

Gabby's father wasn't there when they were surrounded by demons. When Cain had seriously hurt Colt and Gabby. When Arielle's mother was bound to a sacrificial altar, her life force steadily drained from her.

But Reign and Mac were. And they fought with everything they had. If it weren't for them, Arielle wouldn't be here, nor would her mother.

Which means Arielle has no desire to be in the same room as someone who just treated them like trash, demon or no demon. She spins on her heel and yanks open the door. She'll have to take a guess that they've gone to their new place. If she runs, maybe she'll be able to catch up.

She stops short when she finds Reign and Mac on the steps. "Oh, hey. I thought you'd gone."

Reign's hair is mussed, like he's been spearing his fingers through it. "Are they finished already?"

Arielle shakes her head. "No. I don't want to be part of any talk that excludes you two."

His eyebrows twitch, as if they were just about to shoot up. "You need to go in there and be part of whatever's going down."

"So do you," she counters, crossing her arms.

The days of Arielle Hartley being pushed around because people believe they know what's best for her are over.

Reign rubs his chin, those green eyes of his almost looking... impressed. "You could fill us in afterward," he suggests.

But that's not the point. She wants Reign and Mac to know they belong.

"Ari?" Gabby's voice startles her from behind. "What are you doing out here?"

Arielle turns around, bracing herself. "Your father's wrong." She doesn't care how immaculate and impressive he looks. "Reign and Mac aren't here to cause trouble."

Gabby sighs. "I know that. But it's going to take time for him to do the same." She steps through and half-closes the door behind her. "And I suspect whatever he has to say is important."

Arielle hesitates, then shakes her head. "Not without Reign and Mac."

"Please, just give him a chance? This is my dad we're talking about."

"You should go," urges Reign. "We'll be right here."

Waiting outside to be passed second-hand information because they're not allowed in.

"How about Reign can come in?" Gabby says quickly, no doubt seeing the next rejection hovering on Arielle's lips. "I don't want them out here any more than you do."

Mac smiles brightly. "That's a great idea."

"But—" Arielle starts.

Mac shakes her head emphatically. "I'm not too keen to be

in the same room as Douche Dude, anyway." She turns to Reign. "And if you try your own little mutiny to stand up for me, I'll kick your ass."

Reign grins. "There's my bestie."

She turns him around and pushes him. "Yep, and this bestie wants you to give her the low down on what Douche Dude has to say."

Gabby nods, looking relieved. "Thanks, Mac. We'll certainly do that."

Arielle still hesitates, but when Gabby holds the door open, looking at her a little desperately, she walks through, Reign behind her. Although this is a pretty lame compromise, her cousin is hurting after just losing her mother. Arielle doesn't want to add to her heartache right now.

Inside, Gabby's father is standing in the kitchen as if he's never really been in one. He stands beside the island bench, not touching it, frowning at the yellow walls. He straightens when he sees his daughter return with Arielle. He frowns even deeper when he sees Reign with them, but he doesn't say anything.

Arielle stays by the doorway, Reign remaining beside her.

"I don't like him," he mutters under his breath.

Arielle leans in. "Me neither."

Her mother enters the kitchen with an empty platter, then stops. "Hello, Gabriel."

Gabby's father straightens. "Hello, Sierra. You look well."

Her hands clench around the platter, the knuckles turning white. "Did you know? That Shell was an Innocent?"

He shakes his head, the first sign of sadness tugging the edges of his lips down. "I did not. But it explains why I was drawn to her."

Gabby shuffles, her gaze flickering to Arielle and Reign. "Dad, I think introductions are in order."

He nods. "Greetings. I am the Archangel Gabriel."

Arielle blinks. Then blinks again. Another secret. And a great big one at that. Will there ever come a time when she's trusted with the truth?

"Gabrielle's father is the Archangel Gabriel?" Reign mutters, and Arielle's not sure if he's impressed or unimpressed. "Do we start calling her Junior?"

She elbows him, quickly curtailing the movement when she feels the hardness of his chest. Her arm burns, despite the brief contact with steely muscles.

Reign rubs the point where they touched. "Fine, I won't then."

Her lips twitch, and she has to stop herself from shaking her head. Reign's irreverence is a balm to her aching soul.

"I've come to Earth to collect Shell's Grace," says Gabriel.

Arielle frowns. "But you said you oversaw the reapers taking her soul to Heaven."

"Her Grace, her angelic essence, is separate. It is a pure energy that cannot be destroyed."

Gabby wraps her arms around herself. "Do you know where it is?"

The archangel shakes his head. "I'm sure it was used to open the first Gate of Hell. It must be returned to Heaven." His gray eyes turn grave. "Otherwise it could be used to track the next Innocent."

Flashes of Arielle's vision flare through her mind. Another obelisk cracking open. Dead, naked bodies sprawled all around it. She quickly replaces the horror with determination.

Cain won't succeed again.

"You must find it," says Gabriel.

"Wouldn't you be better placed to do that?" Reign asks, mirroring the same thought Arielle just had.

But Gabriel is already shaking his head again, his golden curls brushing his shoulders. "I cannot interfere with matters of

Earth. Even coming here and telling you this is against the rules." He looks to his daughter. "I had to do it. For Shell."

She nods, tears glistening along her lashes. "We'll find it and get it to you."

"Thank you, daughter."

He disappears, the space suddenly empty as if he was never standing there, making Arielle realize that knocking on the door and asking to enter had all been out of courtesy.

"Can we trust him?" Arielle asks the room.

Gabby startles. "Not only is he my father, he's an archangel. Of course we can trust him. If he says we need to find the Grace, then that's exactly what we need to do."

Sierra frowns. "I'm going to Veritas Library to see what I can find out about all of this. Maybe Blaise and Nim know something." She leaves the kitchen, brushing Arielle's arm as she passes, an almost absent-minded gesture of affection. "I'll be back soon."

Arielle nods, but she's already gone. She turns to look at Gabby, finding her following Arielle's mom out of the kitchen.

She rubs her upper arms as if she's cold. "I need to talk to Colt."

As she watches Gabby head back up the stairs, Arielle wonders how much it's been a battle for her cousin to juggle the differences between Gabriel and Colt. Guilt clutches at her gut. Maybe she shouldn't have been so suspicious. She should be more supportive.

But then she suppresses a frown. She doesn't know the answers to any of these questions. Gabby was never going to tell her any of this—that Gabby's an angel. That her father's an archangel. That her boyfriend is a demon. Her whole family knew about that, except Arielle.

She intends on showing them that she was strong enough to handle it. That she's as strong as them.

Mac appears in the doorway. "So, I hear Douche Dude's gone."

"That's Archangel Douche Dude, thank you very much," says Reign.

"Whoa, no wonder he's so smug." Mac pulls up a bar stool beside the island and sits down. "So, what's the low down?"

Reign quickly gets her up to speed, telling her about Shell's Grace and the importance of finding it.

"If Cain doesn't have it, he will soon," Arielle adds once he's done. "He's going to do everything he can to get his hands on it."

Reign nods thoughtfully. "Makes sense."

"Which means we need to find him."

"Which ain't as easy as it sounds," Mac points out. "Cain is far more powerful than any of us realized."

"But not impossible," says Arielle. "We have to try."

Cain is the one who killed Shell. They can't let him take another Innocent. Tearing someone's mother, sister, aunt from their lives.

Mac rubs her brow. "Shouldn't we talk this over with the others?"

"Mom's researching and Gabby's grieving," Arielle points out. "And they'll both focus on finding Shell's Grace. That leaves us to do this."

She looks to Reign, seeing his thoughtful expression. She's already decided this is what she's going to do. But the thought of doing it without him...

"Find Cain. Take him out of the equation. Find the Grace," he says slowly. He smiles a little, the motion making something flutter low in Arielle's abdomen. "Sounds like a blast."

CHAPTER 4

REIGN

R eign shuts the door behind him as Mac flops on a couch in the large, open plan living room he's now standing in. Although he's been in this place a few days, he still hesitates before he enters.

The cottage is small but somehow still cozy, with twin couches, a recliner, and way too many bookshelves. A big TV is mounted to the wall on his left, a wide hallway on his right leading to the small kitchen and two bedrooms further down. It's what a middle-class place should look like.

It's cute. Comfortable. Clean.

And Sierra insisted Reign and Mac move into it.

Reign's first instinct was to refuse, even though he and Mac were eighteen and were only staying with Avril for a grace period while they found somewhere to live. The foster system didn't have to do that, which Avril pointed out frequently. They were there on borrowed time. If they had somewhere else to go, Reign and Mac would've packed and left before Avril could say "Damnation awaits!"

And yet when Sierra offered the guesthouse behind her place, Reign had hesitated. In part because of his pride. He's spent his life not taking any more handouts than he has to. He doesn't like owing people.

But it was far more because of the intense way Sierra always seems to be watching him. Like she's waiting for him to say or do something. What that is, he has no idea, but it's a whole lot of pressure he could do without.

And then there's Arielle...

By staying here, he's cementing whatever connection is building between them. And that's something he's avoided most of his life, for damn good reason. If he's not close to anyone, he can't let them down.

And yet, the desire to see where that connection could take them had been far more powerful than he'd expected it to be.

In the end, it was the way Mac's eyes lit up at the offer that had him grudgingly accepting. His best friend is tough, but she also craves some level of stability. And probably clean sheets.

He enters, knowing that, deep down, he likes this place but he doesn't want to get attached to it. Just like all the good things that have passed through his life, it won't last. He turns on the TV, uncomfortable with the silence, and the sound of a news anchor outlining a fall in the stock exchange fills the room.

Mac picks up the book she'd left on a side table then puts it straight back down again. "I'm not sure Ari's plan is the best one I've ever heard."

Reign jams his hands in his pockets. "She wants justice," he says simply.

Cain took someone Arielle cared very much for. Mac is the only person he's ever let close, and he imagines that if someone hurt her, he'd go to great lengths to ensure that person paid.

"Which makes me wonder if she's thinking straight. She's still grieving."

"Not to mention Cain is one evil bastard," he adds. They

should be doing everything they can to take him out of the equation.

"A powerful evil bastard," says Mac. "We've seen first-hand what he's capable of."

Murder. And a lot of it.

Reign sits on the arm of the couch, not quite comfortable enough to sit on it properly. "Cain felt pain when he touched me. If I'm given the chance to face off with him again, he'll lose."

Reign will make sure of it. He's already been training even harder any chance he gets.

Mac nods, although she doesn't look convinced. "If you say so." She shrugs. "And you know I'll have your back, no matter what."

He grins. "And with a demon for a best friend, how could I lose?

She picks up a cushion and throws it at him. Reign catches it, chuckling.

"We don't talk about that, remember?" Mac frowns, the motion only half joking.

Reign's smile fades. Mac has determinedly side-stepped any attempts at a conversation about what happened in the crypt. About the fact she's a demon. But before he can try again, there's soft chiming music and he looks around, realizing it's coming from the door. It's a doorbell.

He's never had a doorbell.

He frowns. And he's not expecting any visitors.

It seems Mac isn't either because she shoots to his side. They approach the door cautiously and Reign looks through the peephole.

Colt crosses his arms on the other side. "It's good to see you're being cautious," he says, no doubt his exceptional hearing telling him Reign and Mac are peering at him. "You should be."

They glance at each other, wondering what he's doing here. Without Gabby.

Reign opens the door. "That's your house warming gift?" he asks with an arched brow. "A doomsday warning?"

Colt pushes past him, entering the cottage. "You're welcome."

Reign closes the door, another glance passing between him and Mac. It can be hard to tell when Colt's joking.

He moves to the center of the living room, his arms still crossed, and Reign realizes he's holding something. Rolled up parchment is clenched in his fist. The kind that looks ancient. And generally people didn't write down good news back in those days.

"Gabby found you?" Mac asks, coming to stand beside a couch but not sitting down.

Colt nods. "She told me what her father said. Gabby's determined to find her mother's Grace."

"Understandable," says Reign as he joins Mac. "Especially if it can lead us to the next Innocent."

"Yes," Colt agrees. "But that's not why I'm here."

Reign angles his head. "You want to have a slumber party?"

Colt's eyes narrow. "Sure. Although I find pajama's a purely human invention. I don't actually own any."

Mac bites her lip. "I wanna see who's going to be the big spoon when you two curl up in bed."

Reign elbows her, the memory of Arielle doing the same thing to him earlier today flashing through his mind. It had been an affectionate gesture. One between friends. And yet the contact had burned like fire.

Colt shakes his head, and it's unclear whether he's amused or disgusted at Mac's suggestion. "I've come to warn you, Mac."

She tenses. "I think I'd prefer the slumber party."

"As you've learned, Gabby's father is an archangel. He's not one to accommodate demons."

Now it's Reign who tenses. "We kinda got that impression."

"Yes, but he implied he's here alone, and that's a great big pile of *pisiti*." Colt's gaze sharpens on Mac. "He'd be here with an army of angels."

"That sounds...ominous," Reign says, having no doubt it's an understatement.

"Does Gabby know this?" Mac asks quietly.

"I doubt she'll ask too many questions," says Colt. "She and her father only recently reconciled, which meant a lot to her."

"But you don't trust him," observes Reign.

Colt seems to harden. "I hate him." He looks away. "But Gabby doesn't know how much."

Mac's arms wrap around her middle. "I'm not exactly a match for a horde of angels."

"I would suggest not underestimating yourself, Mackenzie." Colt steps forward and passes her the roll of parchment paper. "But until then, I recommend you put these into effect."

Mac takes it and Colt heads to the door. "Probably sooner rather than later."

He's gone before they can ask any more questions, and Reign wonders if Gabby knows that Colt was planning this little visit. Deciding he'd best not mention it, he turns to Mac.

"So, is it a recipe for hummus?"

Mac unrolls the parchment, glances at it, then lets it roll back up. "I can't read it."

Reign grabs it before she tucks it in her back pocket, taking a look himself. "This looks like the gobbledygook that was on the parchment Arielle had at her house," he observes. He looks at Mac. "The one that you read."

Because it was in the language of demons.

Mac sighs, and she looks like she's gritting her teeth. "It's a warding spell. From angels."

He points the papers at her. "Which I'm pretty sure we might need."

She sighs again, this time even louder. She stomps over and snatches it from his hands, unrolling it once again. Her eyes scan the strange symbols and she flicks to the second page. Then she stomps to the door. She holds up the parchment, huffs, then commences outlining a large circle on the timber surface.

Reign watches, eyes a little wide as, with quick sharp movements, Mac draws strange shapes inside the circle. He thinks one looks like an arrow, another maybe a crescent moon. Several don't look like anything he has a hope of recognizing.

But it's the words that Mac mutters in a low, husky tone that really has him stunned. Thick and guttural, they sound ancient. And demonic.

Finished, Mac turns to frown at him. "I have to do every door in the place."

He smiles. "Good thing we didn't move into an apartment block, then."

She doesn't smile back as she stomps past him to the back door. Attached to a laundry that Reign had to google in order to use the washing machine.

"A warding spell from angels, huh?" he calls after her. "Now that's one way to make a place your own."

"Zip it before you get put on the Douche List," she snaps from down the hall.

Reign chuckles, settling himself onto one of the couches. He's about to put his feet on the coffee table when he stops himself. Dammit. He's going to have to grow some manners.

The TV anchor on the news has her serious face on as she stares at him and he grabs the remote, more for something to do than anything else. "Our local reporter is on the scene now," she says somberly.

An older woman appears on the screen, a microphone held in front of her. "I mean, we're a nice neighborhood." Her hand flutters to her chest. "I never would've thought something like that could happen here."

"Something like what?" Mac asks from behind him. She drops the parchment on the coffee table. "I'll finish in a sec."

"Dunno," he shrugs, figuring Mac's probably had enough teasing for now. He'll try to bring up the whole demon thing again later. "Only just turned it up."

The camera pans to a pretty brunette. "Three lives gone," she says sadly. "Brutally murdered in the quiet suburban house you see behind me."

The image zooms onto the single story home. It has a lush green lawn with topiary roses lining the driveway.

"And yet, all the blood in the world couldn't cover the compromising position the couple were found in with their neighbor," says the news anchor as the camera returns to her. "Two families torn apart by three people's lust for pleasure and another's lust for blood."

Reign changes the channel, frowning. They have enough to deal with right now with Cain and Innocents and angel armies. He doesn't need to know about the awful things humans can do to each other.

Mac's also frowning as she curls up beside him and picks up her book. "Seems someone else was having a slumber party."

CHAPTER 5
ARIELLE

Arielle trudges the footpath home, scrunching up the essay she was just handed back. She doesn't think she's ever got a D before, but then again, she's never been through the whirlwind few weeks she's just experienced.

Even as she wrote it, Arielle couldn't see the relevance of exploring the unending clash between religion and politics, ensuring she referenced right the whole way through. Not when her mom was abducted by demons so she could be ritually sacrificed. Not when her aunt was killed so a Gate of Hell could be opened.

Every lecture on politics or social science or how to write a great essay feels like a waste of time.

Not when Cain is out there, hunting the next life he's thirsting after.

She reaches her home and stops, staring at the front door. Her mother and Gabby should be home, and Arielle wonders what they've been discussing while she's gone. And whether they'll share everything they've talked over...

Arielle frowns and she scrunches the essay even further. She pulls her backpack around and shoves the crumpled ball in the front pocket. She'll throw it in the trash when no one's looking. It seems she can have secrets, too.

Straightening her shoulders, she's conscious of the anger that's simmering. An anger that was born alongside the grief of losing Aunt Shell.

An anger that wants justice.

And it's just what Arielle will use to prove that she's not some flimsy, fragile flower that will fall apart at the first sign of a few demons. She can handle the supernatural, and she's going to prove it.

Entering the house, Arielle wonders whether Reign's around. Hooking her bag up, she realizes she's looking forward to seeing him. Even Mac wasn't convinced the plan to go after Cain is a good one, but Reign was willing to support her.

And that means everything.

"Ari? Is that you?" her mom calls from the kitchen.

Arielle enters, eyebrows hiking when she sees her mom's made muffins. Her mom has many talents—many that Arielle never knew about—but cooking isn't one of them. She suspects that because her mom had her so young, she was too busy juggling an infant and schooling to hone how to make an omelet that isn't burned underneath, but still runny on top.

Her mom beams. "I made choc chip muffins."

Gabby's there, too, grinning. "And I had one and I'm still alive."

"Thanks, Mom," says Arielle, meaning it.

Ever since her abduction, her mother's been doing little things like this—cooking instead of takeout, hugs instead of goodnights, soft smiles in abundance. Almost losing her mom made Arielle realize how important she is to her. It seems her mom has realized the same thing.

Her mom wrinkles her nose. "Gabby said they didn't kill her, not that they taste good."

Arielle sits on the barstool beside her cousin. "They're made with love, and that's what counts."

Her mom smiles, reaching over to pat Arielle's hand. "That's what others say to people who can't cook."

The three of them burst into a fit of giggles, and warmth wraps Arielle's heart like a heated blanket. Their first laughter since the loss of Shell. And it's because they're together, as a family.

Gabby sobers, glancing at the photo of Shell with two blonde toddlers that sits on the wall. "We were just talking about what my dad said. About needing to find Mom's Grace."

Arielle takes a muffin and breaks a chunk off. "And?"

"I think that's what we should focus on right now."

Arielle's hand pauses on the way to her mouth as she recognizes the turning point she's at. The old Arielle would've nodded and asked what needs to be done.

But a new Arielle emerged from Sinclair Mansion that night. That Arielle decided to forge her own destiny, rather than let others mold it for her. She doesn't need protecting.

"And you're sure your father is telling us everything?" she asks quietly.

Gabby stiffens. "He's my father, of course I trust him."

Except Arielle isn't so sure he has. She wonders if Gabriel would even have come if he wasn't looking for the Grace.

"So, he gets the Grace, and then he goes back to Heaven to hang out with all the other archangels? That's it?"

Gabby's eyes narrow, flicking to Sierra, then back. "Yes, that's it."

Arielle sits the piece of muffin back down, considering her words. "It's just that if we focus on the Grace, we're letting Cain get away."

"Cain is going to go deep underground," says Gabby. "Finding him could take months."

"All the more reason to get started on it ASAP."

Gabby shifts on her barstool, as if it's suddenly uncomfortable. "We can't afford for Cain to get his hands on the Grace. He'll use it to track the next Innocent."

Except it's also her mother's Grace. It would hurt knowing it's out there, lost, rather than home in Heaven.

"Which is why we go straight to the source of the threat—Cain himself," says Arielle. "No deadly demon trying to open the Gates of Hell, no one hunting the Innocents."

Gabby shoots to her feet, her pale face suffused in red. "This is my mother's Grace we're talking about, Ari," she almost shouts. "Her angelic essence. It belongs in Heaven, with her soul."

Arielle stands, too, her own anger rising to match Gabby's. "Catching Cain will make sure he can't do this again," she urges. She's seen the obelisk destroyed. "That's how we can honor Shell's memory."

Arielle's mom clears her throat. "Let's all take a breath, shall we?"

Arielle blinks, seeing Gabby do the same. She can't remember the last time they fought.

"A lot's happened in a short space of time," her mom says gently. "Everyone's a little worked up right now. Why don't you two sit down?"

But Arielle and Gabby gaze at each other. They move simultaneously, clasping each other in a tight hug.

"Sorry, Ari," Gabby whispers. "I just really miss her."

Arielle's arms tighten. "Me, too. We were always two sisters with two moms."

Gabby pulls back, nodding. She sniffs as she wipes at her eye, then sits back on the stool. Arielle does the same, glad the conflict has resolved, but conscious they haven't reached an agreement.

"The others are coming over soon," says her Mom. "We'll talk about our next steps then."

Arielle smiles weakly. "Sure." She stands. "Actually, I might go have a rest beforehand."

She picks up the plate with her muffin and exits before any more questions are asked. In her room, she places it on her bedside table, no longer hungry. She flicks on the TV, wanting a little background noise. She sits on the bed and pulls her pillow into her lap.

Should she have kept her mouth shut? Everyone's still grieving, meaning the timing probably isn't great. Except Cain won't be waiting for them to grieve. To come to terms with what he cold-heartedly stole.

Arielle's hand tightens around the soft material. Yes, she feels awful.

But she also feels like she's emerging from a cocoon. Like she's finding her wings, whether she's supernatural or not.

A flash of naked skin on the screen has her gaze pulled back to the TV, wondering if she somehow tapped into one of *those* channels. But a news logo quickly replaces the strategically pixelated image, a red banner running along the bottom saying *Breaking News*.

She turns up the volume.

"Another multiple murder has occurred," says the gray-haired news anchor. "Five bodies were found naked at the Multiplayer Love Lounge, brutally killed." His lips thin. "The Multiplayer Love Lounge is popularly known as a polyamorous club. The victims appeared to be partaking of the services offered at the time of their deaths."

Arielle sits up, pushing the pillow away. This is why she didn't stay silent. This is why she has to fight for what's right.

The murders are starting again.

Cain is already rearing his demonic head.

CHAPTER 6

REIGN

Reign stuffs his hands in his pockets and hunches his shoulders as he stands in Sierra's living room, conscious it's a defensive move, but not bothering to change it. He's in a room with a whole bunch of people, and it's...weird.

He's never worked as a *team* before.

Sierra stands beside a wall covered in pretty tiles, scanning the room. Gabby is sitting on one end of the couch, Colt standing beside her. Reign suspects it's rare for him to sit down anyplace that's not his own.

Mac is beside Reign, after elbowing him three times in the middle of the back as he tried to hang back beside the doorway. They're now beside an armchair, Reign standing behind it like it's some shield.

Arielle is on the other side of the couch to Gabby, hands clasped tightly in her lap. It's obvious something is on her mind and he wonders what that is. When Cain killed Shell, he also stole Arielle's innocence. Her belief that everything can turn out okay.

Reign never had either of those, but he imagines it's just as great a loss as her aunt. And he also suspects that changes a person.

Sierra's gaze falls on each of them. "Thank you for coming. In light of Gabriel's visit, we need to discuss what our next steps are going to be."

Arielle pushes to her feet. "I have something to share," she says in a quiet but firm voice.

The room stills.

"I had another vision just before Gabriel arrived." She seems to draw in a steadying breath. "It was of an obelix cracking." She shudders and Reign has to stop himself from going to her. "With dead naked bodies scattered around it."

Everyone is silent as they digest the information.

"Well, that sounds kinda crap," says Mac. "It means another Gate of Hell could be opened."

And they don't even know what the first Gate of Hell is going to mean.

"Then there's the spate of murders," says Colt, his hand coming to rest on Gabby's shoulder as if he's expecting someone to jump out right now.

Arielle's face hardens. "Which has got to be Cain's handiwork."

But Gabby shakes her head. "I'm not so sure," she says. "He targets people specifically to do with the Grail."

"I think Gabby might be right."

Arielle's head snaps to the person who just said those words —her mother.

Sierra looks at her daughter, her gaze steady. "Think about it. Cain doesn't operate that way. He's not about killing for the sake of killing."

Gabby smiles a little, possibly grateful that Sierra backed her up, possibly trying to soften her words to Arielle. "I think these murders are due to something else."

"What?" Reign asks, conscious of the tension climbing in the room.

"I'm not sure," Gabby says with a shrug. "We'll need to find out." Her hand falls on Colt's as it rests on her shoulder. "Once we get my mother's Grace back."

Colt nods. "It's how we'll find the next Innocent."

Reign frowns. "Hang on a sec. We need to find Cain." They need to make him pay for everything he's ever taken. "By finding the bastard, we stop more people from being killed. The Innocent won't have anyone hunting them."

"We find the Grace and the next Gate of Hell stays closed," Gabby points out, her own frown creasing her forehead.

Reign almost points out that her mother's angelic essence will also be returned to Heaven, but he keeps his mouth shut.

"And tracking Cain is dangerous," adds Colt. "He's a very powerful demon. Far more powerful than I've ever seen."

"One that's out there, on the loose," Reign points out. "Working to peel back another layer between us and Hell, having a little killing spree along the way."

Colt doesn't reply, but his steady gaze says he's said his piece and he won't be changing his mind. Reign grinds his teeth, wondering why these people can't see that Cain is at the center of this shit fight. People are dying, for fuck's sake. Arielle glances at him, her gaze full of gratitude, and a strange warmth pools in his stomach.

Sierra shakes her head. "Going after Cain is too dangerous."

Arielle stiffens as if her mother just slapped her. Reign can feel her hurt from here.

Mac clears her throat. "I agree. We should focus on finding the Grace."

Reign's hands tighten on the back of the chair. Right now, he has an inkling of how Arielle's feeling.

"Majority says we go after the Grace," Sierra says, her gaze on her daughter. "To save the next Innocent."

"Well, we are a democracy," Reign says, injecting a lightness into his tone he doesn't feel. He just realized why he's never worked as part of a team. "So I suppose we go with that."

Arielle's hands clench and unclench three times—Reign counts—before she nods and sits down.

Gabby pushes to her feet and takes Colt's hand. "I'll find out what I can."

They walk to the door, leaving the room heavy with silence.

Sierra's gaze falls on Reign, her eyes full of the weight they always seem to carry when she looks at him. "I'd like to talk if you have a moment."

He steps away from the chair. "Sorry, no can do," he says with a smile. "Got laundry to do." He walks to the door. "Ari, do you mind showing me how that darned machine works?"

Arielle looks surprised, but she nods, rising to follow him. "Sure. They're pretty straight forward."

Reign snorts, continuing to make his way to the back door. "If you know whether you can put denim in a cotton wash, you're one step ahead of me."

Her lips twitch. "Denim is made out of cotton."

"See! I knew you'd be all over it."

He opens the door and indicates for her to pass through. Once they're on the back porch, Reign stops, glancing to make sure Mac didn't follow. They need to be alone for this conversation.

Arielle returns back up the steps she just walked down. "Reign? Did you forget something?"

Once he confirms they won't be overhead, he turns back to face her. "If you want to find Cain, I think that's what we should do."

She blinks in surprise. "You do?"

"Yep. I just said we'd go with the majority to save the headache. I'm behind you one hundred percent."

Arielle's face softens. "Wow. That means a lot."

Reign shrugs, not meaning for it to have had such an impact. "He's a murderous bastard who needs to be stopped."

She studies him for long seconds. Long enough that Reign has to stop himself from squirming. "Do you know, when I first met you, I thought you were a total jerk."

Reign stills at the soft, reflective note in her voice. "Sorry to disappoint, but I'm still a jerk."

Arielle arches a brow. "Are you also saying I'm wrong?"

He opens his mouth only to quickly shut it again. "Cain won't know what hit him," he mutters.

She grins. "All we have to do is find him, first."

Reign finds himself smiling back before he realizes it. "Have you thought about how?"

"The crime scenes," she says simply. "We need to go where he's gone."

Reign nods, his eyes narrowing in thought. "That won't be easy, considering the police presence that will be there."

Arielle's face lights up in a way he hasn't seen since Shell's death. Her blue eyes sparkle with purpose. "I've already thought of that, too." She glances around, making sure they're still alone. "Can your laundry wait? Because I have a plan."

CHAPTER 7
ARIELLE

Veritas Library still takes Arielle's breath away. As she steps through, Reign right behind her, she tries to keep the awe from her face, and fails miserably. The arched ceilings are so high that she feels tiny. The sheer number of books overwhelms her with the vast amount of knowledge they must contain. The magic that hangs in the air weighs it down and yet seems to lighten her chest.

"I'm surprised Mac ever leaves this place," says Reign.

Arielle smiles. "I think she asked Nim about putting an extra couch in here so she could sleep on it."

Reign snorts and shakes his head. "Of course she did."

Glad to see there's no one around, Arielle grabs Reign's hand before she's realized what she's doing. She senses him still and she wonders if he feels the same flash of heat shooting up his arm. The sound of a soft *bump* doesn't give her time to mull over the thought.

"Quick, this way."

She pulls Reign to a row of shelves on their right. She's only just started investigating the wealth of information stored in this supernatural library, but one book recently caught her attention. It's what gave her the idea.

There's something they could use. Something that could help them.

She walks about half way down and stops. "This one," she says in a whisper.

"Are you thinking of stealing it?" Reign asks in a quizzical whisper, possibly wondering why she's being so secretive.

"No. I just want to read it in peace." Without prying eyes.

Arielle pulls a book down covered in deep red leather and sits on the floor cross legged. "There's something I saw in this one that could help us."

Reign sits down beside her, peering at the pages she just opened. "Like what?"

She runs her finger down the text, stopping when she sees what she's looking for. "An object that can pick up demonic auras and verify the signature imprint left by demons."

"Now that's cool," he breathes.

Arielle looks up, finding him much closer than she realized. Her gaze roams over his dark brows, the strong features, the lush looking lips... Her eyes snap up, trying to not acknowledge the heat that just flared through her veins, only to connect with his gaze.

Jungle green ensnares her with all its intricacies and layers, and she can't move. What's more, she doesn't want to. What would it be like to explore the maze that is Reign? To touch him...

"Ah, what are you doing?"

They jolt, turning to find Nim wheeling toward them. She stops a few feet away, raising an eyebrow as she registers the tome Arielle's holding.

"With that book?"

Arielle stands, quickly closing it. "Just reading."

Reign grins as he shrugs. "Surely that's pretty normal in a place like this? I mean, it's practically expected."

Nim's eyebrows stays where they are. "Most definitely. But it's the *what* they're reading that's always interesting." She nods at the book Arielle's now clutching like a shield. "Like chapter two of that particular text."

Arielle's mind works quickly. Surely Nim can't know what's inside most of the books with that level of detail. "I just thought I saw something that might help with the murders happening throughout the city."

"I wouldn't have thought that would be your focus right now. The police would be taking care of that."

Arielle grits her teeth although she smiles. "We're just doing a bit of research while the others are trying to find out what they can about the Grace."

Nim watches them for a long second. "Well, you're playing with fire with that book. The object it's talking about isn't one any old person can use."

"They can't?" Reign asks.

"Nope. It's a very powerful magical object. And magic always has a price. Something it wants in return."

Arielle shifts her weight. "What sort of price?"

Nim shrugs. "I don't know. There's a lot of mystery surrounding that particular...entity. Even if anyone knew where it was, it's not something you should be messing with."

Arielle slots the book back into the space on the shelf, not liking the sense of discouragement sinking through her insides. "I think you may be right."

"I know I'm right," says Nim as she turns her wheelchair around. "Why don't you go back home and see what the others have come up with?"

"Great idea," says Arielle, trying to keep the disappointment out of her voice.

Reign indicates with his head that they should probably leave. She nods, frustrated that her one idea has been thwarted. The object is not only dangerous, but no one knows where it is.

Nim looks relieved as she bids them goodbye. She also doesn't leave the aisle as Arielle and Reign walk out.

Outside the library, she squints in the sunlight. "Now what?"

Reign angles his head. "You wanna call Gabby or your mom?"

"No," she snaps. "I don't."

But then she sees the smile playing at the edge of his lips, softening their lines. He's teasing her. That sweet warmth in his eyes, the one that's as far from jerk as it could get, tugs at her chest.

"I'm not going to stop." The images of the dead, naked bodies seemed to have stained her mind. "We have to find another way to locate Cain and put an end to the murders."

His almost-smile grows into a near-grin. "Well, it's good that I have an idea, then."

"You do?"

He spins on his heel, heading toward her car. "I most certainly do," he drawls. "And no magic involved so no price to pay."

Arielle watches him walk away, realizing she's smiling. Reign was checking if she was going to see this through. And when she said yes, he already had a plan on how to help her.

It's him.

She startles as Trinity's voice slides through her mind.

"Who?" she whispers.

Except her childhood friend doesn't answer.

GABBY

The map before Gabby stares blankly at her as she stands in Colt's basement apartment, as if it holds no clues as to where her mother's Grace could be and it's not even apologizing for it. As frustrating as that is, she's not surprised. No one knew where the obelisk was, just like no one knows where the next one will be.

In the same way they had no clue who the Innocent was... until her mother was brutally killed.

Colt's hands land on her shoulders and she leans back into his warm strength. "We can't be too late this time," she mutters.

"That's the plan," he says in his low, sure voice.

Gabby turns around and presses her face against his chest, breathing in his familiar, sexy scent. Colt is her anchor when everything tries to overwhelm her. Was it only really a few months ago that they defeated the Grigori?

"I'm here for you," he says.

"I know. And I love you for that." She squeezes his muscled torso. "Among other things."

Colt shakes his head. "It's just that you haven't really given yourself time to grieve. And you know your emotions can get the better of you."

Gabby looks up, her fierce gaze connecting with his. "I'll wallow in the pain of losing my mother when her Grace is where it belongs, not in the hands of evil."

Her mom would be heartbroken to think that someone could use her essence to track and kill another Innocent.

He watches her in that steady, wordless way of his. "Okay. But I don't think it was Cain who did it."

"What?"

"I mean, Cain ordered it, but can't have been the one who killed her. He was fighting us."

Gabby realizes Colt's right. Cain was in the crypt and they were desperately trying to defeat him, assuming it was Sierra who was the Innocent.

"It means Cain had a partner in crime," she breathes.

Colt nods. "It makes sense that he has someone doing his dirty work for him."

She steps back, pressing her fingertips to her temples. "There's so much more going on, I can feel it."

"There usually is," he says, his lips twisting. They've both found that out the hard way.

Gabby straightens. "You go and check on Ari and Reign, I'm not convinced they're going to sit around and wait for more news. I know what I need to do to track down the Grace."

Colt's brows plough down as he realizes what she means. "You don't have to go it alone."

She smiles as she presses her hands to his chest. "We both know I'm better off doing this part solo."

"You know he can't be trusted, despite the truce. Not after everything he did."

But Gabby shakes her head. "I can trust him when it comes to his love for my mom. I believe him when he says he's here to collect her Grace."

Colt grunts. "I respect your faith in him."

Gabby can't help but smile. Colt could almost go into politics with his carefully considered words. Of course, he'd probably raze them all to the ground...

She presses up so her lips hover close to his. "It will be fine."

His hands tighten around her waist, pulling her a little closer. "It had better be."

Their mouths touch, a vow that begins at their lips and ends in their souls. Gabby melts against the demon who holds her heart, tasting the passion that sparked between them right from the beginning. Just like every other time, she wants to dive into it with everything she has. She loves the soft groans he makes when she—

She pulls back, grinning sheepishly. "You're trying to distract me."

He smiles, a cheeky glint in his chocolate eyes that she doubts anyone else has ever seen. "A little. Although, it's a win-win situation for both of us, if you ask me."

Laughing softly, she peels herself from his delicious body. "We both know it is."

Their love is the only place that she knows is safe. True. And eternally beautiful.

Gabby turns and heads to the door. "Keep an eye on Ari." Her chest tightens. "I can't afford to lose anyone else."

Colt nods, understanding heavy in his eyes. She exits, squaring her shoulders.

It's time to see her father.

CHAPTER 8
REIGN

Arielle drives them through the streets of Mercy City, looking lost in thought. Reign leaves her to it, surreptitiously glancing at her profile.

Just like the first time he met her, he's struck by her beauty. Smooth, pale skin, blonde hair the color of cornsilk, lips that are an alluring shade of rose. But unlike that unfortunate crash in the middle of a sidewalk, she's no longer angry. He's no longer defensive.

In fact, he suspects she passed through the mental armor he keeps around himself during all those times he was busy checking her out.

Which means she's not only beautiful, she's now fascinating. Captivating.

Tempting.

Reign snaps his head to look out the window, not sure what to do with these thoughts. They make his pulse trip and his breath catch, but he's not sure if it's in a good way. These feelings for Arielle are new, powerful in a way he hadn't known existed, and strangely moving.

And yet, they're terrifying.

Arielle pulls up at a set of lights and Reign almost chokes on his inbreath when he sees a couple on a bench seat at a bus stop.

"What?" she asks, turning to see what he's looking at. "Oh."

The woman is straddled across the man, kissing him passionately as she writhes on his lap. The guy's hands are roaming over her back, each time pulling her shirt up a little higher. It feels like another few minutes or so and it'll be thrown to the ground.

A middle-aged woman with too-bleached hair frowns at them as she takes a wide berth around, shaking her head. Except Reign's pretty sure the red that's suffusing her neck and face isn't embarrassment. In fact, she wafts her face with her hand once she's several feet away.

"Well, that takes a public display of affection to a whole new level," Reign murmurs, feeling a little warm himself.

The light turns green and they pull away. Reign looks back to see Arielle's gaze firmly on the road, a pink flush creeping up her cheeks.

One that's far sexier than anything he just saw. And without the 'ew' factor that the couple had.

Reign shifts, his jeans suddenly feeling a little too tight. The near-porn exhibition was the last thing he needed right now.

The rest of the car trip is as silent as it was before stopping at the lights, and yet the air feels thicker. Warmer. Full of awareness.

They reach Arielle's house not long later and Reign's almost relieved to exit the vehicle. Images that involved himself and Arielle sitting in the very same position on the bench seat had climbed into his consciousness and refused to leave. A little part of him hadn't wanted them to.

They circle the main house, making their way to the guest house.

"You know, Mom had this place built when I was pretty young. And yet it's stayed empty ever since," Arielle muses. She angles her head, as if she's looking at the cottage in a new light. "It's like she was waiting. Like she built it for you."

Reign snorts and shakes his head as he opens the door. "Or she feels indebted."

It's the only reason he can think that Sierra would offer them somewhere to live—because he and Mac helped defeat Cain. No one has been waiting for him to come into their lives, he knows that for sure.

"Maybe," says Arielle, not sounding convinced. Her lips twist. "But I doubt she'd tell me anyway."

Reign pauses in the living room. "Being excluded really hurt you, didn't it?"

She pauses, chewing her lip. "I know they were doing it to protect me," she hedges.

"All this is pretty freaking dangerous," he agrees, conscious that she didn't really answer his question. "And yet, here you are anyway."

Her sweet features harden. "Exactly. Whether they like it or not." She looks around. "So, what have you got to show me?"

Reign's about to ask what she means when he remembers why he invited Arielle here in the first place. Rather impulsively. All because he didn't like the disappointment clouding her features at Veritas.

"Ah, well." He shoves his hands in his pockets. "It's in my bedroom."

The moment the words are said, Arielle blushes. He feels heat stain his cheeks as the images of the couple return, full force.

"For crap's sake," he mutters, turning on his heel and striding toward his room. He's just making things even more awkward.

Inside, he opens the closet and rummages in the back corner, pulling out the box he tucked under a stack of blankets. He turns with it in his hands, finding Arielle standing by the door.

"Here," he says, dropping it on the bed. "I've been collecting this stuff for a while now."

Arielle enters and he steps back, conscious that he's keeping space between them. Even more conscious they're in a bedroom. Technically, his bedroom.

She lifts open the flap of the box. "What is it?" she asks, pulling out a pair of black framed glasses.

Another flush threatens to creep up his face. "Just some PI gear I've been collecting. Those glasses have a hidden camera in the frame." He sits on the edge of the bed, finally looking at her. "Don't ask how I paid for any of it."

She shrugs. "Probably the same way anyone else without parents to provide for them do."

Reign focuses on picking up the pen tucked in the bottom. It has a voice recorder installed in it. He used to mistake Arielle's compassion for pity, and he kind of wishes he still did. He doesn't need to be reminded that her heart is as beautiful as the rest of her.

"Well, I'm thinking we could use this stuff as we loiter around the crime scenes, see what we can pick up."

Arielle sits on the other side, pulling out a GPS tracker. "Have you ever considered getting your PI license?"

"No."

And the few times his stupid brain went there, he quickly shut it down.

"You should." Arielle's eyes trap him with their excited light. "You'd be perfect for it—you're unflappable. Nothing rocks your boat."

"Because I've seen way too much shit in my time."

"You're smart."

"A carefully crafted illusion," he counters.

Arielle narrows her eyes, a twinkle now in her gaze. "And you're hot. Housewives are going to be tripping over themselves to hire you to follow their cheating husbands."

Reign's mouth was already open with his next shoot-down, except no words come out.

Arielle thinks he's hot?

She arches a brow, this new, determined Ari unwilling to back down. It's one of the sexiest things he's ever seen.

Reign looks away. "Not exactly what I had in mind," he says, more to fill in the silence.

"I still reckon you should think about it." Arielle puts the glasses back in the box. "And this stuff is great, but they're still not going to let two teens hang around a crime scene."

He shuts the box. "Yeah, you're right. It was a stupid idea."

As stupid as him being a private investigator.

Arielle draws in a sharp breath, her face lighting up once more "What if we weren't teens?"

"I think waiting until we look thirty-five is a little extreme."

The slow smile that curves her lips up seems to be directly connected to something in his chest.

"We're not going to wait, but we're definitely going to look like adults."

Great. They're going to try and use magic again.

MAC

Mac rises from the shrub she's tucked behind, wondering if she should go inside. Something has the hairs on the back of her neck prickling, and she spins around.

Colt raises a brow as he materializes from around the corner of Sierra's house. "Your demon senses are strong."

She frowns at him. "Or you're heavy footed."

"No demon is heavy footed." He comes to stand beside her, glancing at the shrub in front of them. "So, you're spying, too, huh?"

Mac shifts a little, wondering if she should tell him. She's kind of been avoiding Colt, particularly since that little 'moment' down in the crypt where she discovered they have far more in common than she would've liked.

"They're up to something, aren't they?" Colt says, the words more of a statement than a question.

Mac sighs. "I may or may not have already done some spying." In fact, she followed Reign when he went out to talk to Arielle. She'd tucked herself on the other side of the back door and listened with everything she had. "They're planning on going after Cain on their own."

Colt nods, his eyes narrowing. "Cain has taken much from Ari's family." He sighs. "But they're wasting their time."

"They're two smart kids," Mac says, realizing she sounds like she's ancient. "They know something's up with those murders." She crosses her arms. "It's investigating them on their own that's the issue."

"Do you know what their plans are?"

"No," she huffs. "They came back here a little while ago, and went inside. I have no idea what they're doing in there."

Colt snorts. "Maybe they're finally acknowledging their true feelings."

It's Mac's turn to snort. "Not Reign's strong point." She thinks he's spent a lot of his life pretending he doesn't have feelings.

In fact, she's not sure which part of his anatomy he was thinking with when he promised Ari he'd help her with this...

"You know, you could use your demonic hearing," Colt points out.

Mac stiffens, crossing her arms tightly. "I doubt it."

"You took care of Cain's men in the crypt. A dozen of them, without any training. You're a powerful demon, Mackenzie."

"That was because it was an emergency and Reign is all I have," she says through gritted teeth. Although she'll never regret keeping him and everyone else safe, she could've done without learning the reason for her...quirks.

"I could train you."

"No, thank you," she snaps before he's even finished.

Nope. Not happening. Not a chance.

Colt sighs. "Then I suggest we watch these two. Make sure they don't get into any trouble."

Mac unfolds her arms, nodding once. "Exactly what I intend to do." If Colt wants to come along for the ride, then all the better.

But she plans on doing it as a human.

SIERRA

Another wave of sadness engulfs Sierra as she steps through the doors of Veritas Library. She pulls in a deep breath, drawing in the comfort of the familiar scents of wood and truth. Shell's the only person she can think of who never really liked this place.

"This is...too much," she'd whispered.

"It's definitely overwhelming," Sierra had agreed. "But knowledge is power. It's what will keep Gabby safe."

"Easy enough for you to say," Shell had grouched. "Your daughter is none the wiser about this dangerous new world Gabby's now in."

But Sierra hadn't taken exception to her sister's tone. She knew she was worried. Actually, she was terrified. Her worst nightmare had come true—her daughter is supernatural.

"Maybe it's better for Ari to know—"

"Most definitely not!" Shell had shouted the words so loud, they'd almost made the chandeliers shudder. "Ari deserves a normal life, as far from this as she can. You owe her that much." Shell had frowned, turning her back on the shelves of magical tomes lining Veritas. "Haven't we lost enough already?"

Gabby's father.

Ryder.

Sierra sighs, shaking her head as if she can shake away the past. She'd agreed with Shell at the time—she wanted nothing more than to protect her daughter from the sort of pain that's both a dull ache and a sudden, white-hot knife that slices when she least expects it.

But now that she's seen the hurt that Ari's trying so hard to hide, she's not so sure...

Nim appears, a stack of books on her lap as she wheels toward Sierra. "Hey, thanks for coming."

Sierra nods, glancing at the texts and glad for the distraction. "Is there something you wanted me to look at?"

But Nim stops beside a desk and lifts the books onto it before coming closer. "No, I just thought there was something you should know."

"Oh?" Sierra doesn't mean to sound cautious, maybe a little

defensive, but she's feeling, well, cautious and defensive. Nim didn't invite her here to exchange herbal tea recipes.

"Arielle was here earlier."

Sierra stills. "She was?"

"She was researching," Nim says, her heavy voice belaying the matter of fact statement.

Sierra waits, wondering what else her choices all those years ago have put into motion.

"She was looking for the Seeker."

CHAPTER 9
ARIELLE

"So, we're going to find a witch?" Reign asks dubiously.

Arielle nods, turning to face him a little better. "Well, yes. I'm sure they can glamor us to look as old as we want." She grins. "We could be an elderly married couple."

Reign's eyes widen imperceptibly. "Ah, yeah. Sure."

She chews on her lip. "We could ask Blaise?"

"You mean, one of your mom's closest friends?" he asks, one black eyebrow raised into his bangs.

"Yeah, I thought you'd say that." It was something she'd already considered herself, but thought it was worth mentioning. "We could dig around on the internet?"

"And get the people who can predict who your soulmate is with the help of a few chicken feet?"

She wrinkles her nose. "As long as they don't have spiders."

"They will definitely have spiders," says Reign, straight faced.

"Definitely a bad idea then."

Reign grins and she smiles back, enjoying their banter. In fact, she likes spending time with him, period.

"What if we found a hacker?" he suggests. "They don't use chicken feet or spiders, and could get us the information."

Arielle lifts a pretend phone to her ear. "Yeah, hi. We're looking for someone to hack into the Mercy City Police database, no questions asked." She schools her face in mock shock. "You want to charge how much?"

Reign's lips twist. "Okay, fine. And selling one of my kidneys will probably take too long."

"Not to mention a little extreme."

He rolls his eyes. "And probably not worth much, either."

Arielle frowns. "Poppycock."

Reign blinks, but quickly recovers. "Hey, whoa back with the potty mouth," he says jokingly as he stands and picks up the box. He turns away and opens his closet. It's empty apart from a handful of clothes and a pile of blankets in the back corner.

But she's not ready to let it go yet. "You talk poppycock, I'm going to call out poppycock."

He busies himself, tucking the box under the blankets. Arielle notes the way he hides his PI possessions. Reign has dreams, he's just not willing to admit it.

Or maybe the guy who thinks his kidney isn't worth anything doesn't even realize he has them.

He turns around sharply. "Maybe Veritas has some sort of a directory of witches!"

Arielle straightens. "They'd have to!" If there's anywhere that records the existence of witches, it would have to be Veritas.

"Do you think they include the length of their broomsticks, kind of like a Tinder profile?"

She giggles, pulling her car keys out of her pocket. "There's only one way to find out."

They head back out and climb into her car. Arielle pulls out of the driveway, noting her mom's not home.

Reign must, too, because he comments on it. "I wonder where she's gone."

"She'd be more likely to tell you," she says under her breath.

"Well hello passive-aggressive-Ari. I'm asks-too-many-questions-Reign. Nice to meet you."

She turns right, realizing a smile is playing at the edge of her lips despite the sour taste in her mouth. "Yeah, I know. I need to get over it."

"Or talk to her about it."

Arielle checks the odometer to make sure she's not inadvertently accelerating over the speed limit as the muscles in her body wind tighter. "There's nothing left to say."

"As someone whose parents are dead, I'm pretty sure there's always something else to say," he says softly.

His words leave her silent and thoughtful. A few weeks ago, when her mom was missing, she would've forgiven her anything if it meant getting her back.

And yet, she's holding onto this anger and resentment with everything she has...

"Wow," Reign says under his breath. "Is there something in the air?"

They're passing the same bus stop they did on the way here, but the bench seat is empty. Arielle knows the sense of relief she feels is going to be short lived by his tone. She braces herself for the images the last couple ignited—images of herself crawling onto Reign's lap, his eyes closed with the same ecstasy that the guy had. She shifts a little in her seat, hoping she'll be able to contain her rising body temperature this time around.

Except the man pressing a woman against the brick wall of the shopping mall isn't young and good-looking like Reign. In fact, he's balding and portly. The woman he's ravishing with his mouth is gray-haired and about two feet taller than him.

Arielle looks away, feeling they need privacy, even if they don't seem to care. "Seems no one's immune from desire."

"Whether they like it or not," Reign mutters.

Arielle glances at him from the corner of her eye, wondering what he means, only to quickly look away. Reign has tipped his head back, resting it against the seat, and closed his eyes. The image is way too close to the one that was in her head a moment ago. His lips look as if they're arching up to be kissed. His eyes are closed in anticipation. And she could be the one to—

Reign frowns and opens his eyes. "So, I'm all for a good adrenalin rush, but do you know how to drive at high speeds?"

"What? Oh!" Arielle lifts her foot off the gas, blaming the heat in her cheeks on embarrassment.

She shakes her head. There are three words printed on her right boot, right beside the laces.

Get a grip.

"Sorry," she says. "I was just…thinking."

"What were you planning on strangling?" Reign asks jokingly.

The question has Arielle bursting into laughter. It bubbles up her throat, unfamiliar yet welcome, and fills the car with happy noise. Reign chuckles, caught up in the moment despite the quizzical look on his face.

"Anything you want to share?" he asks.

"Heck no," Arielle says quickly.

She has no idea where these sudden thoughts of Reign have come from, but now's not the time to explore them. For all she knows, he sees her like a friend just like Mac. From what she can tell, he's into gorgeously primped girls like Lizzie. Apart from ensuring she's wearing her boots, Arielle pays very little attention to what she's wearing, let alone applying makeup.

"I doubt it's anything I haven't heard bef—"

"And here we are," she says with extra brightness.

Reign's no doubt had girls tell him he's part of their fantasies. Possibly several guys, too. Anyone who's seen his face has probably had their pulse flutter. But Arielle's little brain glitch isn't one he needs to know about.

She pulls up to the curb and turns the car off. "So, we're going to have to do this off the books, so to speak."

"I'm pretty sure most things I've done shouldn't be recorded, so I'm in."

Arielle hops out and he follows. She pauses at the door. "Thanks for doing this with me, Reign."

He stills, not seeming to have expected her to have stopped. "Like I said, I'm with you, all the way."

Her gaze connects with his and her breath evaporates. The sculpted lines and delicious features fade into the periphery. All she can see is the sincerity in his jungle green eyes. The commitment to do this with her.

Does he realize how sexy that is?

His gaze dips down a split-second before he pulls back. If she wasn't so close, so intently captured by the moment, she wouldn't have seen it. But she did. It's as if Reign's as drawn to her as she is to him...

"Yeah, well, Cain has to be stopped."

"Of course," she murmurs as she turns away, wondering what in the world is happening to her. She glances at her right boot.

Get a grip.

She pushes open the door, intending on walking to the ancient index cards that Veritas still uses, hoping she can go through them before Nim turns up again. Each is sorted according to subject rather than in alphabetical order—angels, demons, vampires, fae, shifters. The Holy Grail is the section with the least amount of books.

But it's the witches category that they want today.

Arielle's taken three steps into the library when she stops, Reign having to halt himself in a hurry again.

"Maybe just—" Except Reign stops too, seeing what has Arielle unmoving.

Her mother is a few feet away, Blaise and Nim beside her.

And all three look unimpressed to see Arielle back here.

GABBY

Gabby's back tingles the moment her father arrives. How odd to think that she spent so long denying her true nature. Hating her wings. Wishing she was...normal.

But if she was just the average teen, she never would've met Colt.

Or her father.

And the Grigori would never have been defeated.

She turns as she senses him approach, letting the cool breeze of the beach brush her curls back from her face. She tucks her mother's pendant, ironically the one of an angel, beneath her top. This is always where she calls him. Where he meets her. He either loves the sea, or prefers to be away from humans.

Gabby suspects it's a bit of both.

"Daughter," he says warmly. "I was hoping you'd call me sooner rather than later."

She angles her head. "What are you really here for, father?" she asks flatly.

He draws in a slow breath, hopefully accustomed to her bluntness by now. Possibly realizing she inherited it from him.

"You're an archangel," she says in a low voice, conscious of the joggers several yards away. "You have people to do your running around for you." Even if it's her mother's Grace.

He nods in acknowledgement. "You're right. I'm not just here for that."

Although Gabby's not surprised, his words still sting. Will there always be these undertones and secret motives she won't be privy to?

Probably.

"I'm here to clean up the mess after a Gate of Hell was opened," her father says grimly. "Cain must be stopped."

"Ari said that, too," she breathes, realizing her cousin was right.

Her father snorts. "Humans are no match against Cain. I have my angels looking for him as we speak. Once we capture him, we'll imprison him."

"Imprison him?"

Her father's smile is slow and cold, a contrast to his angelic beauty. "He will be trapped in a world of our making."

Gabby suppresses a shudder. Few people know that angels are just as vengeful as demons.

She takes a step forward. "I want to help." They need to make this right.

She stops when her father shakes his head. "You have a life now, Gabrielle. That's what you should focus on, especially after the Grigori."

She shakes her own head so hard, her curls whip across her cheeks. "Ari is like a sister to me. I can't lose her, too." She clenches her hands. "I won't."

"I understand that, but—"

Another step and she's pressing her finger into his steely chest. "And I won't stop until Mom's Grace is restored to Heaven." She knows she's being pushy, possibly overstepping her bounds even though she's his daughter, but she doesn't care. If he says no, she'll just find a way to do this on her own. With Colt.

His lips twitch, his face softening in a way she's recently become familiar with. He's proud of her. He was hoping she'd respond like this.

Gabby steps back. He was testing her. He's always testing her. She pulls her shoulders back a little. And she's always passed, and with freaking flying colors.

"Very well, daughter." His gaze sharpens. "But you cannot involve your mortal or demon friends. This is strictly angel business."

Gabby instantly opens her mouth to object. She doesn't keep secrets from Colt. They've learned their strength is in being united. And Arielle's had so much kept from her, already.

But the lines on her father's face look like they've been carved from marble. He straightens to his full height, becoming every part the archangel he is. He won't be compromising on this. There will be no negotiating. She accepts it or not.

Unsure whether she's making the right decision, but doing it anyway, she nods. Once. Sharply.

"Okay. Tell me what I need to do."

CHAPTER 10

REIGN

Reign feels like he just walked into a battlefield.

He steps around Arielle and stays beside her, wondering how this showdown's going to go. Sierra, Blaise and Nim are Marvel. He and Arielle are DC.

Each with strengths of their own. Each fighting for what they believe in.

"What are you doing here, Ari?" Sierra asks.

Reign holds his breath, wondering if Arielle's going to hedge or—

"Cain is killing again. He needs to be stopped."

Or, she's going to throw a truth grenade into the space between them. He braces himself. When he said they should talk about it, this isn't exactly what he had in mind.

Sierra draws in a sharp breath as Blaise and Nim move a little closer together, as if they're planning on shielding the other.

"I told you that's too dangerous."

"Because I can't handle it?" Arielle demands. "Because I should be at home, letting everyone else deal with all this?"

Sierra shakes her head. "You don't know what you're up against—"

"Because you kept it from me!" Arielle shouts.

Her mother pulls back as if the words were a blow. "I'm trying to protect you!"

"Because you don't believe I can handle it!"

"I never said that, Ari!"

"You didn't need to!"

Mother and daughter step forward with each hurled accusation or defense. But now that they're only a couple of feet apart, Sierra deflates.

"I lost your father to this centuries-old search. Do you think I could stomach losing you, too?" By the time she's finished, she's almost whispering.

Reign's gut clenches. He can feel Sierra's pain from here. She lifts her hand, only to drop it again.

"You're my world, Arielle."

Arielle's shoulders tense, and Reign resists the urge to go to her. She has a decision to make. A tough one. Her mom loves her. She wants to keep her safe.

And yet Arielle wants to forge her own destiny. She has something to prove.

Reign gets that.

Arielle holds her mother's gaze. "I won't stop," she says softly. Firmly.

Although the motion is silent, Reign sees Sierra draw in a sharp breath. It's there in the way her mouth opens an inch, the way chest inflates on a jerk.

Seems Sierra now has a tough decision to make.

"Your daughter's as stubborn as you are, Sierra," Nim says quietly, possibly with a hint of admiration. "And she has your courage."

"Karma is a beautiful thing," Blaise murmurs. "Unless she's

being a bitch."

"And Arielle's not alone in this," Reign adds, speaking for the first time since they entered.

Arielle looks over her shoulder at him. Her lips flash a brief smile, but a smile nonetheless. This time there's not just gratitude, but a promise in her eyes. The realization that they're in this together.

The knowledge that he'll protect her with everything he has, even his life, slams through Reign, coming out of nowhere. It's so powerful, so primal, that it practically feels like a vow. He blinks, feeling a shift that's both subtle and seismic.

For some reason Joseph takes that moment to appear, hovering to the left of Arielle and her mother. Reign doesn't glance at him as he grits his teeth. He has enough revelations to deal with at the moment.

He has feelings for Arielle. Strong ones.

Crap.

Shit.

Double crap.

Sierra sighs. "Okay. I'll support you."

"What?" Arielle asks, jamming a whole lot of incredulity into that one word.

"You heard me," her mother says, smiling a little. "It's not like I can stop you." Her gaze sharpens. "But you don't take any unnecessary risks."

"Of course."

"And you need to get Mac and Colt on board. That way you'll have help. I'd include Gabby, but I know her focus is on finding Shell's Grace." She glances at Reign. "No offense."

"None taken." He wouldn't recommend anyone leave their loved ones in his incapable hands.

Plus, Colt and Mac are supernatural. They can do things he

never will—like fly and kick serious demon ass. That is, once Mac accepts her true nature.

Arielle pauses and Reign can see her chewing her lip. She's been given the green light, but with babysitters.

MAC

"We should've followed them," mutters Mac as she paces the living room of the cottage.

Colt puts down the book he was reading as he sits on the couch. "And if we were caught? What could Reign say to you?"

Mac's gaze slides away. "Well, it wouldn't be thanks."

"Exactly. And Arielle already feels undermined by her mother. In an ideal world, they'd come to us and ask for help."

She snorts. "Maybe they'll bring a mermaid with them."

"They rarely leave their underwater homes," Colt says, shaking his head as if she's not terribly bright.

Mac's mouth snaps closed. Mermaids are real?

Colt raises a brow. "We could train while we wait."

"No," she counters instantly. "And the answer won't change, no matter how many times you ask."

Colt grunts, obviously not liking her answer. Mac's about to swivel and resume her pacing when he throws the book at her.

Mac's hand reaches out and catches it before she's even realized she's done it, stopping it right in front of her face. "Hey! The book wasn't that bad."

Next comes a mug that Mac catches just as instinctively. Then a vase.

"Hey, you'll break something!" This is Sierra's place. Mac owes her too much to go trashing her guesthouse.

"See those reflexes, Mac? They're demon reflexes."

He picks up the small side table beside the couch and hurls it like a frisbee. Mac catches it and sets it down with more anger than she intended. "Stop it. I know what you're trying to do and it won't work."

Colt takes two steps and lifts the recliner as if it's a beach chair.

"Put that down!" Mac shouts.

"You're right," he says, returning it to its spot on the carpet. "I need to step it up."

Step what up?

But before Mac can ask, Colt is moving. Straight toward her. Holy shit, with his wings extended!

His eyes flash a deep crimson as his lips twist in a grin, as if he's looking forward to this.

Just like the hurled objects, Mac doesn't have time to think. All she knows is she's being attacked.

The same sensation from the crypt sears down her back. There's the feeling of something bursting free, of power rushing through her. Of being strong in a way she's only ever imagined.

Colt stops in front of her. "Hello, Mac."

She goes to say something, but then catches a glimpse of herself in the mirror on the opposite wall. Her own red eyes blink back at her. And a massive set of black wings are stretched out behind her. She looks terrifying.

And yet, kinda awesome.

She shakes her head, turning away from the reflection. "I'm not evil," she says through clenched teeth.

She's spent her whole life trying to prove she's not inherently bad.

Colt shakes his head. "Any power can be used for evil, whether it's demonic or angelic. It's the intent that makes it evil."

Mac mulls this over, unsure if she totally believes it. "I never wanted this."

"It's not a curse, Mac. It's a responsibility, one that has its challenges. But it's also an opportunity."

"To what?" Mac half-shouts, her arms flying out. "To be more of a freak? To be even more different? To carry a truth I wish didn't exist?"

Colt's mouth shuts and his lips thin. He looks as if he's considering his words. Or he's wondering whether he'll be able to convince her that being a demon is a good thing.

Mac jams her hand on her hip and juts it out.

He won't.

"Look, Mac—"

The front door bursts open and slams against the wall. Mac's heart surges into her throat as four large men pour in, their faces hard and resolute.

One by one, powerful white wings unfurl from their back.

Colt jumps in front of Mac. "I gave you an angel warding spell!"

"I didn't finish it."

She really should've finished it...

There's no time to think, let alone regret, because the angels leap, covering the distance between them. Before Mac's realized what's happening, Colt jumps too, meeting the first one midair.

The two powerful bodies clash, black wings colliding with white. Colt slams his fists into the angel's chest over and over, ignoring the blows raining down on him. But a second angel joins in, driving his shoulder into Colt's side.

He grunts, the only sign it hurt, except a third angel comes from the other side, his elbow slamming into Colt's jaw.

"Stop!" Mac screams.

The first angel grabs Colt and spins, throwing him against

the wall. Colt hits it with a *thud* and a *crack*, his wings flaring and flexing before he crumples to the ground.

Colt! Sierra's house!

The first angel straightens. "We're not here to kill you." His lips twist. "Well, not this time."

The second steps to the side, flanking his friend. "Although there will come a time when you have to leave your human vessels and go back to Hell, where you belong."

"If you are foolish enough to stay, we will ensure you are extinguished," says the third, moving to the left. He smiles and it's one of the coldest things Mac's ever seen. "Permanently."

The fourth remains at the back, his face impassive even as his eyes glow silver.

Colt leaps to his feet, his eyes flaring bright red. "Unless we finish you first."

But the angels work in unison again. One spins, his wing arcing out to strike Colt. The second lifts into the air, his foot a missile for Colt's chest. The third picks up the end table Mac only just sat down a few minutes ago, ready to smash it over Colt's head.

And the fourth ducks and runs.

Straight at Mac.

She expands her wings, ready to use every ounce of the power she has yet to harness. But the angel changes direction at the last second, tucking his wings close to his body he executes a graceful twist. He sails over Mac, reaching down with one hand.

His fingers brush her forehead, the touch gentle. Almost a caress.

Her legs give out. Her body turns to lead.

And everything goes black.

KEEPER

SIERRA

"You just let her go?" Blaise asks, and Sierra's not sure if she's impressed or incredulous.

She takes a few steps back as she lets out a breath. She's never really argued with Arielle. And never like that.

But then again, the supernatural has infiltrated their lives. She should've known it was inevitable.

Sierra spears her hands into her hair. "I didn't really have a choice, did I?"

Blaise nods. "True. She was going to do this, anyway."

"Like I said, stubborn like her mom," says Nim.

"And Ari's right," Sierra says on a sigh. "I have to believe in her."

Arielle's strong. Smart. Special.

And all Sierra has in the world.

Her gaze settles on Blaise. "I want you to track her. To make sure nothing happens to her."

"I thought you were going to trust her," Blaise points out.

"I do. It's the forces we're up against that I don't trust." The very same forces that Sierra shielded Arielle from, meaning she's not prepared for what she's undertaking. Sierra's chest constricts. "I just want to make sure she's okay."

Blaise nods, her face softening with understanding. "I'll go cast a tracking spell now."

With a quick kiss on Nim's head, she leaves. Sierra walks to the nearest chair and flops on its velvet seat. Her head suddenly feels too heavy for her neck, so she lets it hang down, her hair curtaining her face. She has shopping to do. A house to clean. Meals to cook. But she doesn't move.

She wants to cry.

She wants to scream.

She wants to go get her daughter and run away from all this.

Nim's feet resting on the footrests of her wheelchair appear at the edge of her vision. "I'm here if you need me."

Sierra looks at her, grateful for the support. Nim and Blaise and Shell were her family once her mother passed away. They were Ari's extended family.

Sierra straightens as a thought occurs to her. "Arielle wanted the Seeker to find Cain, didn't she?"

"I'd say so." She frowns. "I told her how dangerous it is. Each time it's used, it drains the person, creating an opening for dark magic to infiltrate."

Nim's words make Sierra feel sick. "We need to make sure she doesn't find it, then."

Nim's face turns thoughtful, almost unconvinced, which Sierra didn't expect. Her hands move to the wheels of her chair, like she's bracing herself.

Or ready to shoot out of here.

"I've been getting a sense from the Other Side," she says slowly. "Whispers. The spirits are warning against interfering with Arielle's destiny."

Sierra shoots to her feet. "What? I'm not going to sit back and wait to see what happens."

"I know. She's your daughter and you love her. I'm just saying...Arielle's destiny must run its course."

Denial is like a white hot flare. Ryder's destiny was to not see his daughter grow up. For them to have little more than a few weeks together. For their love to never explore the depths they barely tasted.

"You were around the same age when you discovered the

supernatural," Nim points out. "And the supernatural gave you your daughter."

Sierra frowns, unable to separate the circular logic. Magic took so much from her. And yet it gave her Arielle. She spins on her heel, striding for the door. Ryder may have been taken from her, but Arielle won't be. She'll make sure of it.

"I'll do everything I can to stop the Seeker from falling into my daughter's hands," she calls over her shoulder as she steps through.

The door is just closing when Nim's words reach her, soft, but with the impact of a wrecking ball.

"You can try."

CHAPTER II
ARIELLE

"Y ou sure you're okay?" Reign asks as they walk toward the guesthouse. "That was quite the fireworks there back at Veritas."

Arielle shrugs. "I think so," she says thoughtfully. "I mean, Mom said she's going to trust me, so that's something."

He pauses with his hand on the door. "You really stood up for yourself there. Good on you."

A pleasant warmth expands in her chest at the compliment. Reign is one of the strongest people she knows—he's practically fearless—so it means a lot.

But before she can say anything, brilliant white flashes within the guesthouse, blasting from the windows and framing the door.

"What the hell!" Reign shouts.

He covers the last few feet to the door, yanks it open and runs in, Arielle right behind him. They stop just inside and she gasps.

The living room is chaotic. There's a hole in the wall to their right. Furniture is overturned like there's been a fight.

And Colt is kneeling over an inert form.

"No! Mac!" Reign cries, running forward.

Colt moves back as Reign falls to his knees. Mac's lying on her side, her eyes closed and her face lax.

He grasps her by the shoulders. "Mac! Can you hear me? Please, wake up!"

Arielle moves toward them, feeling like this whole moment is surreal. There's no blood on Mac, no obvious injury. And yet, she flops in Reign's arms like she's lifeless. Arielle claps her hand over her mouth. Surely she's not—

"It was angels," Colt says gravely. "Four of them. We tried to fight them off."

Reign scoops Mac into his arms. "What have they done to her?"

Colt's shoulders drop. "They said they didn't intend on killing us. Just that they were putting her to sleep."

Reign stands, bringing Mac with him. "Mac, please wake up."

But she's a rag doll in his arms, her head and arms flopping down like they're barely connected. He takes her to the couch and lays her down. Her chest rises slowly and evenly, the only sign she's alive. "What...what do we do?"

Arielle's chest aches at the lost note in his voice. She looks to Colt. "Why would the angels attack her? Why now?"

He shakes his head. "Their schemes are beyond me."

"Bastards," Reign growls. "Mac's not a danger to them."

Arielle pulls her cell phone out of her pocket. "I'm going to call Gabby." She's an angel, if she doesn't know what's going on, surely she can find out.

But Colt leaps forward, his hand extended to stop her. "No. Gabby's trying to find her mother's Grace with the help of her father. She'd be furious to learn angels attacked Mac. It could sabotage her quest for justice."

Arielle's hand tightens around her phone. Dammit, Colt's

right. Finding her mother's Grace is important to Gabby. They can't get in the way of that. She tucks it back in her pocket, feeling helpless again.

Colt walks past her and stands beside Reign. "Let me try. I'll see if I can sense any spells."

Reign nods, but looks like it hurts him to move away from Mac. Colt kneels down, looking pointedly at him. "I'll need a little room."

Grimacing, Reign stands.

"Mac's a fighter," she tells him as she moves closer. She's about to say she'll get through this but she stops. Reign doesn't need empty promises. Nor does he respect them. "And she has you."

"Damn straight she does," he growls.

"Well, I certainly find the two of you intimidating," she says, nudging him with her elbow. "You two are one heck of a team."

Their bond is so close, it makes Arielle envious. Sometimes, almost a little jealous...

Reign looks a little surprised, but before he can respond, Colt stands.

"The angels seem to have trapped her mind within her," he says pensively. "And the only way to reach her is for a consciousness to connect with hers."

"So how do we do that?" Reign asks, his voice a poignant mix of desperation and determination.

"I tried," Colt replies heavily. "But there's a...wall. A powerful one that I couldn't get past."

"A wall?" Arielle echoes. "What does that mean?"

"It means whatever consciousness they've trapped her in, they don't want anyone getting in. It's like Mac's mind is surrounded by a supernatural fortress."

Reign strides back to Mac, sitting on the edge of the couch

and picking up her hand. "Then how do we bust that fucker down?"

Arielle's phone is already out of her pocket. "I'll call mom. Surely Blaise can get past it."

BLAISE ARRIVES MUCH QUICKER than Arielle expected, but she puts it down to the worry in her mom's voice when she told her what happened to Mac. Plus, she's relieved.

Mac's chest is barely moving, as if it could stop any moment.

Reign looks like he's about to tear every hair in his head out. Vomit. Punch a wall. Then take on every angel in existence.

Blaise's long hair is all white, along with her flowing dress, making her look like a bride of the spirit world. Arielle blinks as she stands in the doorway, adjusting to the change. Blaise tends to stick to her black and white coloring or purple.

"I was working on a protection spell," she explains when she notes Arielle's surprise. She glances over her shoulder. "Seems fated, now."

She enters, and Arielle breathes in the familiar scent of incense. It calms her a little. Blaise is a powerful witch. Possibly *the* most powerful witch. If anyone can get through this block, it's her.

Blaise's gaze falls on Mac, unconscious on the couch, and she approaches her carefully. She frowns. "This is powerful angelic magic."

Arielle follows her, noting the way Reign scowls at Blaise's words. "But you're more powerful, right?"

The thought that Mac will lie here, motionless like this indefinitely isn't one she wants to entertain.

Blaise doesn't answer, instead kneeling beside Mac. "I'll need a moment."

"Take all the time you need," Reign says in a low voice. The strain in his face tells everyone in the room he'll do whatever it takes to get Mac back.

It's an intensity that seems to spear straight through Arielle. Reign obviously loves with everything he has.

Blaise raises her hands, hovering them just above Mac's body. She closes her eyes, her face developing a calm, serene expression. Her hands move up, drifting to Mac's head, then move around in slow circles. She draws in a deep breath, looking like she's fortifying herself.

Reign leans forward, as if he wants to get closer but doesn't want to move. Arielle almost goes to him, wanting to give him a hand to grip. To somehow share the tension that's thrumming through his taught body.

Blaise's eyebrows twitch and her hands stop. Her shoulders tense, and then she's cupping Mac's face, her fingertips resting on her temples. Blaise drops her head, the serene expression gone.

She looks like she's digging deep. Working hard.

Arielle holds her breath. Surely that has to be a good thing. It means she's breaking through the wall holding Mac's mind captive.

Blaise sags, her hands falling to her sides as she breathes heavily.

"Did you get through it?" Reign asks desperately. He falls to his knees beside her. "Mac? Wake up."

But Mac doesn't move. She remains the living shell she is.

Blaise looks at Reign. "I couldn't get past. It's far stronger than I could've imagined."

"No," Reign snaps. "I won't believe we can't reach her."

"We have two options," Blaise says heavily. "Either we do nothing and hope Mac finds a way to break herself out."

Reign's already shaking his head. "Not going to happen. What's plan B?"

Blaise stands, her gaze moving from Reign to Colt then Arielle. "We find a way to break through the wall."

Arielle suppresses a frown. Isn't that what Colt and Blaise just tried to do?

"Damn fine idea," says Reign. "Where do we find the wrecking ball?"

Blaise sighs. "I'll have to do some research." She glances at Mac then back to Reign. "I'll do everything in my power to bring her back."

Reign nods. "Thanks. That makes two of us."

Blaise grasps his shoulder and gives it a squeeze. "I'll call when I know something."

Blaise heads to the door. Not waiting to see her out, Reign scoops Mac up. "I'm going to take her to her room. Make sure she's comfortable."

Arielle watches, Blaise standing at the door and Colt remaining where he is with his arms crossed, as Reign carries his best friend close to his chest. His jaw twitches as his throat works.

As he disappears down the hall, Blaise and Colt exchange a glance.

Arielle waits until Reign has disappeared into Mac's room. "What?" she hisses. "What was that look?"

Colt's face shutters, telling her he has no intention of answering that question. But she knows something's up. That glance said they both know something. And it ain't good.

Arielle turns to Blaise. "What? What didn't you tell Reign?"

Blaise's shoulders slump a second before she jerks them back upright, as if she's injecting determination down her spine. "I didn't tell him because I don't intend for it to be an issue."

"For what to be an issue?" Arielle asks, her stomach clenched tight.

"The longer Mac spends trapped in her own mind, the harder it is for her to escape."

"But that means—"

Colt crosses his arms even tighter. "It means if we don't get her out soon, she'll die."

GABBY

Gabby's father tucks his hand behind his back, his blue gaze intense as the beach breeze plays with his golden locks. "All you need is something of your mother's to track her Grace."

That's it? It's that simple?

Gabby tugs her mother's necklace from beneath her top. "Something like this?"

Her father blinks. "Yes," he says softly. "That will suffice."

Grief drags at Gabby's heart at her father's tone, but she pushes it away for now. Like she told Colt, there will be time to free the millions of tears that are progressively accumulating within her when her mother's Grace is home.

Turning her face to the sea, she draws in a deep breath of salty air and closes her eyes.

She sees her mother's cherished face. Gabby focuses a little deeper and her mom's familiar qualities are there—generosity, kindness, the tendency to be a worrier. And then there's her soul, a gleaming, pulsing energy every human has at their center.

But it's the next level beyond that Gabby's seeking. The angelic essence that no one knew she carried will be tucked within it, a core of pure power from Heaven.

Except Gabby finds...nothing. She draws in a sharp breath when she realizes there's something—a barrier of some sort. A pitch black crust that's encased the Grace like a fist.

Frowning, Gabby tries to get past it, only to be repelled back. Her eyebrows sinking even lower, she focuses harder. But the blackness only seems to contract more, tightening defensively.

She opens her eyes, turning to her father. "Something's stopping me," she says, her own soul aching. "I can't get past it."

A muscle in her father's jaw twitches. "Cain has put a cloak on it."

"He can do that?" she asks, realizing the talk of Cain being powerful has been more true than she realized.

"Cain was not only the first murderer, but he was also the first living being to be turned into a demon."

Gabby's eyes widen. "Making him the oldest demon in existence." She shakes her head, confused. "But demons are the spawn of Lucifer and Lilith. Cain is the eldest son of Adam and Eve."

"Yes, but Cain murdered his own brother," her father says. "As a punishment, Lucifer put the Mark on him, now known as the Mark of Cain. It turned him into a demon, rather than being born into it." His face hardens. "As far as I know, he's the only one of his kind."

Gabby's hand clutches her mother's pendant. "Why is he doing all this?"

Her father shrugs. "The Mark made him immortal, I suspect that curse is wearing thin." His lip curls. "Although why anyone would choose to be human, is beyond me."

Gabby ignores the jibe, as much as she wants to point out that he thought she was half-human for most of her life. "And he wants Mom's Grace to destroy another Gate of Hell. To find the next Innocent and kill them."

Her father nods, but his face tells her that's not all. "As you know, Grace is nothing but divine or celestial energy. It's very powerful. It could be used to do a great many things."

The ominous words have Gabby's chest constricting. The damage Cain could do is almost limitless. It's not just her loved ones at risk and the Innocent, but everyone's on Earth.

"But Cain disappeared after the last fight," Gabby points out. "He could be anywhere."

Her father shakes his head grimly. "I suspect he's not far away. He's planning something. I know it."

Gabby's hands clench. "The others need to know about this. We could work together to find him."

Except her father's already shaking his head, his face turning thunderous. "We will not involve humans and demons in matters of angelic importance. You are the only one I can trust."

Gabby goes to argue. Cain's actions affect humans and demons just as much as the angels. But she knows the truce she reached with her father, the fledgling relationship they've only just forged, is too fragile.

She needs him to trust her or her one link to her angelic ancestry is gone.

"Okay, I'll do this," she says, holding his gaze.

He nods, that flare of pride back in his eyes. "Excellent." He turns away, ready to return to his place in Heaven. "If you find Cain, the angels under my command will do the rest. They'll retrieve Shell's Grace."

Gabby nods, knowing he's about to stop time for the briefest of seconds. Just long enough for him to disappear.

Anyone who may have noticed her talking to a man will blink, maybe rub their eyes, then tell themselves they need to lay off the caffeine or sugar or get more sleep.

According to angels, those few moments of confusion are a small price humans pay to have angels among them.

Gabby frowns. She'll do as her father asks, because she has little choice. She has no doubt her father loved her mother.

But she's not going to forget that her father is an archangel.

That his loyalties lie with Heaven first.

CHAPTER 12
REIGN

"Look, if this is about the time I swapped your happy herbs with chopped parsley, I'm sorry, okay?" says Reign past the lump in his throat. He has to consciously loosen his hand around Mac's, as if he's physically trying to pull her out of this coma.

Except she doesn't move. It's been hours and she hasn't moved.

"Plus, you've got to admit. It was pretty funny watching Rico as he thought he'd smoked the real thing."

Mac's chest continues its slow rhythm. Up. Down. Up. Down. Nothing else twitches.

"Come on, Mac," he pleads. "You'd prefer to do makeup than sleep."

When the silence gets too much, Reign stands, tucking the blankets around her a little tighter. Then fluffing the pillow her head rests on. Then he tugs on the sheets to make sure there are no wrinkles.

"We're going to need some tunes or something," he mutters. "And if you keep this up, I'll resort to playing country music."

There's a soft knock on the open door. "I could offer to sing, but I think even country is preferable to that," says Arielle.

Reign straightens. "Hey, what are you doing here?"

She lifts the bag he didn't notice she was holding. "I made some dinner. Thought you might be hungry and figured you won't be leaving Mac's side."

He stills, not sure how to take that. She's right on both fronts, but he hadn't expected her to be so...considerate. "Ah, thanks."

She flushes. "It's no big deal. I just made some pasta, salad, and garlic bread."

"Is that all?" he asks dryly. He's never made any of those, let alone all at once.

Arielle takes a cautious step in. "Any movement?"

He shakes his head heavily. "I tried the blink once for yes, and twice for no but it seems she's not ready to talk."

Arielle nods, not looking too surprised, before sitting cross legged on the floor beside the bed. "Does she like lasagna or garlic bread? Maybe the smell will wake her."

"Actually, Mac's two primary food groups are carbs and books."

Arielle smiles. "I knew there was a reason I liked her." She pats the space in front of her. "Why don't you pull up a piece of carpet and we'll remind her what she's missing out on?"

Reign sinks down, sitting across from Arielle. He watches as she focuses on pulling out several takeaway tubs, each holding something different. The soft light in the bedroom curves over her lashes, strokes her cheek, caresses her lips. It's a beauty that starts deep in her soul.

He clears his throat. "Thanks for, ah, making all this."

She shrugs as her gaze falls away, her cheeks pinking again. "This is what friends do."

Friends. Why does that word have his heart smiling and frowning all at the same time?

Arielle pulls a lid off what must be lasagna and passes it to him, along with a knife and fork. "Here. It was Aunt Shell's recipe." Her lips tip up. "It wasn't until I made it a few years ago that I discovered how it tastes unburned."

Reign shakes his head, sitting it on the floor so he can cut it up. "I'd take a burned home cooked meal over most of my dinners any day."

Arielle's fork pauses on the way to her mouth and he realizes he just let slip the reality of living on the streets. He glances up, tensing himself for the pity he'll see on her face. He hates it, but for some reason, he knows pity coming from Ari will sting even more.

But she's looking at him, her head angled. "So you've never smelled burned broccoli?"

He blinks. "No one should do that to broccoli."

She bites her lip as she suppresses a smile, returning the fork to hover before her mouth. "You have no idea what I've had to endure."

Arielle's making light of everything he's experienced growing up. Saying her blissful childhood could compare to his. Like she knew that's exactly what he needed her to do. Something warm and sparkly bubbles up through his chest. It tumbles out of his mouth, and Reign finds himself laughing, the sound loud and yet so light it seems to float straight to the ceiling.

Her fork dips as her own giggles almost have the slice of lasagna slipping off. Arielle's eyes widen and she quickly scoops it into her mouth before it lands on the carpet. Red sauce splatters over the edge of her lip.

Chuckling, Reign reaches over and brushes it away with his thumb. Before he's realized what he's done, he sticks it in his mouth and licks it off. The laughter instantly dies and something else enters the room. Something a whole lot warmer. And decidedly heavier.

Awareness.

No. Desire.

The flame blue of Arielle's eyes kindle in a way he's glimpsed and always craved more of. His gaze dips to her mouth, and his thumb burns. He just brushed those lips. And he wants to do it again. Take the time to feel their plumpness, their softness.

To taste them.

His breath hitches when her tongue flicks out to moisten her bottom lip. Almost as if she's tasting the place he touched. Tasting him. The reaction in Reign's body is instantaneous. His pulse skyrockets. His blood heats. His urge to kiss Arielle becomes a burning need.

He jerks back, shocked at the intensity. Shit. What is he doing? His best friend is lying in a coma right next to him, and here he is, considering pouncing on Arielle. Could he be any more of a douche?

He glances around and sees some napkins in the bottom of the bag Arielle brought. He pulls one out. "Here."

Arielle takes it, and he tenses as her fingers brush his. How can so much heat be contained in one touch? "Thanks," she says in a husky voice.

Reign resists looking at her, even though the raw edges of that one word seem to tug at something deep within his gut. Instead, he picks up his lasagna, scoops up a piece and shovels it in his mouth. "Wow, it's really good!" he says loudly, glancing at Mac.

"Family recipe," Arielle chimes in, her gaze focused on her food.

As he chews, he almost wishes he hadn't made the joke. The

lasagna is delicious, but Arielle won't believe him, now. She'll think any compliments he makes are for Mac's benefit.

Arielle clears her throat, her gaze on Mac, too. "I bet you two got up to a lot of mischief."

"Mischief is one word you could use," he says, glad for the change of topic. "Most of it wasn't terribly legal."

"Stuff like that act you put on at Sinclair Mansion? The one where Mac pretended she had an upset stomach?"

Reign isn't sure where this line of questioning is going, so he decides to be honest. This is a good time for her to remember he's nothing but a street rat. "It's our go-to. We tell restaurants the public restrooms are all full. We managed to snaffle an entire rotisserie chicken from a place called Chook Nook once."

Ari pokes at her lasagna. "Do you always pretend you're boyfriend and girlfriend?"

That has Reign stilling. That's the part she's going to focus on? "It's an assumption that people kept jumping to, probably because we're so close. At first, we didn't bother correcting them. Then, we just went with it."

"And because you've been that in the past?"

Reign barks out a laugh. Except, despite Arielle's casual pose, her gaze is focused. Her fork is no longer poking the lasagna.

Shit. This answer matters.

Except this has gone too far. Helping Arielle find Cain is the right thing to do. But letting her think that he's anything more than a short-term guy is wrong.

He shakes his head. "We've never been more than damned good friends. Plus, even if Mac felt anything more than BFF or sister status, she's smarter than that." Arielle blinks at his harsh words, but Reign ignores the stabbing feeling in his gut. "If she was awake, she'd tell you—I'm not boyfriend material."

MAC

Mac rubs her forehead as she enters Mercy City University library, not entirely sure why she's here. She looks over her shoulder as the automatic doors slide closed, wondering where she just came from. In fact, she can't seem to remember much of anything at the moment. "Hello, Mackenzie." Mac spins around to see the librarian smiling at her from behind the counter. "Did you get that essay on the Human Rights Act done in time?"

"Ah, yeah," she says, wondering if she's being pranked.

Quickly walking past so she doesn't have to answer any more weird-ass questions, Mac makes her way to the back of the library. That's where all the couches are, the place she likes to curl up and read.

She frowns. That library looks like it always has. She's visited it countless times before. And yet, she sure as heck has never written an essay, let alone one on the Human Rights Act.

What the flippety-flock is going on?

The couches are ahead, dark blue with purple cushions, and she sees there's already someone on them. Someone she recognizes!

The sense that all is right in her world soothes her, blanketing the tension that was climbing up her nerves. Reign is looking at something on his left, grinning widely, meaning he hasn't seen her.

Before Mac can take another step, a blonde leaps onto his lap. "I missed you!"

Reign chuckles. "It's been thirty seconds."

Mac pauses, knowing the blonde is also someone she knows, but not quite placing her. She draws in a startled breath as she realizes who it is.

Lizzie arches like a cat on heat, pressing ravenous kisses to Reign's mouth. "Longest thirty seconds ever," she murmurs.

A queasy feeling climbs up Mac's throat and she clears it. Reign and Lizzie don't seem to hear it, so she does it again, louder.

Lizzie peels back, a satisfied smile already curving up her face. "Sorry, Mrs.— Oh, it's you, Mac." She loosens her lean limbs, curving into Reign. "I thought the cranky librarian was back."

Mac ignores her, glaring at Reign. "What are you doing?"

He grins like the Cheshire cat. One who's about to get laid. In a library. "You're the one studying law. I'm just here for the...atmosphere."

Lizzie giggles with her hand over her mouth and the sound grates over Mac's frayed nerves. "You're not with her," she grinds through clenched teeth, pointing a finger at the thin girl. She can't remember why this feels so wrong, only that it does.

Lizzie rolls her eyes. "You're the one who introduced us, Mac. In fact, you hooked us up on a blind date."

Mac's arm drops to her side. "I what?"

Reign shakes his head, the amused affection he's regarded her with so many times before sparkling in his green eyes. "Maybe that sci-fi book you've been reading on parallel universes has messed with your head."

Mac frowns. How does so much of this feel familiar, and so much of it doesn't make sense? She rubs her forehead again. "I think I have a headache."

"You did pull an all-nighter getting that essay in," says Reign. "Why don't you go home and get your mom to make you one of those herbal teas you like so much?"

Taking a quick step back, Mac bumps into a bookshelf. The impact sends a jolt through her, telling her this is all very real. "Actually, I think that's a good idea."

Lizzie uncurls, an arm slinking around Reign's shoulder. "You do that. I'll keep Reign busy."

Mac spins on her heel, not wanting to see their lips lock. The sight makes her ill, and yet apparently she was the one who introduced them.

Outside the library, she draws in a deep breath. Reign's right. She must've overdone it. Snapped something in her brain. She'll go home and rest.

But as she sets off, her body seeming to know where to go, she realizes she can't seem to remember what home looks like. Or her parents. In fact, she's not even sure she likes herbal tea.

"Come back, Mac."

Mac spins around at the sound of the familiar voice. It wasn't Reign, or even Lizzie, but she's sure she's heard it before. Except there's no one there. The pavement is empty, the dappled shade of the trees beside it the only thing touching the gray cement.

Who the hell's talking to her?

And come back to what?

SIERRA

Sierra raps her fingers on the wooden surface of her desk, staring out the dark window. Arielle brought the food to Reign almost an hour ago and she hasn't been back. It's good that they're friends...

Sighing, Sierra leans back. The open book stares at her, the words she's read over and over again unable to give her the answers she needs.

Mac is trapped within her own mind. Locked in there by angels. Her heart aches for the girl. It seems others knew she was special, too.

Sierra thinks back to the day she ran into Mac at the library.

The curly-haired, caramel-skinned girl had absorbed knowledge like a dry sponge, except she'd never reached saturation point. Sierra had discovered this when she invited her back the following week, and all the times after that. She'd recognized Mac's potential. Her thirst for information, her curiosity about the fantastical. She knew Mac could be the first in the next generation of Archivists.

She'd made Mac promise their meetings were a secret early on. The girl had shrugged, saying there was no one in her life to tell. It turns out she didn't even tell her best friend. Reign.

Sierra wipes her hands down her face. She has to talk to Reign. Tell him the truth, every glorious, painful part of it. He was the Grail Keeper they saved all those years ago. He was also the orphaned baby she sent with David and Mikki…who somehow ended up in the foster care system.

Guilt coils and tightens around her ribs. She failed him. Just like she did Arielle.

It's how to make this right that she needs to figure out. The first thing she needs to do is talk to Mikki so she can fill in the gaps. As for Arielle… She's about to push to her feet when Nim's words slide through her mind.

The spirits are warning against interfering with Arielle's destiny.

The words are ominous. They feel like a prophecy.

And they make every maternal instinct in Sierra's heart quiver and tighten. She won't lose her daughter to this, she vows. She won't.

The backdoor opens, and she hears Arielle enter the kitchen. Sierra stands, about to walk over only to find her daughter already exiting.

"Hey," she says warmly. "How was dinner?"

Arielle's face tightens briefly. The movement is so fleeting that Sierra doubts anyone but her mother would've noticed.

Her daughter smiles. "Great. It's a great recipe. Everything was great."

Sierra doesn't point out the triple use of one word...which suggests it wasn't so 'great.' "Is everything okay?"

Arielle yanks up a blinding smile before she turns and runs up the stairs to her room. "It's fine," she calls over her shoulder. "I was just helping a friend."

Although the assurance is said lightly, Sierra pauses. Why did it feel like her daughter just spat the last word out?

CHAPTER 13
ARIELLE

When Arielle arrives back at the guesthouse the
following morning, she's done a lot of thinking.
She's attracted to Reign.

Reign's attracted to her.

And yet he's making sure she knows he's not boyfriend
material.

Now, she has to decide what to do with that. She'd bet her
boots that she has far less experience in the casual hookup
department than he does. In part because Reign obviously
resists forming connections, and he would totally have girls
throwing themselves at his hot, brooding self. But mostly
because she never has.

The truth is, she's never wanted to. She only commits if she
knows there's a connection that has the potential to last. She
feels things too strongly to be able to do anything but that.

Which leaves her at an impasse. It means that no matter
how bright and hot whatever's sparked between her and Reign
burns, he'll walk away. They'll never know if it would've
snuffed itself out, or continued to simmer...

Arielle pauses with her hand on the doorknob, a burst of frustration making her huff.

She wants to see exactly how hot and how bright. She's starting to imagine what it would look like. Dream of it.

But she also knows her heart wouldn't stay separate. It doesn't have walls protecting it. And the last thing she needs right now is more heartache.

Not after losing Shell.

Not with Mac in a coma that has a timer.

Not with Cain on the loose and another Innocent's life at risk.

Arielle pushes open the door, her resolve strengthened. She and Reign are staying firmly in the friend zone. It's the best thing for everyone.

Except the first thing she sees as she enters is him. Blaise and Colt are there at the table, too, but she barely registers them. He's leaning over a large book, a thick lock of black hair caressing the frown on his forehead. He looks up and their gazes connect.

And the way Arielle's heart trips. The way heat curls low in her belly. The way she likes how his eyes widen imperceptibly. None of those say friendship.

Dammit.

She drags her gaze away, noting the stacks of books on the table. "No change?"

"No," says Reign tightly. "She's doing a damned good impersonation of Sleeping Beauty."

Blaise sighs. Today her hair is a golden yellow, as is her dress. "It's a very powerful spell that they've used. Our best bet is to channel an angel." She glances at Colt. "And Gabby's an angel."

"No," says Colt flatly and Arielle suspects this is a conversation they've already had. "We're not involving Gabby."

Blaise sighs again, not looking surprised, but also not bothering to argue. "Then we need to keep reading. These books were cleaned out from the crypt at Sinclair Mansion. We haven't had a chance to look at them too closely."

Arielle walks over and lifts one of the heavy tomes off the pile. "Research it is."

Reign does the same, taking the next one down. "I'll read while sitting in Mac's room," he says, already heading to the hallway. He slips into the room without a backward glance.

Colt watches him, frowning. "I get the feeling he won't be leaving the house until Mac wakes up."

He glances at Blaise and she quickly looks away. Arielle suspects they both thought the same thing.

If Mac wakes up.

Arielle pulls her book to her chest. "I'll go read with him."

She ignores the next glance that passes between the two as she walks past. This is what a friend would do. Nothing more, nothing less.

She enters Mac's room, seeing that just like Reign said, Mac hasn't moved. He's sitting on the floor beside the bed, the book already open on his lap. He looks surprised to see her. "Hey."

"Hey," she says softly, sitting on the floor, too. Even after promising to help her, he's surprised that she's here, helping him. "I just want you to know, I'll do whatever I can to help get Mac back."

His lips part, a soft breath huffing past, before he quickly pulls himself upright. "You don't have to do that. You want to find Cain."

Arielle shakes her head. "This is important." Reign's important. So is Mac. She lifts her hand as he tries to speak. "And I want to."

Reign studies her. "Why, Ari?"

She blinks at the blunt question. There's an intensity in his green eyes that tells her this answer counts. She wraps her earlier decision around her like a cloak. "Because we're friends." She shrugs a shoulder, struggling to hold his gaze. "You did the same for me. Was that just as friends?"

It's his turn for his lashes to flutter, the thick black seeming to be the only thing that moves on his face. "Yep, that's why I did it," he says after a long second.

Arielle pulls up a bright smile. "Great. It's settled then."

Friends.

It's the best thing for everyone.

Arielle opens the book she brought in, and immerses herself. She's got the outcome she wanted. She should be happy.

And yet the smile she dialed up falls faster than she'd like. In fact, it feels like a frown would be far more comfortable right now.

Shaking off the unwelcome feelings, Arielle focuses on the carefully printed words before her. From the corner of her eye, she sees Reign do the same.

Yep. Friends researching together. Focusing on Mac. Just the way it should be.

Arielle frowns when a word catches her eye. "Hey, look at this."

Reign's by her side in an instant. "What? What is it?"

"According to this Mac's consciousness has been trapped within her subconscious. And this spell has been used before."

His eyes widen as his gaze follows the same line. "On Shakespeare."

"Surely not..." Arielle breathes as she continues reading. "The angels trapped him within his subconscious, allowing him to find the ideas for his plays. There's nothing about what he discovered, just that the archangel Uriel woke him and afterward is when Shakespeare gained popularity."

Reign sits back, stunned. "His subconscious came up with the tragic love story of Romeo and Juliet? That guy needed to see a shrink."

Arielle shakes her head in amusement. "He kinda did."

"Do they say how the spell can be broken?" he asks, his face once again turning serious.

Arielle keeps reading, but there's nothing. The book moves onto other angelic spells, and a quick skim shows there's little that can be done about those, too. "No," she says heavily.

Reign sits back with a frustrated sigh.

Arielle frowns. "But the spell *was* broken. By an angel."

"Colt said we can't involve Gabby, and he's probably right. She needs to focus on getting her mother's Grace."

"Although, we do actually know another angel," Arielle says slowly. "In fact, this one is a captive audience."

Reign's eyes widen a second time. "You mean Dumah?"

She shrugs. "Well, he *is* an angel, which means he could have the answers we need."

"Arielle Hartley, I can't believe you just suggested that."

She lifts her chin. The old Arielle never would have. She played strictly by the rules. But look what happened when she did that... "I would've done this to save Shell."

His face hardens as his green eyes blaze. "I'll fight for Mac with everything I have."

The intensity of Reign's words have her breath catching. What would it be like to have this passionate, strong guy fighting for her? The promise that he'd die for Mac is blazing through his body.

A pang, hot and tight, contracts through her chest.

Arielle blinks in astonishment. She's jealous.

She shrugs, pushing away the confusing feeling. "I don't see any harm in asking a few questions. We need answers."

Reign's gaze falls on his best friend. The one person in this world he loves. "You're right." He pushes to his feet. "Let's go."

Arielle stands up. "Now?"

He grins, the flash of the old Reign taking her breath away. "I'm not much for books."

With a grin of her own, she turns for the door and walks out of the room. She doesn't stop when she reaches the living room where Blaise and Colt are reading at the table, Reign right behind her.

Blaise looks up. "Where are you going?"

Reign reaches around and opens the door. "We're going to get some snacks. We won't be long."

Arielle follows him out, ignoring Colt's raised eyebrows. Whatever reason he's attributing Reign leaving Mac's side, it's not what he thinks it is.

The drive to Colt's apartment is short and quiet, and she wonders what Reign's thinking. Is he having second thoughts? Is this too far, even for him?

They're just pulling up to the curb when Reign speaks. "It's fine if you wait here."

Arielle turns to him. Even with everything that's going on, he's worried about her? "Or you could."

His brows twitch in surprise. "Well, that's not going to happen."

"Neither is me sitting by and playing it safe."

Reign sighs. "I had a feeling you'd say that."

Arielle opens her door, telling him the conversation is over. "Let's go get some answers."

He follows, quiet once again, a pensive look tightening his handsome features. She uses the key Colt gave her to enter, knowing this isn't why Gabby's boyfriend gave her a copy. His place is supposed to be a safe haven if they ever need it. They're supposed to stay well away from Dumah. The decision of what to do with the angry angel has yet to be made.

Inside, the place is quiet and dim. Gabby's clothes are strewn over a few chairs, while there's very little sign Colt even lives here. Reign falls beside her, his gaze roaming over the space as if he's expecting someone or something to jump out any second.

Dumah's been moved to a small storeroom at the back of the basement. Arielle opens the door and switches on the light. The angel blinks, the only sign he's been sitting in darkness, but his hard gaze zeroes in on his visitors.

He waves his chained hands. "Arielle. Reign. How wonderful to see you."

The lack of any warmth in the angel's words almost has a shiver running down her spine. If it weren't for the massive white wings behind him, she'd have thought he was a much darker being.

Reign steps forward. "Mac's been put under a spell."

One of Dumah's black eyebrows twitch. "That's too bad."

"She won't wake up," Arielle adds. "She's trapped in her own mind."

Dumah straightens. "An angelic spell, no less. I wonder which faction has an interest in her," he muses, his eyes glinting.

"Factions?" says Reign. "What do you mean, factions?"

Dumah waves his hand dismissively. "That does not concern you." He angles his head. "I'm curious, why the update?"

"You're an angel," Reign points out. "We're giving you a chance to make this right."

Arielle nods, her gut feeling tight. "This is your chance to do something good. How do we break the spell?"

"I will never tell you that."

Reign steps forward. "So, you know."

"Of course, I know." Something flares in Dumah's dark eyes, something that makes Arielle uneasy. "I can save Mac." He lifts his bound wrists, the metal softly clinking. "But you'd have to release me first."

"You're the one who was trying to kill her in the first place," Reign growls, anger vibrating through his words.

"I was hired to do a job," Dumah says coldly. "Although, if she's under an angel spell, I can't actually kill her." He lifts his hands again. "Release me and I'll tell you how to free your friend."

"Not. Happening," Reign bites out.

Dumah sits back. "Well, humans," he draws the words out, disdain dripping from each one. "Good luck using your nonexistent magic."

Arielle and Reign glance at each other, disappointment heavy between them. This visit got them nowhere but even more frustrated. In silent agreement, they turn and leave.

"Who knew angels were such assholes," Reign mutters loud enough for Dumah to hear.

"You need me," he calls after them.

Arielle shuts the door with force, letting him know what she thinks of his offer. They don't speak until they're back on the other side of the living room.

"We can't trust him," says Reign.

She sighs, knowing he's right. She pulls her cell phone out of her pocket. "I say we call Gabby."

Reign looks at her, the same surprise stamped across his face as when she suggested they talk to Dumah. "I'm feeling threatened. I'm supposed to be the impulsive one among us."

"I know why Colt doesn't want to contact her, but we're running out of options."

And Colt knows that the longer this takes, the less chance

there is of being able to free Mac. If they don't do something, she could be trapped in her mind forever.

Reign rubs a spot above his eyebrow. "And I suppose if Gabby can't help, maybe her father can."

Arielle nods, even though the suggestion makes her deeply uncomfortable. She's not sure why she doesn't trust Gabriel, but she can't shake the feeling of unease at the mention of the archangel's name. She frowns. If Gabby had ever trusted her with any information about her angel ancestry, maybe she'd understand it better.

Reign drops his hand, his face grim. "We don't have a choice. It's her or Dumah."

GABBY

Gabby pushes away the latest book of spells her father brought her with a huff. She pulls her caramel frappé closer and takes a sip, letting the sweetness envelop her senses for long seconds.

The noise of the cafe she's sitting in ebbs and flows, somehow distant yet close. She suspects her father has something to do with that. She opens her eyes, noting the way he's watching her as he sits across the small table. No one has sat at any of the tables around them, like an invisible wall has been built. If anyone considers sitting at an adjacent spot, they frown in puzzlement, then quickly find somewhere else to go. Most seem to remember somewhere they have to be.

She's not sure whether that's because she's reading a sacred text from Heaven, or whether he'd rather humans not get too close. As per usual, probably a bit of both.

She puts the frappé down, wishing the dopamine hit could've lasted a little longer. "Nothing. I can't get past it."

No matter what spell she's tried. No matter how hard she's concentrated. Each time she tries to locate her mother's Grace, she hits the wall of nothing. Frustration gnaws at her insides. Every failure is counting down the hours to when Cain uses it for his own ends.

Her father nods sagely. "I suspect Cain's using something very ancient to power the spell. Possibly himself."

Gabby leans forward, an idea striking her. "If I can't find the Grace, maybe I can find Cain himself."

But her father is already shaking his head. "Cain is too powerful. He's warded himself against angels, which includes you."

She lets out another huff. Even a caramel frappé isn't going to help with this. She's about to ask what she's supposed to do now when her cell rings. She picks it up, her heart jolting that it might be Colt, but it's her cousin's name lighting up the screen.

She glances at her father as she takes the call. "Hey, Ari."

"Gabby, I need a favor."

That has her sitting up a little straighter. Things have been weird between her and Ari lately, and she hates it. They grew up as sisters, and it's a connection Gabby doesn't want to lose. "What's up?"

"Have you heard about Mac?"

Uneasiness weaves its way down Gabby's spine and she glances at her father. He's watching her with the same intense stillness. "No. What's going on?"

Gabby listens as Arielle tells her everything that's happened. A clamp tightens around her heart with every word. Mac's in desperate trouble.

And no one told her.

That hurts far more than she thought it would. Her gut

clenches as she realizes she just got a taste of how Arielle must've felt.

"An angel can break the spell," Arielle finishes. "You could save Mac."

"I'll do whatever I can to help," Gabby promises. "Let me see what I can find out."

"Thanks, Gabby. I was hoping you'd say that."

Arielle hangs up and Gabby stares at her phone. She could sense there was more Ari wasn't telling her. She looks up at her father. "You heard that?"

He nods. "Yes."

She asks the question that's been burning in her mind since Arielle told her. "Was it your men?"

Her father holds her gaze as he answers. "I had nothing to do with what has happened to the demon."

Gabby flinches at his choice of word. Of course that's how her father would view Mac.

"Yes, I have no love for demons," he continues, having noticed her reaction. "Angels are sworn enemies of those born in Hell. But you fell in love with one, and although this has caused issues for me in Heaven, your happiness is important to me, daughter."

The indignation that was about to erupt dissolves. She knows her relationship with Colt is hard for her father to accept. She hadn't considered that it would make his life hard upstairs.

Her father leans forward. "I will find out who did this," he says in a low voice.

Gabby can't help but smile. For all his aloof ways, he tries to show his love in the ways he can. "Thank you."

"But it won't help your...friend. The angels cannot undo the spell."

"What?" she gasps. "Why not?"

"These spells are powerful and carry great risk. If anything goes wrong, the girl could be hurt." He shrugs. "Or permanently damaged."

The ominous warning makes Gabby feel ill. "Then she's trapped?"

He shakes his head. "The best way to break the spell is by the victim themselves. She can will herself out of the reality she's trapped in, but that can only happen when she finds the answers she's searching for."

Gabby's back curves as she sags into her chair. "But if she doesn't..."

"Her mind will be lost to the reality she's trapped in, and her body will slowly degenerate. It will eventually die."

"And yet, if I try to help, I could make it worse?" she whispers.

"It is highly likely that's what will happen."

The caramel frappé feels like it's curdled in her stomach. She wants to help, but she can't.

Her father leans forward another inch. "You can't be distracted by this. You must focus on finding your mother's Grace."

Gabby nods, knowing he's right. There's nothing she can do, anyway.

And yet, the decision only makes her feel more alone.

CHAPTER 14

REIGN

R eign holds his breath as he waits for Arielle to hang up. The way she spoke, it sounded like good news, but he's learned hope likes to play tricks on him. He tends to avoid hanging out with the fickle emotion.

"She said she'd help in whatever way she can," Arielle says, her face alight. "She's going to find out what she needs to do."

He lets out the air trapped in his lungs with a whoosh. "That's good news."

"It's great news! Mac could be giving you her usual sass by this afternoon."

The knot in Reign's chest loosens. "Mac would be pissed to know we spoke to Dumah."

"Or, she'd know the lengths you'd go to save her," says Arielle.

There's a softness to her tone that has Reign stilling. The way she's looking at him...like she admires him for it. She's looking at him like he's some sort of good guy.

Except, he's not. Which is exactly why he pointed out to her he's not boyfriend material. He's not respect material either.

But before he can think of something to say that will remind her of that, Arielle's cell rings.

"It's Gabby," she says excitedly. She flicks the screen and brings the phone to her ear. "Hey, Gabs. You've got news already?"

Reign can make out Gabby's voice on the other end, but not what she's saying. But as the light slowly dims in Arielle's face, he knows he screwed up.

The disappointment that flashes through him tells him he was stupid enough to hope.

"Okay, thanks anyway," Arielle says quietly. She hangs up and her heavy gaze drags up to meet his. "She says it's too dangerous. That there's a risk Mac could be damaged during the process of breaking the spell."

"Right."

"She said our best bet is to be patient and wait to see if Blaise can find anything else out. Or, for Mac to snap out of it herself."

"Right," he says again, knowing he's repeating himself, but finding it hard to squeeze anything else past his numb lips.

Wait? Hope? That's what they're asking him to do?

Arielle shifts her weight "There's something else. Something Blaise and Colt didn't want you to know."

Reign tenses. He knows that tone. Most people in his life have used it at one stage or the other. It's always slightly deeper, a little strained. As if it's struggling under the bad news it's carrying.

She draws in a deep breath. "The longer Mac stays under, the more cemented the reality she's in will be, and the more her mind disconnects from her body." Her lips twist. "The deeper she goes, the less likely she is to wake up."

Even though he knew bad news was coming, the words still gut him. "You're saying we don't have time."

Arielle shakes her head, her blue eyes swimming with pain.

Which means they can't wait. Just like he's not going to depend on hope.

"Ari, do you mind waiting for me in the car? I'll be there in a sec."

She jolts in surprise, her eyes narrowing a moment later. "Actually, I do. If you're going to free Dumah, I want to be there."

Reign hesitates. Arielle's so hell bent on proving she's strong. That there's nothing she won't back down from.

Before he's realized what she's doing, she strides past him and back toward the storage room.

He rushes after her. "Ari, hang on a sec!"

But she's already opened the door. "If we free you, will you do it?"

Dumah sits back in the chair, a smug smile curving up his lips. "You returned sooner than I expected."

Reign stands next to Arielle, hating that they're having this conversation. "Gabby said breaking the spell is risky, is that true?"

Dumah shrugs. "Everything has a risk. In fact, it can be just as dangerous for the angel, themselves."

Reign's gut clenches. The irony that he wishes Mac was here to help him make this decision isn't lost on him.

Dumah shifts forward, not-so-subtly moving his bound hands so they're more visible on his lap. "But I'll take that risk if it means being free."

"And you leave Mac alone," says Reign. "It's her who gave you the opportunity to have this conversation."

Dumah nods. "She's more powerful than I thought. And far more popular, it seems. I have no interest in being caught up in whatever this is."

Reign swallows, still unsure. There's nothing he won't do to save Mac, but he doesn't trust Dumah. And he doesn't want to do what he usually does—make things worse.

"It's a deal," Arielle says before he has a chance to speak.

Two steps and she's in front of Dumah. She reaches down, working quickly as if she's worried she'll change her mind. Or, that Reign will stop her.

"Arielle—"

But she steps back, the deed done. "Now, tell us how to help Mac."

Reign moves close enough that their shoulders are touching. He can't believe she just did that. For him just as much as Mac.

Dumah stands slowly, expanding his wings in a luxurious stretch. "Finally," he breathes. He drops his chin. "Fools," he sneers.

Reign reacts instantly, but it's still too late. As he tries to pull Arielle out of the way, Dumah powers between them, his wings knocking them out of the way. Reign's thrown to the left, while Arielle's shoved to the right.

Dumah darts through the open door, half-running, half-flying. In a blink, he's gone.

Reign leaps to his feet and over to Arielle. "Are you okay?"

She nods, pushing her hair back from her panicked face. "We can't let him get away."

He propels himself after the angel, heart already thudding as his mind races. He just did something as stupid as hope. He trusted.

He takes the steps out of the basement two at a time. He can't see Dumah, but he can hear him. His heavy breathing and light footsteps are just ahead. But just as Reign catches sight of him, Dumah reaches the door.

"Stop!" Reign shouts.

But the angel ignores him, bursting into the foyer of the

apartment building. There's a cry as he must crash into someone, but he barely breaks stride, shoving them out of the way. Reign reaches the door in time to see Dumah exit the building.

In a blink, he disappears.

Reign's about to curse when he sees he's not alone. As he registers who's here he almost curses again.

Nim is on the ground, Sierra already helping her up and back into the wheelchair. They both turn to him, wide eyes registering Arielle arriving behind him.

"What have you done?" Sierra asks, horrified.

Shame flushes through Reign, making him feel like the toilet he is. "Apparently, something we shouldn't have."

Shit. He just made things worse.

MAC

Mac finds herself outside a two-story home, her feet seeming to have carried her here on autopilot. She walks up to the front door like she's done it countless times before, fishes in her pocket and pulls out a set of keys. She's opened the door and entered before she's realized what's happening.

This has to be her world. How else can she be so familiar with it?

"Is that you, honey?" a female voice calls out.

"Yeah, it's me," Mac replies, following it to a large, open plan kitchen.

The dark-skinned woman is just putting a cup of milk and some cookies on the island bench. "Just in time, Mackenzie."

A man enters through another doorway, looking casual in a polo shirt and slacks. "There's that daughter of ours."

Mac pulls herself onto a stool, trying to process that these are her parents. That this is her home. It's a sweet, beautiful picture that she should be happy to be part of, shouldn't she?

"Are you okay, honey?" her mother asks, her face crinkled in concern. "Are you worried about Reign?"

Surprised at her intuitiveness, Mac nods. "Ah, yeah. I just came from the library. He was there with Lizzie."

Her father sits on an adjacent stool, scratching his beard. "Everyone knows she'll be bad news for him. The bit we don't understand is why you set them up on a blind date."

"Me neither," says Mac. "I don't even like the girl."

Her mother comes around, rubbing her back in a soothing gesture. "I'm sure you were just trying to help."

Mac nods. "I think I'm hallucinating or something. I thought you guys were dead," she blurts before she can stop herself.

Her mom recoils, shocked. "No wonder you're so pale. That would be a terrifying thought."

Her father picks up a biscuit and passes it to her. "Why don't you go to your room and have a rest? All this studying and pressure has taken its toll."

Mac takes it, noting that it looks homemade. "Yeah, I think that's a good idea."

She's conscious that her parents watch her as she heads to the stairs. They're worried. Concerned. Just like loving parents should be. Mac finds her bedroom without needing to think about it, entering a room with white furniture and purple and yellow accents. It's light but fun, just what she'd imagine her perfect room to look like.

She sits heavily on the bed, breathing in the scent of fresh linen. Despite her disorientation, this is a good life. A happy one. Maybe she needs to stop thinking so hard.

Mac looks around, wondering if a nap will help. Maybe she has been studying too hard. Her gaze falls on the dresser across the room, a large beveled mirror above it. She gasps, reeling back at the reflec-

tion staring back at her. Dark, curly hair. Caramel skin. And two, red glowing eyes.

She's a demon.

For some reason, that thought feels more real than anything she's seen today. But if she's a demon, she should have wings. Mac squeezes her shoulder blades, glaring at her reflection until her eyes sting.

Nothing appears behind her.

She flops back, staring at the ceiling, feeling both frustrated and relieved. A demon is the last thing she wants to be.

There's a flicker from the corner of her eye and she turns to see two faint figures in the corner of her room. One has long yellow hair and a yellow dress, the other is a guy, broad and red-haired. Their lips move, and although no words come out, Mac knows what they're saying.

"Come back. Please."

Except she doesn't know who they are and where they want her to go.

Or whether she really wants to leave.

SIERRA

Sierra releases Nim's arm, glad to see she's okay. She looks around even though she knows Dumah's long gone. His angelic magic could have him in Australia if he wanted.

She turns back to Reign, still trying to come to terms with what just happened as her daughter steps in front of him, her chin high.

"It was my idea," she says, her blue eyes wide with challenge. "And I'm the one who let Dumah go."

Reign moves so he's standing beside Arielle. "I was the one who decided we weren't going to wait."

Watching Reign and Arielle defend each other is a bittersweet moment Sierra isn't sure what to do with. Luckily, there's more pressing things to deal with. "I think we can agree that you're both at fault," she snaps. "Do you know what you've done?"

"We were trying to help Mac," Reign says softly. "When we learned that Gabby couldn't, wouldn't, do it, we decided it was worth a try."

Arielle nods sharply. "Mac deserves to have someone fighting for her."

Sierra's chest constricts. And this is how her daughter believes that should be done. "We're all fighting for Mac," she points out. "But we're not rushing into anything, either."

Arielle's cheeks flush and her gaze wavers.

Reign frowns. "And you failed to mention Mac doesn't have all the time in the world for us to figure this out."

Arielle straightens again. "You kept that from him."

Sierra's heart feels like it's being squeezed harder and harder with each word. She let down Reign, even though all she wanted was the best for him. And she let down her own daughter, even though all she wanted was to protect her.

How does she make this right?

"Dumah wasn't the answer," she says quietly.

"He's known for his trickery," Nim adds. "I'll see if I can track him."

Sierra nods. "Thanks. We don't know what his next move might be." She turns back to her daughter and Reign. "I think we should have a talk back at the house."

Arielle's jaw works. "Sure."

Reign seems surprised by her agreement, but he shrugs. "I think I can fit that in my schedule."

Sierra spins on her heel, following Nim out of the foyer. It's time.

Time to tell them both the truth.

CHAPTER 15
ARIELLE

Reign sighs, turning to head back down to Colt's basement. "Well, this is going to be fun."

"Except we're not going home," says Arielle as she follows him.

He stops, turning to look at her a couple of steps above. "We're not?"

"Nope. There's no way I'm going home to a lecture about what Mom thinks is best for me. Not when Mac still needs us."

Reign reaches the door and pushes it open so she can pass through, his eyebrows pulled low. "She looked mad, which is understandable, but she also looked kinda...sad."

Arielle crosses her arms, not liking that he's right. "That's because I'm thinking for myself, and she doesn't like that."

Or, because her mom doesn't believe she can do this. Releasing Dumah would've been even more proof of that. But Arielle isn't going to go home, not until she's shown she's just as much a part of this as anyone else.

That she's an asset, not a liability. A strength, not a weakness.

That this is just as important to her as any of them.

"Except we royally fu—stuffed up," Reign points out. "And we're out of leads."

She lifts her left boot, pointing to the side of her calf. One word is printed there. *Perseverance.* "Did you know that Howard Shultz, the founder of Starbucks, was rejected two hundred and forty-two times as he tried to find a bank that would loan him the money to start his coffee chain?"

"Ah, no. I didn't."

"What would've happened if he gave up after the first rejection? Or the two hundred and fortieth?"

Reign's eyes widen. "That would've been catastrophic."

"Exactly. Which is why we're not giving up either." She straightens, drawing a sharp breath. "And if an angel can't help, maybe a demon can!"

"As much as I'm all for the can-do attitude, Colt will give us the same response Gabby did."

"Which is why we try to find another one. A more powerful one." She can't believe she didn't think of this before. "Like Cain."

Maybe this always went back to the bastard.

"You want to catch Cain and use him to break through the wall around Mac's mind?"

Arielle nods. "In a nutshell, yes."

Reign grabs her hand and pulls her to the door, muttering. "I can't believe I've found someone crazier than I am."

He tugs her back up the stairs and out of the building. Arielle's too stunned by the contact to object. Nor does she want to. The warmth, somehow delicious and comforting at the same time, trickles up her arm. Does he hold hands like this with Mac? Even as the question rises in her mind, she pushes it away. It shouldn't matter. Friends hold hands all the time.

Outside, he releases her when they reach the car. Arielle's hand tingles as it falls to her side, suddenly feeling like it's no longer whole. She shakes herself mentally and unlocks the car. "Do you have an idea where we're going?"

Reign opens his door. "Yep. I had the idea before Mac was attacked. I thought we could try it next."

She climbs in, too. "You do?"

"Just like you said, we need to check out the sites of the murders." He pulls out his cell phone and opens the map app, typing something in. "I say we just go have a look around the Multiplayer Love Lounge. Enough time has passed that there will be far fewer cops hanging around."

Arielle puts the car into gear, nodding thoughtfully. "Smart. I like it."

Reign ducks his head and she's not sure, but she thinks a flush creeps up his cheeks. Her own warmth spreads through her chest. She likes that her compliment had an impact. "Multiplayer Love Lounge, here we come."

The club is on the outskirts of the city, as if it wants to be accessible, but isn't quite mainstream enough to hang with the other, more central clubs. It's early afternoon, so the building at the end of the block is still closed, which Arielle isn't sure whether it's a good thing or not. She parks beside the curb, wondering how they're going to pull this off.

Reign turns to her. "So, breaking and entering used to be a hobby of mine, but it's not one I recommend. The law seems to frown on it. So why don't you stay here and I'll see what I can find?"

Except Arielle's already opening her door. "Are we going to have to go through this every time?"

Reign quickly jumps out, looking unsurprised but still disappointed. "Hey, I was doing what your boot says —persevering."

She points to the other side of said boot. "And this part says *don't fight it*."

He shakes his head as he rolls his eyes. "You won't be saying that when we face down Cain."

"Of course not. Then I'll be following the advice on my right boot." She indicates toward a scrawl near the laces. "*Take it to them.*"

Reign snorts. "Those boots have an answer to everything."

"I'm hoping one day it rubs off on me," she says wryly. Maybe she shouldn't have put *think it through* so far near the heel.

She's about to take a step toward the building when Reign grabs her hand. "You did what you did because you care, Ari. It meant a lot. To both me and Mac."

Her own fingers instinctively wrap around his. "I just want to..."

Help.

Make this right.

Kiss Reign.

He steps back as if he just read her thoughts, releasing her hand like it just turned into a red hot fire poker. "You're a good friend, Ari," he says huskily, looking away.

She wipes her palm down her jeans, hoping it'll erase the simmering heat that one point of contact generated. Reign's reminded her of what she keeps forgetting herself. That they're friends.

And yet his voice shows he's not unaffected by their closeness. Their touch. But he pulls away, each and every time. Why?

He steps back, moving toward the side of the building. "I say we try the back door." With a quick glance, he disappears around the corner, calling over his shoulder. "If you've changed your mind, that's totally cool. Actually, I'd encourage it."

Rolling her eyes, Arielle follows him. "And I'd encourage you to reach the acceptance stage much quicker."

She sees his lips twitch as he walks down the side of the

building and around the corner that will take him to the back. With a quick skip, she catches up.

The back of the club is a narrow alley with a dumpster and not much else. They stop by the backdoor beside it and Arielle's pulse starts skipping, too. She's going to break and enter. She never imagined herself breaking the law so brazenly. But then again, she never imagined a world with angels and demons. Or one without Aunt Shell.

Reign must sense her hesitation because he opens his mouth. She narrows her eyes, keeping her voice low. "I've always wanted to do something like this, okay?"

He snaps his mouth shut, even though he no doubt knows that's a blatant lie. She accidentally walked out with a book from a bookstore once. She returned with it the next day and insisted she pay for it.

He grips the door handle, his eyebrows hiking up when it turns in his hand. "Seems you're going to be disappointed, gangsta girl. The door's unlocked."

She lets out the breath that had stupidly been trapped in her lungs. "That's too bad."

Reign shakes his head again, those lush lips of his twitching with humor. He pushes the door open slowly, his body coiled. Arielle gets ready to run. But the dimly lit corridor on the other side is empty.

Indicating with his hand for her to follow, he enters. The carpet muffles their footsteps as they creep in. The walls are painted black and the scent of alcohol and cigarette smoke hang in the air. Small down lights illuminate their way, a handful of doors on either side. Reign surreptitiously tries each one, but unlike the backdoor, they're all locked.

"What are we looking for?" Arielle whispers.

"An office, maybe. Police reports. Hopefully not a room where an orgies in progress."

Arielle's cheeks flame and she's glad for the gloom. Of course that's a possibility in a polyamorous club. Nor is she some flushing sixteen year old who didn't know such a thing existed. It's just that being here with Reign...it has her feeling like all of her blood is pulsing just below the surface of her skin...

They reach the end of the corridor and the space opens out to the club itself. An elevated dance floor is on the right, while a bar stretches across the length of the wall to the right, a long mirror behind it. Everywhere is painted black, including the tables and chairs dotted around.

"Why do I feel they use a lot of neon in this place?" Reign mutters.

Strategic lighting that would create shadows and corners to let passion soar, away from prying eyes. Arielle fans herself, trying to get her wayward thoughts under control. The knowledge that people were killed in this club, that just a few days ago it was a crime scene, has her body cooling. She needs to remember why they're here.

He softly clears his throat. "I don't think we're going to find out much here. We might need to get some fake IDs and come back when it's open."

Reign. Sultry lighting. Dancing bodies.

Arielle's blood temperature jolts up another few degrees. She's about to answer when there's a sound behind them.

Someone else just cleared their throat.

They spin around and Reign shoots his arm across Arielle in a protective gesture. A tall man stands across from them, his arms crossed over his crisply pressed police uniform.

Crap. They've been caught. By the cops.

"What are you doing here?" he demands, glaring at them.

Reign moves forward a little. "This is the Multiplayer Club, isn't it? Where are all the gaming consoles?"

The cop slices a hand sharply through the air. "I'm not in the mood for a smart ass."

"We could have a problem then," Reign mutters.

The policeman ignores him, his gaze snapping back to Arielle. "I'm waiting for an answer. What are you doing here, Arielle?"

Arielle gasps as she realizes he knows her name. How is that possible?

But as she stares at him, the man morphs. Changes. And turns into her curly-haired, frowning cousin.

Gabby jams her hands on her hips. "Well? What are you doing here, Ari?"

GABBY

Gabby has to work hard to keep her anger under control. It's a good thing her outfit was nothing but glamor, because she might've been tempted to shoot Arielle and Reign's asses.

Arielle lifts her chin. "Looking for Cain."

The anger flares hotter for a brief second before dying just as quickly. The Arielle she knew wouldn't have done this. Nor would she have been so headstrong about it. "I was really hoping you wouldn't say that."

"What are *you* doing here?" Arielle shoots back.

Gabby's mouth twists. "Looking for Cain."

After spending more time *not* locating her mother's Grace, she decided she was going to Plan B, no matter what her father said. Right now, finding Cain feels more probable—how desperate things are becoming.

Which means Ari was right in some ways. The ancient demon is who they should be trying to find.

Her cousin's blue eyes flash. "Great idea."

"I'm just going to point out that we all seem to be going after the same thing," Reign points out.

Except Arielle isn't supernatural. The risks she's taking are far higher. And she doesn't seem to care. Gabby can feel the determination pulsing through her. It's a force to be reckoned with.

Gabby sighs. She doesn't want to fight with Ari. She just wants to keep her safe. "And you thought you'd check out one of the crime scenes," she observes.

Reign is watching her closely. "Seems like we weren't the only ones with that idea."

She notes the close way the two are standing together. The feelings between them have grown, she can feel it. She wonders if they've realized it themselves. And how far one will go for the other...

She sighs again. "If we're both here, we may as well work together."

Something flickers in Arielle's gaze and Gabby's chest tightens when she realizes what it is. Suspicion. She's not convinced Gabby's going to let her be part of this. Because none of them did before.

"That makes sense," she says quietly.

Deciding to show she means it, Gabby glances around. "There's definitely traces of demonic aura here, but it's a higher demon. Someone powerful."

Reign straightens. "Cain?"

"No, it's not his signature," says Gabby. She'd know if it was him. "And I don't know who would be capable of doing this." She spins on her heel, eyes closed as she breathes deeply. "Not a succubus, that much I know."

"We need to look at the security footage," says Arielle. "See what happened."

Gabby's stomach clenches at the thought. She's seen death in her time, but it never loses its impact. Pain always clings to the dead. Either theirs, or of those they left behind.

But she nods. That's exactly what she came here for. "Let's go check out the security office."

Arielle steps forward, that determination now stamped across her face, but Reign hesitates. "Ah, maybe you should arrest me or something? It's the only way it'll be plausible that we're with you."

Gabby rolls her eyes as she points to the mirrors above the bar. "Take a look."

Arielle gasps as she sees two more police officers are looking back at them. Arielle's a dark-haired Spanish middle-aged woman, while Reign—

He strides toward the bar to get a closer look. "You made me a chick, too?" he demands, touching the blonde hair pulled back in a shiny bun then glancing down...at his buxom chest.

"Yup! It's time to connect with your feminine side."

Arielle's lips twitch. "It wasn't exactly what I had in mind when I suggested that we find a spell to disguise ourselves, but you've got to admit. It works."

Gabby blinks as she realizes Ari had considered the same plan she did. Before her.

"It's bad enough being a police officer," he mutters. "I think I would've preferred to have been arrested."

Gabby allows herself a smile as she restores her own glamor. "Let's go see what we can find out, shall we"—she glances at Reign's badge just above his breast pocket—"Constable Honeycutt?"

Reign scowls at her. "My eyes are up here, Sergeant."

She slaps his ass as she strides past. "Annoying, isn't it?"

CHAPTER 16
REIGN

Gabby raps on the door of the security office then hooks her fingers on her gun belt. The door opens, the scowl dropping away from the overweight security guard as he realizes who's on the other side.

He straightens, tucking his shirt into the belt barely visible beneath his gut. "Yes? How can I help you?"

He scans Gabby, the grizzled sergeant, then Arielle, the middle-aged Spanish woman, then Reign. His gaze lingers as he takes in the curvy blonde, making Reign bristle. He glares at him, only for the guard's gaze to heat up as if he'd just been issued some sort of challenge.

"Good day," Gabby says in a gravely, male voice, bringing the guard's attention reluctantly back to her. "We've had some evidence come to light and we'd like to review your security footage."

"Again? The other guys who were here yesterday said you were all done. It's not like—"

Gabby straightens. "An investigation such as this is lengthy and nuanced," she snaps. "It's important we're thorough."

The guard glances at Reign again, then smiles widely. "Sure, come on in." He opens the door, waving a welcoming arm.

Reign gives the guy his perfected 'back-off' glare as he walks past. Most people are smart enough to know he means it. The security guard's response is to rake his gaze from Reign's head to toe, pausing at two key areas of his anatomy.

"Consent is a thing, you know," Reign growls as he walks past.

The security guard chuckles. "The name's Tom, by the way."

"As in the peeping kind?"

The man blinks, looking confused.

Reign ignores him as they enter the seedy looking office. Several monitors cover the opposite wall, a desk beneath it littered with coffee cups and takeaway boxes. The place smells of sweat and lecherous security guard.

Gabby sits in the desk chair, focused on the computer screen in front of her. "I see you have the night of the murders already filed on the desktop."

The security guard grunts. "It's been looked at enough times." His gaze slides away. "Not that you've caught anyone," he mutters.

Suddenly, Joseph appears beside Peeping Tom. Reign tenses. Of course he does.

The old man frowns. "Have you sinned?"

"Go away," Reign snaps. He's not going to answer rhetorical questions—his life has been one long sinfest.

Tom's chin jerks back into the folds of his neck. "I beg your pardon?"

Joseph strokes his beard, his face tight. "Sin has been here."

Glad that he has someone to legitimately target with his words, Reign narrows his eyes in the guard's direction. "You heard me. Get out."

Arielle comes to stand by his side. "This is a police investigation," she tells Tom. "We'll let you know when we're done."

Tom looks like he's going to object, but Gabby glances over her shoulder. "We'll take it from here."

With a disgruntled glance at Reign, he lumbers out. Reign unwinds another notch when he sees that Joseph is gone, too. There's too much going on to have to deal with that, too. There's no point worrying about whether or not he's a Grail Keeper when there's no Grail to keep.

"Crap," Gabby mutters. She glances at the other two. "The security cameras were turned off a minute before the murders."

Reign moves in closer, seeing the black screen with a digital clock counting out the time at the bottom. "Great. A smart demon."

Arielle comes to stand on Gabby's other side. "Is it worth looking at the footage in the lead up?"

Gabby nods. "I was just about to suggest that."

She drags the mouse back ten minutes, and the two of them press their faces a little closer. If they weren't glamored, right now they'd look like the sisters they grew up as. Reign wonders if they realize how similarly they're behaving, too. That they're both fighting for the same thing.

And how lucky they are to have family in their lives. One that cares.

"There," Arielle almost shouts, pointing at the screen. "Go back a few seconds."

Gabby does, and Reign sees it, too. The camera pointing at the back door shows a red-haired girl slipping out, glancing frantically over her shoulder.

"She got out," Arielle breathes. "Before the massacre."

Gabby looks up. "We need to find her."

Arielle pulls out her phone and takes a few photos of the image. It's grainy and small, but it's something.

Tom shoves open the door. "So, see anything new on the blank footage?" he sniggers.

"We've learned a lot, actually," says Gabby as she stands and walks out..

"Like men can be total asses," mutters Reign as he follows. "And not even realize it," he adds as Tom goes to speak.

Tom opens his mouth again, but this time Gabby speaks. "Tell me about it."

The fact that Tom sees one of his own backing Reign up has his mouth snapping shut. Arielle arches a brow as she walks past, too. The guard's gaze slides away as he mumbles to himself.

Back in the alley, Reign watches as Gabby and Arielle's glamor slips away. He glances down, relieved to find he can easily see his feet again. "Next time, I want to look like a Sumo wrestler, okay?"

Gabby grins cheekily at him. "Which won't be nearly as much fun."

Arielle angles her head. "And you've got to admit, you were hot."

"The minute I'm out of the sisterhood, you gang up on me?" he asks incredulously.

The two glance at each other, bashful smiles dancing at the corners of the lips like two girls who just met in the playground. Two girls who are looking for a friend and know they just found a kindred spirit.

They look away and Arielle pulls her cell phone out of her pocket. "I say we head home and see what we can find about this girl."

"Yep. My thoughts exactly."

But before they can move, Gabby's cell rings. "It's Colt," she says, her voice smiling and frowning at the same time. She picks up. "Hey, what's up?" The frown wins out as her brows creep down. "Yep. I should be there."

She turns to Reign and Arielle. "Nim thinks she's closing in on Dumah. I'm going to give him a hand."

Arielle's shoulders tense. They're the ones who let the lying bastard out in the first place. "Yeah, that's probably best."

And yet she's still not going to apologize for it.

Gabby nods, the frown firmly in place. "Let me know if you find anything. We'll go after this girl together."

"Sure," says Arielle, but Reign notes that she used the same tone she did when she told her mom she'll head home from Colt's place.

Either Gabby doesn't notice, or she decides to ignore it, because she swoops in and hugs Arielle. "Stay safe, okay?"

Arielle clasps her back. "You, too," she says softly.

Before Reign can blink, Gabby's engulfed him in a hug, too. "Keep doing what you're doing," she whispers in his ear.

She pulls away and walks briskly down the alley, not giving him a chance to respond, which is probably a good thing. He has no idea what to say to that—she wants him to keep being a loser?

"Right," Arielle says, all business again. "More research."

He groans. "My favorite."

MAC

Mac sits up with a gasp, the images of the nightmare that gripped her still burning through her mind.

She was a demon. A deadly one. She was in a library of some sort, but not the one at the university, and she and Reign were surrounded by more demons. Within a minute, she'd ended every single one of them.

And then they were running down to a crypt. Women were lying on altars, their energy being siphoned off. A man was in the center, violence in his eyes. He'd run at them just as Mac woke up.

She pushes her fingers into her hair, tangling them in the thick curls and tugging. Her eyes sting with the sharp pain. She's definitely awake and definitely real.

"I'm giving new meaning to studying like a demon," she mutters to herself.

Because it sure as shit isn't anything more than that.

She gets to her feet and, finding herself on autopilot again, showers and dresses. She's wearing tight black jeans and a cute little red top that shows a glimpse of her belly. Why does it feel like she's always wanted to dress like this but has never been able to?

Coming down the stairs, she finds her parents in the kitchen again. A paper bag sits on the counter.

"I know you won't have breakfast, so I've packed a few extra snacks," her mom says with a smile.

Mac picks it up, smiling. "Thanks."

Her father pulls out his wallet and passes her a twenty dollar note. "And this to get your coffee from that place you like so much."

She takes that, too. "Thanks."

Her mom smiles right back. "We figured you probably didn't sleep very well."

Mac stills, her hand on the lunch bag. "You did?" Did she cry out during her nightmare? Do they know she's having some sort of mental meltdown?

"Of course," her mom says warmly. "You're getting your results for the advanced program you applied for. It's understandable you're nervous."

"Even though we know you're in. Your GPA is more than enough."

"Oh, yes," she says. "Of course."

Another thing she'd forgotten. And yet, how? An advanced program is something she would definitely be thinking about. Maybe that's what triggered the weird-ass nightmare.

With a quick smile, Mac leaves. Outside, the sun is shining and the air is warm and she breathes it deep into her lungs, pushing the uneasiness away. There's no one calling her back, no hazy silhouettes hovering around, and she's living her best life. Something tells her that in a few more days, this will all pass. And so will the unease.

She finds herself at the university cafe, just like her father predicted. Looking forward to a caffeine hit, Mac enters. A quick scan of the place shows just about every other student is here for the same thing, so she takes her place at the back of the line. The excitement at the prospect of being part of the advanced program has her bouncing on her toes. She's not going to let anything mess that up.

A giggle from her left has her turning toward it, already smiling. If Lizzie's here, then Reign might be, too.

The blonde bombshell is sitting at a table at the far corner of the room, her back to Mac as she's tucked beneath a fake palm. Except Reign isn't with her. Some other guy is. And the way they're leaning forward, heads close, has the smile disappearing.

"Yeah, I'm definitely in," Lizzie says in a low voice. Mac stills, glad for the freakingly good hearing she's had all her life. "All I had to do was get myself one blind date."

The line moves forward, and Mac moves with it, tucking herself a little behind the guy in front of her. Surely Lizzie isn't talking about Reign and the date Mac apparently set them up on...

"Luckily Reign's a good kisser," Lizzie giggles, making Mac's stomach constrict. "It makes it fun while I work to get those records for you."

The man chuckles. "Job satisfaction is important." He stands, brushing her cheek with his knuckles. "Keep me posted. We don't have much time."

The man leaves without glancing around, leaving Lizzie at the table. Mac watches in shocked horror as a smile spreads across her painted lips and she pulls a compact out of her handbag. She flips it open, picking up the powder pad sitting inside and angling the small mirror so she can see her cheeks.

Mac has to clap her hand across her mouth to stop the gasp climbing up her throat. Lizzie's eyes are the same hellish red as those in her nightmare.

Mac spins around and darts out of the cafe, hoping the traitorous bitch didn't see her. Her coffee will have to wait. Just like her results.

She has to find Reign and warn him.

SIERRA

Sierra watches as Gabby and Colt leave Veritas, their hands gravitating towards the other the moment they're out the door, off to track Dumah armed with the information Nim gave them. Those two have been through so much, and yet here they are again, fighting for what's right. She's glad they have each other.

Fighting evil alone takes its toll.

She turns back to Nim, the fear that this would all have been for nothing a writhing sack of worms in her gut. She can't have protected Arielle all these years just to lose her now. "We need to find the Seeker. I know Arielle, and she hasn't given up on it."

Not her determined daughter. Not the young woman who needs to prove herself because her family kept the truth from her.

Nim was about to wheel herself away when she stops. "It's

not as simple as that, and you know it. The spirits believe she's destined to find it."

Sierra crosses her arms then uncrosses them. She takes a few steps one way then back again. Too much anxious energy is thrumming through her nerves. "The spirits don't know that for sure, though, do they?"

Please don't let them know that for sure.

"If they do, they can't tell me," says Nim. "They're not allowed to directly influence the living world. But being a medium, I can see what they do—multiple threads of probability that the future can take."

Relief has Sierra able to stand still again. "Okay, so this could go any number of ways."

Nim holds her gaze. "In every possible thread, Arielle finds the Seeker."

Sierra almost doubles over as the words hit her. She paces several steps away only to quickly return, shaking her head as if the motion can stop this. "No, no, no. There has to be something we can do."

"The strange thing is, the Seeker is attracted to magical blood," says Nim, looking perplexed.

Which is just the thread of hope Sierra needs. "Which means Arielle won't find it. She's as supernatural as I am."

Being human is probably one of the reasons Arielle's so determined to show she's not weak and vulnerable. That she doesn't need to be protected. In fact, Sierra felt the same at her age.

"It's definitely a contradiction," agrees Nim. "But I know what I've seen. The Seeker is Arielle's destiny."

Sierra strides forward once again, squatting down in front of Nim. "We can't let it happen," she pleads, injecting the desperation clawing at her heart into every word. "You know how dangerous that thing is."

And Arielle's not ready. Releasing Dumah only proved that. She's inherited Sierra's impulsive streak and her emotions are getting the better of her.

Nim studies her for long seconds before she sighs. "Fine. I'll help you find the Seeker."

Gratitude floods Sierra.

Now, all they have to do is locate it before Arielle does.

CHAPTER 17
ARIELLE

Arielle stops in the doorway of Mac's room, her laptop clutched to her chest. Reign is sitting on the edge of Mac's bed, head bowed as he holds her hand. Her heart spasms at the pain etched across his handsome face. He looks like he's trying to climb into her mind so he can drag her back himself.

"No, I'm not praying," he says without looking up.

So, he knows she's standing there. "It's kind of hard to do that when an angel is what put her there in the first place."

Reign turns, those striking green eyes of his locking with hers. "Seems like some of them are asses, too."

Arielle remembers his words to the security guard at the club.

Men can be total asses. And not even realize it.

Something had struck her at the time but it hadn't been the moment to say anything. She takes a few more steps in. "Not all of them though," she says. "Gabby's an angel."

Reign angles his head in agreement. "Except she made me a chick."

Arielle smiles as she sits on the floor. "That's true." But she's not going to let him use humor to avoid this. "But she's one of the good guys. It's the same with men."

His dark eyebrows contract, wondering where this is going.

"Sometimes they're *not* assholes," she says softly, holding his gaze. "And they don't realize it."

Reign's eyes widen imperceptibly, several emotions flashing at once. Surprise. A flare of instant denial. Vulnerability. And something...warm.

Stew on that, Mr. I've Defined Myself Too Narrowly.

She flips open her laptop. "I'm going to do a search with the images of that girl from the club and see if anything comes up."

"Ah, yeah, great idea." Reign slips off the bed, sitting beside her as he leans back on it. "I'll research." He says the last word dryly, showing how much he's looking forward to that.

And yet, he's doing it anyway. That's what makes Reign far more than the dropkick he's decided he is. No matter what it takes, he stands up for what he believes in. He fights for those he loves.

Arielle blinks as she opens her web browser. The wish that she was someone who falls under that category just wormed its way into her chest and settled in like it has no intention of leaving.

Quickly tapping away, she focuses on her screen. If she ignores the feeling, hopefully it will go away. Right now, they need to find this girl. She's their one connection to the demon on a murder rampage.

But ten minutes pass of scrolling through images. Then another twenty. And nothing comes up.

Arielle groans in frustration. "The image is too grainy. I'm not getting any hits."

Reign looks up from the book he's reading. "Send it to me and I'll get it out to my network. Maybe someone will recognize her."

"It's worth a try," she says, pulling her cell out and doing as he suggested. Her spine rounds as she lets out a breath. "Back to waiting."

"Actually, I think I may have found something."

"You have?" She sits up straight, glancing at the book in his lap.

"Yeah, I'm surprised, too. Who knew this research thing could work?" He lifts the book. "Come and look."

She shuffles so she's sitting beside him with her back also against the bed, conscious of their shoulders brushing. "Is it about the obelisks?"

"It's about the levels of Hell," he says somberly. "And that as each layer is peeled back, demons are let loose on the world."

"Oh."

Arielle leans in a little closer, tucking her hair over her ear when it brushes his arm. "That means Innocents are being sacrificed to free demons."

"Yeah, it does."

She blinks as the page blurs, then fades away. Straightening, her eyes widen as the room falls away. An obelisk appears, cracked and crumbling. Surrounding it is crimson light.

Another blink, and it's gone.

"Ari?" Reign's sounding a little panicked. "Are you okay?"

"Huh? What?" She looks around, finding she's back in the bedroom. "Sorry, I just had some sort of mini-vision."

Reign lets out a breath. "I thought you were going to go visit Mac in coma land."

Seeing the fear fading from his eyes, Arielle shakes her head. "You're stuck with me for a little longer."

His eyes twinkle. "Wasn't that my line to you?" He sobers. "What did you see?"

"The obelisk cracking again," she says heavily. "I don't know if it was the last one or one coming."

"Let's hope it was the former. And the only one."

Arielle frowns. "There was one difference. The sky was pink. A deep fuchsia."

Reign lifts the book up. "Why does that sound familiar?" He skims a finger over the handwritten words. "There!"

Arielle reads where he's pointing to, her eyes widening. "Each Gate of Hell holds a Sin. If a Gate is broken, the Sin is released."

"And pink equates with Lust," Reign breathes. "When the first Gate broke, Lust was released into the world."

She sits back, her mind whirling. "That makes total sense. The murders—they were all associated with sex."

Reign nods, still reading. "Lust amplifies feelings of desire and passion, and when people succumb, she kills them, feeding off the intense energy that's been created."

Arielle shudders. "That's awful."

"And exactly what's been happening," he says grimly.

She clutches his hand as something else strikes her. "If Cain finds the next Innocent, and he uses their Grace to break the next Gate of Hell—"

"Then another Sin will be unleashed on Earth."

Arielle swallows, glancing at Mac. She hopes this is all related. That by finding Cain they end all of this—they keep another layer of Hell trapped...and save Mac.

She doesn't want to have to choose.

GABBY

Gabby wrinkles her nose. "What is it with this angel and alley-ways?" According to Nim, this is the last location she detected Dumah at.

Colt glances around, his gaze sharp. "And demons are the ones who are supposed to be odious."

She giggles. "No one uses that word anymore."

"Well, it's their loss," he says, chocolate eyes twinkling. "It's a..." He angles an eyebrow. "A doozy."

Shaking her head, Gabby moves in to press a kiss on his lips. "I think doozy went out of fashion at about the same time as odious."

Colt's gaze drops to her lips, his breath hitching as his body softens. She loves the way he does that. It shows he's melting right along with her.

Except he straightens again, then frowns. "I'll see you soon."

"What?"

But he's already gone, the space in front of her now nothing but air. Gabby spins around, knowing that can only mean one thing.

Her father appears at the entrance of the alley, four others behind him. Although their wings aren't visible, she knows they're angels.

He's brought backup.

He stops in front of her, his chiseled face stern. "You were hiding Dumah."

Gabby crosses her arms. "I figured you'd hear about that eventually."

"And now he's on the loose again," her father accuses.

She narrows her eyes. "He was sent here to kill Mac."

One of the angels behind him bristles, but her father ignores her. "Dumah belongs to a rival faction of angels who were ordered to kill the demon girl. I don't know why."

"But you won't help her," she points out. "Which is why Dumah was released."

"Fools," mutters one of the male angels.

Gabby glares at him. "They're trying to help Mac, which is more than you're all doing."

"And what of your mother's Grace?" her father asks. Although his voice is soft, there's a hard edge to it.

"I'm not leaving Mac to the mercy of some angelic spell that's doing who knows what to her," she grinds out. "We need him to save her."

"We are here to take care of Dumah. He's no longer your concern."

Gabby's hands clench, knowing exactly what he's saying. "You can't take him to Heaven. Not before he fulfills his promise to help Mac."

Her father steps in closer, meaning she has to tilt her head back. She makes sure she does it with as much attitude as possible. "If more Innocents are sacrificed, more Gates will be opened. Demons will roam Earth, wreaking their havoc. And when that happens, more angels will arrive. It will mean war."

"No," she breathes. "It would be carnage."

And humans will be collateral.

His blue gaze is piercing as it holds hers. "The fate of the world is at stake. A powerful demon is already killing according to the power they wield."

Gabby gasps. "It's Lust, isn't it?" That was the demonic aura she sensed at the club.

"Yes, it is. And another Sin will be next. Which is why you must leave Dumah to us."

The angels behind him nod, their gazes just as piercing.

"But—"

"No, Gabrielle," her father snaps. "You cannot do both. You have a choice to make—help Mac or find the next Innocent."

Denial tears through Gabby, as powerful as it is impotent. So is the anger that quickly follows. And the deep sadness that she's going to be letting Arielle down again.

Her shoulders drop, acceptance far heavier than she expected. Too many people's lives are at stake.

Her father nods once, and he and his posse disappear. He knows she's made her decision.

She has to find the Innocent.

CHAPTER 18

REIGN

Arielle's hair brushes his arm as she looks closer at the book, a sweet caress Reign tries to ignore. They're researching. Studying. Nothing more.

But then she turns her head, her gaze rising to meet his. Except it never reaches that far. Her eyes fasten on his lips, making his mouth go dry. A silent groan rumbles through his chest. She needs to move away.

Except she doesn't. In fact, with a smooth flick of her leg, Arielle's straddling him. Her blue eyes, electric and alive, capture his and don't let go. Reign's breath is trapped in his lungs, evaporating under the blazing heat that's scorching his body.

"Ari...what are you doing?"

She smiles, and it's one of the sexiest things he's ever seen. "Taking." She slides up his lap an inch, and he almost spontaneously combusts there and then. "Giving," she whispers.

Her chest presses against his a moment before her lips do, and his control snaps. He grips her head, angling it so he can get better access. The hunger to taste Ari has become a primal need. An ache.

And it's the heaven he knew it would be.

She moans into his mouth, her hands sliding over his shoulders. He gasps and draws back, shocked at the sensation. It's like her hands burned straight through his shirt.

Fuck. She's naked. And so is he.

They're skin on skin. Flame feeding flame. Passion multiplying passion.

With nothing between them. No barriers. No ability to stop.

Strident ringing slices through the image and Reign's eyes fly open. Arielle shoots up, her head lifting from his shoulder. She blinks groggily as she pulls out her phone. "It's Mom," she says in a sleep-slurred voice.

Shit. He was dreaming.

He goes to stand up, a new wave of heat flushing through his body, burning away the desire. But he stops when he sees that a certain part of his anatomy doesn't care about the embarrassment incinerating the desire that gripped him a moment ago.

It's still seeing Arielle's sweet, pale flesh. Still feeling her body pressed against his, trembling and tight. Still hard and throbbing with need for her.

Reign jams his hand through his hair, the next flood of shame even worse than the first.

"Yeah," Arielle's saying into her phone as she sits straighter. "We must've fallen asleep in Mac's room."

Quickly grabbing the book that they'd been pouring over, he slips it onto his lap, trying to get his breathing under control. It was nothing but a dream, he tells himself. He's being a freaking randy teen.

Arielle frowns. "That's not far from here." She pauses listening. "Yeah, we'll be careful. Thanks, Mom."

She hangs up, looking at Reign. "There's been another

murder, only a few streets over. Four people. They died just like the others."

The mention of demonic murders is like a dousing of ice. "Shit."

"Yeah. Lust strikes again." Her face scrunches. "We need to find this girl. She's our only lead."

If they don't, more people will die. Arielle's words remind him of the messages he sent last night. Knowing it's a long shot, he looks at his own cell, seeing a message from Darnell. He opens it. "Whoa."

"What?" Arielle shifts back, and he instinctively shuffles to keep a little distance between them as flashes of his dream pepper his consciousness.

"They've found her," he says, tightening his hand on his phone as he mentally pushes the luscious images away.

"They have?" she says, clearly excited. "No way!"

His eyebrows hike up, his attention well and truly captured by the words on his screen. "Her name's Rachel, and she's been hiding at our old hangout."

THE HANGOUT IS as dingy and dilapidated as when he left it, looking as if the only thing holding the rundown house together is graffiti. Reign hesitates, realizing Arielle is about to see how he used to live. The muscles in his back constrict, pulling at his shoulders. Maybe this is exactly what she needs to see.

That he's a street rat. Living in a filthy, forgotten house that society discarded, just like it did him.

Maybe then the moments between them will stop.

Moments that fed the sizzling dream he had. A dream that means he can barely look Arielle in the eye.

He stops at the bottom of the stairs leading up to the saggy porch. "Avoid the second step. Termites."

She nods, following him. Darnell slips through the gap left by the hanging door, grinning when he sees Reign.

"Hey, man." He greets him with a fist pump and brief hug. "Been living it up, huh?" he says, stepping back to take in Reign's clean clothes and washed hair.

"Something like that."

"Hi, I'm Arielle." She steps forward, extending a hand.

Darnell raises a brow as he shakes it. "Hey, I'm Darnell."

"You're a friend of Reign's?"

"Yeah," he says, slapping him on the back. "He's the one who gave me a place to stay."

Arielle smiles, her gaze flicking to Reign. "Wow, that's a very un-asshole thing to do."

He grits his teeth. "I let him stay in a shit-box, one that's not even mine. I wouldn't be sainting me."

"You shared what little you had," she replies with an arched brow. "Want to negate that, too?"

Darnell chuckles. "I can see why she's your home slice—hot *and* sassy."

Reign's pretty sure his jaw is about to snap. "She's not mine, or anyone's, slice of anything. We're just friends."

"Yep," says Arielle. "We're helping each other out."

Darnell glances between them. "Okay," he says in the most drawn out drawl possible. Reign wonders how many years he's aged before he's done.

"Where's Rachel?" he asks.

Darnell juts his thumb over his shoulder. "She's upstairs, in your room. But I gotta warn you, she's a bit freaked out."

"Poor thing," Arielle murmurs. "What she must've seen..."

They enter the house and Reign glances around the living room. He knows he shouldn't be surprised by how little things have changed—the saggy mattress, the rubbish, the plastic bags that function as shelves, storage containers, luggage if they have to move—but he is. Probably because so much else has changed...

He watches Arielle's face as she follows him in. She takes in the graffiti on the walls, the stairs with no bannister, the sense of hopelessness that hangs in the air. "A bit of a fixer-upper, huh?"

Darnell snorts out a laugh as Reign's lips angle up before he can stop himself. Damn this girl and her sweet heart and smart mind. He walks quickly to the stairs, as if he can escape the thought. A thought that violates the friend-zone they're in as much as the dream did.

They make their way up, the stairs creaking as they ascend. They reach the room that was once his and Reign glances inside. His gut clenches at the sight that greets him.

A young woman, maybe a little older than them, is curled up with her knees to her chest on the musty mattress he used to call his own. Her short red hair is a tangle around her pale face, her eyes too big in her panicked face.

"Who are you? What do you want?" she demands in a shaky voice.

They stop in the doorway and Reign's throat tightens. He's been on the streets long enough to see the effects of trauma, and right now, Rachel is the poster child for the life-changing impact it has on a person's world.

"Hi Rachel, my name's Arielle, and this is Reign. We're here to help."

Rachel scoots further back, pressing herself against the grimy wall. "There's nothing you can do." Her eyes well with tears. "She's coming for me. For all of us."

Reign and Arielle glance at each other. Rachel's talking about Lust.

He squats down, making himself smaller. "We know you've been through a lot. That's why we're here."

"There's nothing you can do. There's nothing anyone can do."

Arielle shakes her head, also lowering herself down. "We want to stop this. So you'll be safe as well as everyone else."

Rachel shakes her head, her limp bangs brushing against her lashes. "I just want to go home," she says tearfully.

"And we'll take you there," Reign assures. "We just need to know what happened at the club."

Rachel glances past his shoulder as if she's expecting Lust to come storming in any second. "Is...is it safe? To go home, that is?"

"We're pretty sure the woman who did this isn't after you. She's moved on." To other victims. And Reign doubts Rachel is going to be losing herself to lustful emotions anytime soon.

Rachel's arms loosen around her legs a little as she chews her lip. "You want to know what I saw?"

"Yes," Reign says quietly. "We want to stop this."

Rachel raises her watery eyes to him, to Arielle, and then back again. Suddenly, they widen as her gaze leaps to something behind him and a scream is torn out of her throat.

Reign shoots to his feet as he spins around, heart thundering and muscles ready to fight. But it's Gabby standing behind them, her hands slipping off her hips as she realizes how scared Rachel is.

She turns her gaze to Arielle. "You were supposed to tell me if you found anything," she says under her breath.

Arielle narrows her eyes. "How did you find me?" she asks, neatly avoiding Gabby's accusation.

"I placed a tracking spell on you," Gabby hisses. "I was hoping I wouldn't need it because you'd be honest with me."

"But you didn't trust me enough not to use it," Arielle points out in a soft voice, and Reign's not sure if it's the hurt or the anger that she's trying to contain.

Reign clears his throat. "Gabby, I'd like you to meet Rachel. She's the one who witnessed the murders."

Two sets of blue eyes turn to him, then guiltily snap to Rachel. "Hi, Rachel. Sorry to scare you like that."

Rachel nods. "Did you say tracking spell?"

"Ah, I meant a tracking device," says Gabby. "Definitely meant tracking *device*."

"No, you didn't," says Rachel, certainty flashing in her eyes. She straightens, her legs shifting to a cross legged position. "I heard exactly what you said. Which means you might actually believe my story."

MAC

Mac's just heading to a parking lot so she can leave the university campus when she sees Reign. He's climbing out of a dark blue truck, smiling when he sees her.

She waits as he approaches, hoping she makes sense as she tries to explain what she saw.

"Hey, big day today," he says cheerily. "How many hours till you get your acceptance into the advanced program?"

"What? Oh, yeah, not long now. Look, I need to talk to you about Lizzie."

Reign's grin grows. "I'm just heading to see her now. We're going to the library to study." He says the last word with so much innuendo that Mac feels nauseous.

"I don't think you should go. She's bad news."

His eyebrows shoot up. "What? You're the one who convinced me to go on a date with her. You said, and I quote, she's totally your type." He grins again. "And you were right."

"No," says Mac, shaking her head furiously. "I was wrong. I just overheard her, she was with another guy. She's trying to get something from you. Some sort of information."

He leans a little closer. "You've been studying too much."

"This has nothing to do with that. I'm telling you, she's bad news!" Mac's about to tell him about the red eyes, but she stops herself. She saw the same when she looked in the mirror. It will only reinforce his belief she's losing it.

He shakes his head. "Not from where I'm standing. She's really into me and I'm really into her."

"But—"

Reign steps around her. "After you find out that you're in, why don't you go home and read one of those sci-fi books you like so much? Maybe that one on parallel universes you spent three weeks talking about."

Mac watches as he walks away, tears stinging her eyes as she wonders what she's supposed to do next. Nothing makes sense, but she saw Lizzie with that guy, she heard what she said. Reign's in trouble.

Jolting into action, Mac sets off to follow him. She needs to tell him everything. She needs to make him listen.

But she's just rounded the building when Lizzie steps out of the recessed entry.

"I heard everything you said," she sneers.

Anger flashes through Mac. "Leave him alone."

Lizzie laughs. "It's too late for that." Her eyes flare, reminding

Mac of a lioness closing in on her prey. "Thank you, by the way. The good word you put in for me made my job so much easier."

"What job?" Mac demands. Everything feels like it's spiraling out of control.

Lizzie straightens her skirt. "You can't stop me," she says dismissively. "Now, if you'll excuse me. I'm off to see my boyfriend." She flips her hair over her shoulder as she sashays away. "We're really into each other."

Mac watches her leave, the anger coursing through her unable to find an outlet. There's a bench seat nearby and she drags herself over, flopping onto it. She leans forward, her head dropping into her hands, watching as hot tears drip onto the pavement.

She's so confused. What's real and what's not? How does she fight this when no one believes her? She's not even sure she believes herself...

"Mac?"

She sits upright, surprised to hear her name, and finds two girls standing in front of her. They're both blonde, although one has straight hair, the other curly. The girl with the straight hair is wearing an impressive set of knee-high canvas boots, while the curly haired girl is wearing the cutest mini-skirt Mac's ever seen.

But she doesn't recognize either of them. "Yeah? How do you know my name?"

"Mac, my name's Gabby. This is my cousin, Arielle."

Arielle smiles, the motion gone almost as soon as it's begun. "We need to talk."

CHAPTER 19
ARIELLE

Arielle turns back to Rachel, pushing away the thought that's shredding the fabric of her faith in herself.

Gabby doesn't trust her. She put a tracking spell on her.

Arielle sits all the way down, conscious that the floor is covered in dirt and dust. Her heart is being constricted, and it's not just because of the scared young woman in front of her.

This was Reign's room. Bare. Dirty. Unloved and unwanted.

Coming to this house has given her a whole lot of insight into the guy who's danced on the wrong side of the law for most of his life. No wonder he pushes everyone away. That's all the world has done to him.

She glances at his strong profile, noting the gentle way he's looking encouragingly at Rachel. Everything he's been through has hardened him, as it would. But under that armor, is honor, courage and honesty. Like a protector. Or a knight.

She flushes, looking away. That's also something to consider later. Right now, they have to find Lust.

Rachel draws in a trembling breath. "I went to Multiplayer that night because I'd heard about it. It was exciting to learn that there's somewhere that caters for people like me." She lifts her chin, looking each one of them in the eye. "I'm attracted to a person, not their gender. Nor does a relationship have to be limited to two people."

Arielle nods. "You don't live by the status quo. I respect that. It shows you're strong enough to stand up for what you believe in."

Exactly what Arielle's trying to do, even though no one seems to believe she can do it.

Rachel blinks, her spine straightening a little as her shoulders pull back. "Yeah, I suppose so."

"Ari's right," Reign agrees. "You got this."

"Well, I met a guy and a couple of girls who I hit it off with pretty quickly. We just had that instant chemistry, you know?"

"Yeah, I know," says Gabby as Arielle thinks the same. Seeing Reign had stopped her world, and that was even when she'd realized he was the one who almost ran her over.

It's him, Trinity whispers.

Arielle stiffens, and Reign glances at her out of the corner of his eye. She instantly relaxes, ignoring the voice that just joined her consciousness. She can't afford to scare Rachel.

Rachel's eyes unfocus as she remembers the night. "We danced and things only got hotter, so we were going to head to one of the private rooms. I quickly ducked into the bathroom to make sure I didn't look like a sweaty rag. I was so excited." She flinches, her gaze returning to the room as if she's pulling away from the memory. "And then I heard screams," she whispers.

Arielle moves closer as a single tear trickles down Rachel's pale cheek. She reaches out and grips her hand. "I know this is hard."

Rachel studies her for a long second, her hand tightening around Arielle's. "You're a Pisces, aren't you?"

"Ah, yeah. How did you guess?"

Rachel smiles a little, the tear glistening on her cheek. "Pisces care about others. They're uber kind-hearted and very good at making connections."

"Oh," says Arielle, a little nonplussed but still touched. "Thanks."

"I'm a Sagittarius," says Rachel, scrunching her freckled nose. "I'm not so good at focusing on any one thing."

"And this is painful to focus on," says Arielle gently.

"Definitely a Pisces," says Rachel playfully, although the gratitude in her eyes touches Arielle. Rachel draws in a fortifying breath. "I sneaked a peek, thinking some mass shooting was happening or something. But it wasn't."

"Everyone was naked, as if in just those few minutes, their sex drive had exploded..." Rachel's lip trembles and she falls silent.

"There was a woman, wasn't there?" Reign asks quietly.

Tears pool in Rachel's eyes. "Yes. She was wearing a waitress uniform as if she worked there. Except she had red glowing eyes and huge black wings," she confesses in a whisper.

"That bitch," growls Gabby.

Seeing that her audience has unquestioningly accepted her account, Rachel continues. "Her mouth was open, and she was sucking people's energy like some awful black hole. Everyone was writhing. First in ecstasy, then in pain."

The room's silent and Arielle suspects Reign and Gabby are imagining the horrific scene along with her.

"I was terrified," whispers Rachel. "I ran out the back door and didn't look back. I ended up here when Darnell said he had a spare room."

Because Reign's now living in the cottage. And because Reign showed Darnell the same kindness that was extended to Rachel.

"Did you get a good look at the woman?" asks Gabby. "Can you give us a description?"

"She was beautiful, tall and curvy, with long red hair." Rachel wrinkles her nose. "Not my carrot-colored hair, but a deep wine color. But I can do better than a description. I saw her name tag."

Arielle almost gasps in excitement, but Reign speaks. "Most people would use a pseudonym in a place like that?"

"Yeah, I doubt Geshek is a real name," says Rachel. "But they'd have employee files with that info."

Gabby steps away as she pulls out her cell phone. "I'm going to ask Colt what that name means. It sounds middle eastern."

Arielle nods then turns back to Rachel. "So we need to go back to the club and get a look at their files?"

"I already have."

"You did?" Reign asks in surprise.

Rachel shrugs. "I wanted to know this woman's name if she's coming after me. Darnell had a laptop lying around, said it belonged to a friend. So I hacked into the club's server. The woman's real name is Luna D'Mello."

Reign and Arielle look at each other. They have Lust's name.

"We have to find her," Arielle says decisively. She looks back to Rachel. This girl is not only smart, but far tougher than the terrified bundle of nerves they walked in on. "The information you've given us is invaluable. Thank you."

Rachel leans forward. "I tried to find her details. I knew I couldn't go to the cops with what I saw, so I wanted to know this woman's name myself." Her lips twist. "But I couldn't get into the city's records. Not from here."

Reign looks at her thoughtfully. "Where would you need to be?"

"Inside their firewall. As in, inside the city administration building."

"And then you could get the information?" Arielle asks, her muscles tense. "We'd have her address?"

Rachel nods. "We sure would."

"And you'd be willing to do that?" Reign asks cautiously, no doubt knowing it's a lot to ask.

"Heck yeah." She looks around as she grimaces. "I can't keep living here, and until she's gone, I can't go home."

Arielle winces, knowing this is exactly where Reign lived for months. She's glad her mother had that cottage built. At least he now has somewhere safe and clean.

She pushes to her feet, dusting off her jeans. "Let's do it."

Reign does the same, his eyebrows pulling down. "Maybe we should talk about it—"

"I knew it, Geshek means lust in Hebrew," says Gabby as she enters, stopping as she realizes what Reign just said. "Talk about what?"

Arielle steels herself, remembering that her cousin put a tracking spell on her. That she still doesn't trust her. "We don't need to talk. We've decided. We're breaking into the city administration building to get Lust's details."

Gabby's face instantly darkens. "No. That's illegal."

"With each day that passes, more lives are lost." Arielle's hands clench. "We can't let that stop us."

"Maybe Colt can find a way in," says Gabby, shaking her head. "Let's see if there's another way." She turns to Reign. "Tell her it's not worth getting on the wrong side of the law."

Arielle holds her breath, waiting to see what Reign will say. He stands, holding Gabby's gaze. "Arielle is stronger than you give her credit for. You could try having a little more faith in her."

Arielle's breath hitches as sweet warmth fills her chest and clogs her throat. Reign's words are like a song through her veins.

Rachel also stands. "And I have no idea who you guys are, or why you know this bitch had wings, but I'll spend every day of my life looking over my shoulder unless I know she's been taken care of."

Gabby's frown is the deepest Arielle's ever seen. A muscle in her jaw twitches. "You need to slow down and think through the consequences."

Arielle's shoulders sink. "One day, you'll believe in me," she whispers.

She turns and walks out the door, Gabby's doubt in her only making her more determined.

Which means she's going to break into Mercy City Hall.

CHAPTER 20
REIGN

As they stand behind some trees at the back of the large, white building, Reign isn't so sure this is the best idea they've ever had.

He wasn't when Arielle suggested it. But then Gabby came in and undermined her all over again, and he couldn't bear to see the flash of uncertainty cross her face. She needs someone to believe in her.

Even if this is risky as fuck. Arielle doesn't have a rap sheet. She's someone who would've gone through life without ever accruing a stain on her record. He doubts she's ever got a parking fine.

Which means he'll be the one to take the rap if anything goes wrong. He decided that two seconds after Arielle suggested this highly illegal scheme. His future was on a one way track to jail, so it's no big deal.

Rachel tucks her hair behind her ear as she readjusts the strap of the messenger bag carrying the laptop. "So, a fire alarm should be going off in the west end of the building in about"—she checks her watch—"thirty seconds."

Reign arches a brow. "You're quite the hacker, aren't you?"

She beams even as she shifts nervously. "I just didn't realize I'd be using the skills to fight the paranormal."

In the hours between leaving the hangout and night falling, Reign and Arielle filled Rachel in on why she saw a being with red eyes and black wings. Rachel had been pale, but relieved to hear she's not nuts, as they'd told her that angels and demons exist. That they're fighting to find the Innocent because its Grace can open the next Gate of Hell. That Lust has already escaped from the first.

Reign made sure he never mentioned the Grail, and he was glad to see that it seemed to slip Arielle's mind. It's a complicating factor they don't need right now. One he'd rather not think about.

Not when he's about to break and enter into City Hall. After hacking into the security and fire alarm system. So they can steal sensitive data.

Arielle hoists her own backpack, the lines of her jaw tight in the gloom. "Should be straightforward enough."

He grins, pushing away his misgivings. "Piece of cake."

Just as he says the words, a high-pitched wail sounds from the building. Lights go on down the right side and the security guard who was standing outside the back door rushes in.

"Let's go," says Rachel. "We need to get in before the fire department gets here."

Heart hammering, Reign breaks into a run as he keeps low. He'll be the first to enter. The first to face whatever they'll be up against. Gravel crunches and he finds Arielle beside him, shooting him a determined glance.

Of course she is.

Just as he reaches the door, Rachel whispers. "They're unlocked."

Trying the handle, he finds she's right. Another marvel of her hacking skills. Inside, they find themselves in a dimly lit corridor. Beyond the walls, the fire alarm continues in a strident pulse.

"Straight ahead. Fourth door on the left," says Rachel.

They move as silently and quickly as they can, although Reign's not sure how his thundering pulse doesn't give them away. Just as they shut the door, the wail of two fire trucks can be heard from outside.

The room they're in is a large office space, desks clumped together in groups, gray dividers creating individual pods.

"Bingo," breathes Rachel.

But Reign stops her, blocking the view of Arielle as he points out the security cameras tucked into the corners of the room.

"What do you take me for?" Rachel scoffs. "I turned them off before we even came in." She slips onto the chair of the first one and pulls out the laptop. "Now, to work some magic."

"Will it take long?" Reign asks tensely.

She keeps her gaze on the screen as she types. "It'll be quicker if I don't have to answer rhetorical questions."

Grinding his teeth, Reign paces several feet away and then returns. He finds Arielle watching him, her teeth peeking out as she chews her lip.

He makes a conscious effort to loosen the muscles knotted through his jaw. And shoulders. And gut. "Sorry. I think it's the sirens." He smiles weakly. "I've been conditioned from a young age."

Arielle smiles faintly at his lame joke. "I would've thought you'd be calmer, that's all."

That's because in every other illegal little jaunt, there was a part of him that thought it was a good idea. That it was worth the risk. It seems that part of his brain fled the moment he agreed to do this.

He shrugs. "I'm more of a petty crimes kinda guy. It's just taking a little time to get in the groove."

She nods, frowning a little. "Did you want to do this, Reign?"

He freezes, that question locking his muscles far more effectively than his futile efforts. What does he say to that? He promised he'd always be honest.

Except you haven't told her how you feel about her...

Reign ignores the snarky comment. His brain is being a right royal pain in the ass today. "I want to show you you're as strong as you're hoping you are," he says softly.

As strong as he knows she is.

Arielle blinks, her lips parting in a way he wishes he didn't notice. But then she frowns. Shit. She's realized he avoided the question.

"Bingo," says Rachel, her fist pumping the air. "I'm in."

Reign and Arielle quickly join her, seeing that the screen of the laptop now sports the Mercy City coat of arms.

Rachel grins. "So much easier when I'm directly connected to the network. Now, to find Luna D'Mello."

She types, her fingers fast and familiar with a keyboard. Reign has no doubt this girl has spent a lot of time in front of a computer. Doing who knows what...

A small, whirling icon appears and she sits back. "This is an impressive laptop." She strokes her fingers over the silver case. "I kinda like it."

"It's stolen," mutters Reign. He can't believe Darnell kept one so he could have his share of the haul. He's mortified and touched all at once.

And no wonder the guy at the store was so pissed—it seems Rico and Darnell stole some state of the art computers. Man, they're lucky they weren't caught...

Rachel rolls her eyes. "Oh no. You mean having it is illegal?"

He snorts, acknowledging everything that's happened in the

last twenty minutes is on the wrong side of the law. About three miles past the line of right and wrong. He glances at the door. The sooner these two can get back to lawful citizens, the better.

Arielle places a hand on his arm, making him turn back as the soft touch blazes his skin. "You're worried."

"I'm being vigilant," he points out.

"Nah," replies Rachel. "You're freaking out. Which is unusual for a Taurus. They're usually so steady."

"I've never liked fitting in a category," he snaps back. She's really not helping.

"Reign?" Arielle asks, watching him closely.

"Bring the info to the nympho," Rachels sings happily as the screen fills with four names.

"Really?" Reign asks. "The info to the nympho?"

Rachel shrugs. "It's all I could think up in the moment. Well, that or armadillo."

She copies and pastes the names into a document, then takes a photo with her cell. "Just to make sure." She snaps the laptop shut a second later. "And, we're done."

Thank crap. Reign grabs Arielle's hand. He'll unwind when they're back at her house.

They're about to step around the desk when the door of the office bursts open, slamming into the opposite wall.

"Freeze! This is the police!"

Reign moves instinctively. He yanks Arielle back, grabbing Rachel by the shirt as he goes. He pulls them behind the desk and hunkers down.

Shit.

Shit.

Shit.

They've been caught.

Rachel is shaking her head in bewilderment. "But I disconnected the cameras," she whispers. "I made sure we weren't seen."

They obviously were.

"Stand slowly with your hands up," demands a strong voice.

Arielle's eyes are so wide, the white blazes in the dim room. "What do we do?" she mouths.

Reign peeks underneath the bottom of the desk, watching as multiple legs file into the room and spread out.

Shit.

Fuck.

Shitfuckshit.

"You have three seconds," snaps the voice impatiently. "We're not here to play games."

Reign's about to stand with his hands raised, hoping that maybe they didn't see that there are three people here. He'll tell them he was here alone. Maybe give them some attitude, just to get them cranky so they'll haul him in without asking too many questions.

Except he never gets the chance.

Two seconds have passed when the cops open fire. As the first shot cracks through the air, Reign folds over Arielle before a bullet lodges in the foam divider above them.

"They're shooting at us?" she asks in a terrified whisper.

Reign yanks Rachel closer, moving her behind them as more shots pepper around them. Bullets smash through the computer, ricochet off the desk, clang against the metal legs. It's only a matter of time before they get hit.

"Not again," Rachel moans.

He peeks through a gap between the desk and the divider, his breath freezing when he sees what she must have.

About six men. All in uniform. All with glowing red eyes.

"Demons," he whispers. Having made the decision about how this is going to end, he squeezes Arielle. "Stay here."

"What?" she asks, alarmed. "What are you doing?"

He glances at Rachel, intending to tell her the same thing, only to find her crouched as if she's ready to move. She flicks him a glance. "I can fight."

Before he can ask what she means by that, she leaps away, landing in a roll behind the next pod of desks. There's no time to be impressed. All he can hope is she can fight as well as she hacks.

He allows himself the briefest caress of Arielle's cheek, something piercing his chest when her blue eyes flutter closed. And then he's running, head tucked low, ducking as a bullet whizzes somewhere above his head.

He circles around, using the desks as protection, knowing he's going to have to run at these bastards. He grabs a keyboard on his way through, holding it in front of his head. It's not exactly bulletproof armor, but it'll have to do.

The moment he reaches the final desk, he throws the keyboard at the nearest demon. The man was just swinging his handgun around to aim at Reign when it smashes across his face. Reign uses the moment to leap and slam his fist into the man's solar plexus.

The demon doubles over and Reign brings his elbow down on the back of his head. He collapses, already unconscious.

There's a gunshot and a bullet lodges in the wall behind him. Reign looks up, ice freezing his heart as he sees a gun pointed at him, crimson eyes lining him up. He runs, knowing he'll never get to the demon in time, but unwilling to wait for the bullet to come to him.

He always knew he'd go down fighting.

Rachel appears behind the demon, spinning so fast the strands of her red hair fly out, and cleans him up with a spinning kick. She lands above him, dropping to one knee as she ploughs a fist into his face.

She wasn't lying. She can fight.

Reign keeps running, already focused on the next demon. From the corner of his eye he sees Arielle pop up as she throws a small potted plant. It hits the demon a second before Reign does. He throws punch after punch, injecting all the anger and fear that she's now made herself a target into pummeling the man.

Rachel lets out a guttural shout as she leaps and kicks, never getting close enough to need to punch. She moves so fast she's almost a blur. She takes out the next demon, leaving three more to go. They're evening out the odds.

The laughter that suddenly echoes through the room has his blood freezing. Black smoke pours through the open door, viscous and thick, climbing upward even as it continues forward. It coils and twists, forming a figure. The curves of a voluptuous female appear, colors blazing through. Red hair. Lush crimson lips. Hellish glowing eyes.

Lust.

The demons instantly stop, standing at attention as if they're waiting for their next order. Lust ignores them, her glittering gaze scanning the room. She finds what she's looking for as her eyes fall on Rachel.

"Yes," she hisses.

Rachel snaps out of the frozen terror she was in, running back toward the desk they left. She's taken two steps when she's jerked back as if by an invisible coat hanger. She stumbles and would probably have fallen if whatever's seized her didn't grab her by the throat and lift.

Her eyes widen, terrified and helpless, as she's slowly spun around to face Lust, only the tips of her feet still on the ground.

"You thought I didn't see you?" Lust purrs. "That I'd let you get away?"

Rachel whimpers, and Reign's hands clench. They didn't need to go to these lengths to find Lust. She found them.

And somehow, they have to get away.

"Let her go," shouts Reign.

Lust turns her head slowly to look at him. "Quiet, or your death will be a slow, painful one."

"Bring it on, bitch," Reign snaps. If he can get Lust to focus on him, maybe Rachel and Arielle can run. "From what I can tell, you're all curves and no action."

Lust bristles, her hair twitching in sinuous waves, but then she turns back to Rachel. "This isn't how I like to do it, but this is about necessity, not fun." Her red lips curve up. "And I'll still enjoy it."

Her hand tightens, making Rachel's eyes bulge and she begins to struggle with everything she has. From the corner of his eye, Reign sees Arielle stand up, that determined look on her face that he's wishing he didn't recognize. She's planning on doing something.

His gaze flicks down as she raises something clenched in her hand. She's holding a letter opener. It's somehow absurd and achingly courageous.

But Reign would never let her put her life at risk like that. That's not how this is going to end.

He propels forward, digging his feet into the floor with everything he has. "Run, Arielle!" he screams. "Get out of here!"

Lust's hand squeezes tighter, yanking a strangled gasp out of Rachel. She doesn't even glance at Reign as he shoots toward her, even though he has no doubt she knows he's coming.

Fine by him. He's up for a little hand-to-hand scuffle. Maybe his weird pain power that worked on Cain will work on this bitch, too.

He hopes so. It's the only advantage he has.

"Reign, no!" Arielle screams.

But he only uses the panic in her voice to propel him faster. He angles his head down, ready to become a battering ram. He'll knock Lust over, giving Rachel a chance to escape with Ari.

But a split second before the collision, Lust's other hand snaps out. She doesn't even glance in his direction as she does it, as if he's not worth her attention. As if she's not worried that he's going to touch as much as a blazing red hair on her head.

In a blink, he sees why. A long dagger is in her hand, the tip waiting to slice him. Reign has no chance to slow his momentum. No way to stop.

Pain is its own white-hot knife as the blade impales his chest. Lust's face twists with satisfaction as she pushes it in deeper, the Hell-color of her eyes blazing. Reign drops to the ground, agony like a supernova exploding through his torso.

Lust turns back to Rachel, raising her arm so the girl's feet are no longer on the ground. "I'll finish you all," she growls.

Panting with pain, Reign moves his head, hoping Arielle is doing what she's supposed to—getting out of here. He finds her across the room, and she's definitely moving. She's moving the fastest he's ever seen. But Arielle's running toward him. Toward Lust.

"No," Reign groans.

His ultimate fear is playing out before him. He's watching it as inevitably as he's feeling his blood gush out of his chest.

He's died for nothing.

KEEPER
CHRONICLES

MAC

Mac stares at the two blonde girls, uneasiness slithering up her spine. "Talk about what?"

"About a girl called Lizzie Evans," says Arielle, Gabby nodding beside her. "She has something of ours."

Mac pushes to her feet. "She's trouble, isn't she?"

Arielle and Gabby glance at each other. "Yeah," says Gabby. "Big trouble."

"We believe she works for a very dangerous organization," adds Arielle.

Mac recoils, fear clutching at her throat. "But Reign..."

Arielle stiffens at the mention of his name. "She's got to him, hasn't she?"

"She really has," says Mac, a sick feeling pooling in her gut. "And I saw her talking to another guy earlier today."

The two girls glance at each other again. Arielle nods imperceptibly.

"Lizzie's connected to some people in high places," says Gabby. "She works for a man named Cain, and he works for Mayor Virginia."

"The Mayor?" Mac repeats, realizing this goes far higher and deeper that she expected.

Arielle nods. "She's not who she seems to be, and she's also behind all this. She's consistently won every election she's run for because she has crime money at her disposal."

"And what does Reign have to do with all of this?"

"Cain and the Mayor believe he has something they want," says Arielle, her eyes grave. "And they'll kill him to get it."

Mac wants to run after her best friend right now. She wants to shake him until he sees sense. Instead, she stays where she is, hands clenched. "I tried to tell him Lizzie was trouble, but he wouldn't listen."

Arielle's lips twitch. "He's so stubborn."

Realizing Arielle knows him, Mac looks at her more closely. "He hasn't mentioned anyone called Arielle."

She looks away. "It's...complicated. It's like he doesn't want to *admit I'm part of his world."*

Mac digests this. She's not really sure what Arielle means, but it sure sounds like Reign.

"But maybe he'll listen to me," says Arielle. "It's important that he knows."

It really is. Shit's getting real.

Glad she finally feels in control, Mac nods. *"I'll bring him to the cafe at eleven o'clock."*

SIERRA

Sierra spears her fingers through her hair, flopping back in the chair she's sitting in. "This is just getting depressing."

Nim glances up from the book in front of her. "We're researching the Seeker, what did you expect?"

"Not this," Sierra says, her hand waving to the two other leather bound tomes on the desk in front of them. Even in the ethereal lighting of Veritas Library, they look ominous. "I mean, the Seeker's been responsible for so much."

"World War I, the Mongol Conquests, the Taiping Rebellion, World War II, the Conquests of Timur, the Russian Civil War, the Thirty Years War, the Mughal Maratha Wars, the Napoleonic Wars, the Korean War, the Hundred Years War—"

Sierra lifts her hand to stop Nim. She's already read all that, and it only makes her sicker to hear it all over again. "Yes, all that." Essentially, every tragedy of war and death that's fallen upon humanity. "But we're still no closer to finding it."

Nim chews her lip in thought. "We've also read that the Seeker's power can be harnessed, rather than the Seeker dominating the one who has it for its own purposes." She holds Sierra's gaze. "Arielle could be the person to do that. The spirits certainly seem to think so."

The nausea only multiplies with each of Nim's words. Arielle let Dumah out—an impulsive, dangerous decision. How can she be ready for something as powerful as the Seeker? How could she ever control it?

She shakes her head, swallowing down the acid that's burning her throat. "The risk is too great. If she fails, she'll be the catalyst for any of the horrors you just listed. All because she meant well. I can't let that happen to her."

"But the spirits—"

"Aren't all knowing," snaps Sierra. "Nor do they love my daughter like I do."

Their world won't be torn to shreds if anything happens to Arielle.

Nim sighs. "Okay. We'll keep searching. In the meantime, maybe Ari will surprise us. Maybe she'll show you she's more capable than you thought."

Sierra nods. "Thank you."

"Have a little faith, okay?" says Nim, smiling gently.

Drawing in a tremulous breath, Sierra nods. "Maybe she'll surprise us."

CHAPTER 21
ARIELLE

Arielle falls to her knees beside Reign, her heart splintering. The entirety of his chest is drenched in blood. "Reign," she whispers.

But he doesn't answer. His lashes don't flutter. His face remains soft, almost vulnerable, sweetly beautiful in a way that only fractures her chest further.

Above her come the gagging sounds as Rachel is progressively strangled. Arielle cries out, knowing they're both dying.

And that she's the one who brought them here.

She grips the letter opener, feeling how flimsy it is. It won't kill Lust, but maybe she can wound the demon before she dies, too. Maybe it'll anger her and she'll punish Arielle. It's the least she deserves.

White light explodes in the room, making Arielle throw her arm across her eyes. She curls over Reign, seeing what feels like the explosion of the sun behind her tightly clenched eyelids.

It's gone before the gasp wrenched from her lips is finished. Arielle opens her eyes, seeing that Lust is gone, too. As are the demons. Rachel is on all fours, one hand at her throat.

"What just happened?" Arielle whispers. Angels?

The sound of heels sharply rapping has them both turning around. A woman in a power suit, brown hair pulled back tightly, enters the room. "We'd best call 911," she says calmly.

Arielle blinks, recognition flickering in her mind, but unable to place the woman's face. She knows her...

"Mayor Goodstone?" she asks incredulously.

"Please, call me Virginia." She glances around the room that was suddenly cleared on her arrival. "I feel we're past formalities, now."

She slips out a cell phone from the pocket of her slacks, dialing as she holds it in one hand. "Yes. There's been an incident at City Hall. One person seriously injured."

Arielle turns back to Reign, her mind trying to catch up with what's just happened. Rachel crawls over, looking just as dazed. Mayor Goodstone—Virginia—continues to provide information to the paramedics in a cool, calm voice.

Reign's eyes fly open, a pained gasp drawing into his lungs. He glances around frantically, and she quickly moves so she's in his line of vision. "Sh, it's okay. Everything's going to be okay."

He visibly unwinds, pain drawn in tight lines over his face. "Who...you...convincing..."

Arielle's hands flutter over his blood-soaked chest, unsure whether she should touch him or not. Rachel moves in, quickly pressing a palm over the slice in his shirt. "Pressure will stem the bleeding."

Reign winces, his shoulders curling in as if he's avoiding her touch, but Rachel doesn't pull away, her face pale but resolute.

Arielle nods, a tear unwillingly escaping and tracking down her cheek. She can't fight. She doesn't know basic first-aid. Yet she ran into this anyway.

And Reign is the one who paid the price.

"Now's the time to fight, Reign," she whispers fiercely. "Please. For me."

He nods imperceptibly. "Always."

His eyes flutter closed, those thick, dark lashes of his a stark contrast to his bloodless skin. Arielle clutches his hand, her tattered heart constricting as she feels how cold it is.

"You're going to be okay," she says through numb lips.

He has to be.

The wail of an ambulance in the distance echoes the sound howling through her mind.

ARIELLE WATCHES as Reign's wheeled away down the hospital corridor. The doctors said he'll need surgery. That they won't know what damage has been done to his internal organs until they've had a look.

She clamps her hand over her mouth. What has she done?

Rachel slips an arm around her shoulder. "He's the toughest Taurus I've ever met. He'll pull through."

Arielle nods, even though there's no way Rachel can promise that. No one can.

The sliding doors to their left open and Gabby rushes in. "I came as soon as I heard! Is he okay?"

"He will be," Rachel assures. "They've just taken him into surgery."

Gabby glances at the doors Reign disappeared through then back at Arielle and Rachel. "What happened?"

Arielle screwed up. Again. That's what happened.

But before she can answer, Arielle's mom and Nim enter the room. Her mom looks around frantically, and when she spots Arielle, she rushes over. They hug, holding each other tightly.

Arielle struggles to hold her tears in. She's tried so hard, and yet all she's done is let everyone down.

Her mom pulls back. "What happened? Is Reign okay?"

The same questions Gabby asked. The first Arielle can answer, the second she wishes she could influence the outcome. She can't lose Reign...

Arielle steps away, stacking each vertebra above the other, trying to fortify herself from the inside out. "We went to City Hall to find Lust's address. But she found us." Her gaze flickers to the red marks on Rachel's neck. "We managed to get away, but not before Lust stabbed Reign."

She doesn't share the part about the white light and the Mayor, not because she's keeping secrets, but because she's still trying to figure out what happened. Trying to find the words.

Arielle's mom and Nim glance at each other, and Arielle has no idea what that means, but it only multiplies the guilt that's eating away at her like acid.

"You need to stop, Ari," her mother says gently, her eyes pleading. "You've seen how dangerous it is firsthand."

The words are a slap. A punch to her throat. A wrecking ball to Arielle's gut.

And yet, they're the truth. She's done nothing but make things worse.

"Slow down, maybe," says Gabby. "But not stop."

Arielle's mom spins to face her. "What?"

"You heard me, Sierra. Arielle's shown she's tough. So full of courage, that I'm awed. We shouldn't underestimate her."

Arielle's rooted to the spot in shock. Her cousin's words bring fresh tears to her eyes.

Gabby turns to her. "But definitely slow down," she says with a small smile.

Arielle's mom is already shaking her head. "No. You don't know what you're saying, Gabby. This is bigger than any of us have realized."

And Arielle doesn't have what it takes.

"I need a moment to think," she murmurs, spinning on her heel and exiting the ward. She walks and doesn't stop until she's outside the emergency department they arrived in not long ago. A few steps and she's at the curb, the ambulance bay not far away. She's never traveled in one before.

She always assumed it would be scary. But not so terrifying that her bones shivered. Reign was so pale. So still. There was so much blood...

The cool night air glides over her skin, raising goosebumps. She crosses her arms, rubbing even though it won't make the cold go away. Not when it starts inside her. Frozen indecision somehow sitting alongside the burning guilt.

What does she do?

Mac's in a coma, trapped in her own subconscious, put there by angels. Cain is searching for the Grace, if he hasn't found it already. Lust is murdering because she gets off on it.

And Arielle foolishly thought she could help. Maybe even do something about it. But even Rachel's been more useful than her. Her hacking skills, her surprising martial arts skills, have done more than Arielle's involvement has.

Maybe she should step back. So no one else gets hurt.

And yet, the decision *feels* wrong. She was so sure she's meant to be part of this. Shaking her head, she knows she can't stay out here. She needs to be there when Reign wakes.

If he wakes...

She pushes away the terrifying thought. She's just about to turn back when a limousine pulls up to the curb. Black and shiny, with tinted windows, it screams of money, showing that even the rich aren't immune to accidents or illness.

The door opens but Arielle doesn't wait to see who's coming out. She has enough pain of her own.

"Arielle," says a female voice.

She spins back, shocked to find the Mayor standing beside the open car door.

"Mayor Goodstone?"

"Virginia, remember?" She steps back, indicating the interior of the limousine. "I thought we'd have a chat."

Arielle hesitates. Some answers would be good, but Reign's inside, undergoing surgery. She needs to be there for him.

"It won't take long. And I have some information you may find...helpful."

"Five minutes, tops," Arielle says, quickly jumping in. The Mayor saved all their lives, and they need to know why.

The interior of the limousine is plush and well lit. The leather seat molds to Arielle's body as she sits in it stiffly. She just realized she's put herself in a very dangerous situation. One flick of the Mayor's fingers and she'd be whisked away to who-knows-where.

The Mayor makes herself comfortable across from Arielle, her hair now down and brushing her shoulders in mahogany waves. Arielle goes to jump out as the door begins to close.

"I know about Mac," says the Mayor. "And I can help you with her predicament."

Arielle stills. "How?"

"And I know how you can banish Lust and all her demons." Virginia's eyes sharpen. "You saw what I did back there."

Reeling, Arielle isn't sure what to ask first. Virginia Goodstone is obviously supernatural, but is she angel or demon?

"And, I know where Cain is."

The questions evaporate. "Where is he?" Arielle bites out. Finding Cain can make this all okay again.

Virginia smiles. "Syria."

Arielle presses further into the leather seat as she digests this. Cain's in the middle east. She could never afford to fly there, not to mention she wouldn't know the first place to look.

"I could send you there," says Virginia, as if she read her mind. "All expenses paid and with my best men."

Arielle's mind is working in overdrive. "Why?" she asks again. "Why would you tell me all this?"

Virginia inclines her head. "I want the Gates of Hell to stay closed as much as you do." She leans forward. "And I'd want something in return."

Knowing they've come to the punchline, Arielle holds the woman's gaze. "What?"

"There's a grave in Damascus. I need a spell chanted over it."

Knowing what she's being asked of is not as innocent as Virginia's making it out to be, Arielle chews her lip. What price is worth saving countless lives?

Virginia's lips angle up ever so slightly. "You do this, and I might throw in the one weapon that can kill Lust. Permanently."

"If you want the Gates of Hell closed, why don't you do this yourself?"

"There are...complicating factors. I'm unable to see the grave because of my link to it. Cain mustn't know I'm following him. And ultimately, a person in my position cannot be seen to be meddling in the supernatural."

Arielle nods, chewing on her lip. "How do I know I can trust you?"

"Because you'd be dead without me," Virginia says simply. She pins Arielle with her gaze. "You have a choice. Stay here, losing your battle as people die. Or go to Damascus, get me what I want, and you stop all of this."

Arielle's breath lodges in her throat. She could fix this. Save everyone.

Her mom could actually be proud of her. Reign and Gabby's words could be founded on something more than faith.

"I'll think about it," she says, her heart thudding against her ribs.

Virginia smiles despite the noncommittal answer. "I'll get everything in order, just in case," she practically coos. She presses a button on the leather-clad console beside her and the door opens. "Then I'll contact you."

Arielle climbs out, drawing in lungfuls of cool air as she tries to steady her nerves. She turns back, only to find she has nothing to say. Should she reject this offer?

Or say yes, and finally have a chance to make this right?

The Mayor's hand appears, the red-painted nails holding a business card. "I'd recommend learning to fight, dear. Here's a place with a good reputation."

Arielle takes the card and the door quickly shuts. The limo drives away, as if it's worried she'll change her mind. She can't blame it. She's not entirely sure she's made the right decision just by taking it.

Tucking the card in her back pocket, she turns and quickly makes her way back inside the hospital.

She's found a way to help Mac. Capture Cain. And end Lust.

All she has to do is say yes.

VIRGINIA

Virginia slips off her suit jacket and rolls her shoulders. Humans are so caught up in appearances and facades. For the most part she doesn't mind, it's allowed her to mold herself into someone of power and influence.

But the clothes are far more restrictive than what she

prefers. Than the clothes of her younger years, before everything went wrong.

She presses her thumb to the top drawer of her desk. The scanner blinks and it slides open. She pulls open a smaller, hidden drawer tucked inside and presses her thumb once more to the sensor that appears.

There's a soft *click* behind her.

Virginia stands and walks over to the hidden compartment that just opened in the wall. She smiles as she reaches in and grasps the vial sitting within it. Gently pulsing light bathes her hand as she withdraws it and holds it up.

Grace. Angelic essence, of an Innocent no less. Arielle's very own aunt.

Virginia's smile grows. "It's finally happening," she whispers.

Nothing can stop her now.

CAIN

Cain paces the familiar penthouse apartment, the Damascus heat wafting through the open window. He's not even sure why he's back here. Putting himself through this again.

It's not like he can see the grave. Anyone connected to the body buried beneath the sand is blind to its location. A cruel touch by those who put him there, cursing those who wanted closure to search aimlessly for the entirety of their existence.

And yet he's never stopped trying. And he never will.

There's always one more thing to try.

His cell phone rings, the modern sound feeling alien in the

land of Cain's childhood. It feels like yesterday and millennia ago, all at once.

"Cain," he snaps as he answers it.

"There's been a development," says a male voice. "Lust and her demons were banished by something powerful."

"What?" There are few beings more powerful than a Sin of Hell.

"I don't know. She'll be back, no doubt, but she's out of the picture for the moment."

Cain moves to the window, breathing in the familiar air. "We need to focus on the Grace. We cannot let this distract us."

"Yes, of course."

"I mean it, Xeven. We won't find the next Innocent without it."

There are still six Gates of Hell to be opened, and Cain won't stop until each one is destroyed.

He hangs up, not waiting for an answer. Xeven knows how important this is. He's told him enough times. Fire flares across Cain's arm and he steps out of the sunlight even though it makes no difference. It's always worse when he's closer to home.

Closer to *him*.

Cain glances down at his arm, carefully rolling up his sleeve. The Mark of Cain is burning so fiercely he doesn't know how it didn't scorch the material. It's as impatient to be gone as he is.

He clenches his fist, using the pain to fuel his determination.

There's always one more thing to try.

CHAPTER 22
GABBY

It's the early hours of the morning when they're given the news. The surgeon pulls the scrub cap off his head as he walks toward them, looking almost as tired as Gabby feels.

"He's going to be okay," he says, getting straight to the point. "The blade punctured his lung and there was a lot of internal bleeding. We've drained the hemothorax, and he'll be with us for at least a few days as he recovers." The doctor smiles a little. "He was very lucky, the knife just missed his heart."

Arielle collapses onto the nearest chair, sobs of relief wracking her body. Sierra sits next to her, wrapping an arm around her shoulders. "He's going to be okay," she says over and over, the words seeming to reassure both of them.

The doctor glances at Gabby. "They're family?"

Gabby's about to answer that Reign has no family, but she stops herself. "Yeah. He's everything to them."

Arielle just hasn't realized it yet.

She glances at Rachel, who's standing a few feet away, her own relieved tears trickling down her cheeks. "I'm going to let the others know."

Rachel nods. "I might go home soon. My dad will be worried."

Gabby brushes her arm as she walks past. She gets a sense that Rachel is going to become a part of their lives in ways none of them expected. Outside the hospital, she keeps walking as she dials Colt's number. How she wishes he was here to hold her.

"Hey," he says, his voice full of concern. "What's the news?"

"Reign's out of surgery, and he's going to be okay. He's got some healing to do, but he's a stubborn dude, I'm sure he'll do it three times quicker than anyone else."

Colt lets out a breath. "That's great. We need Reign more than he realizes."

"Yeah," says Gabby on a sigh. She rubs her forehead, glad that she has a chance to work off some of the tension knotting through her muscles. "Things are getting...messy."

"We've managed messy before."

Gabby blinks the sting away from her eyes, grateful for Colt's solid presence. "But this time family's involved."

If only Ari would slow down. Let someone help her instead of trying to do it all on her own.

"Not everything is your responsibility, you know," he says gently.

She sighs. "I know. It's just that Ari's like a sister to me. And Mac didn't ask for any of this. And people are dying."

"Why don't you come back here? Try and get some sleep?"

Gabby glances at the first shades of dawn climbing through the sky. Pale yellow. Soft peaches. Gentle blues. Being with Colt is just what she needs right now. He'd hold her close, those strong arms reminding her of the beauty that exists in this world. That the power of love can conquer the insurmountable.

But then she sees where her unconscious has brought her. Of course this is where she'd come when she's feeling like this.

"I'll be there in about thirty minutes," she tells Colt. "I'm just going to talk to Mom."

"Sure," he says, his voice soft with understanding.

Gabby hangs up. Colt knows the cemetery is only a few blocks from the hospital. He wouldn't be surprised that she ended up here, either. Weaving her way through the tombstones and the large trees shading them, she finds her mother's grave. Fragile blades of grass are only just starting to break through the fresh soil, and Gabby presses her fingers to her mouth at the sight of the new growth. It's proof of life after death, but it's also evidence that time's moving on.

And each one of those seconds has passed without her mother in her life.

Gabby falls to her knees. "Mom," she chokes. "I could really use you right now."

The tombstone stares blankly at her, and she wraps her arms around herself. A dawn breeze rustles the leaves of a nearby tree. "What do I do?" she whispers.

Does she encourage the flame of courage in Arielle? Or does she temper the determination to prove herself?

How much can she trust her father?

Cain.

Mac.

Her mother's Grace at risk of falling into the wrong hands.

It all feels like too much. An unbearable weight she doesn't know how to shift.

There's a sound behind her, and Gabby spins around, instantly on alert. But the cemetery is empty, nothing more than rows of tombstones broken up by carefully tended gardens. Her frayed nerves aren't coping. Standing, she decides it's time to go home. To Colt.

She's taken one step when she sees it.

A symbol has been carved into the trunk of the tree only a few feet away. A glowing, white emblem.

Gabby approaches it slowly, a sense of familiarity creeping over her. Three interwoven crosses are encased by a pentagram. She's sure she's seen it before. But where?

The symbol pulses softly in the early morning light, as if it's willing to wait so she can look her fill.

Someone's trying to tell her something.

Her cell rings and Gabby answers it without looking at the screen, assuming it's Colt and excited to tell him about this latest development.

"Gabby?" asks Nim. "Are you okay?"

Gabby jolts in surprise. "Oh hey, Nim. Yeah, I'm fine. Just went for a walk to clear my head."

"The spirits reached out to you," she says, the sentence a statement rather than a question.

"Yeah, they did. A symbol just appeared on a tree."

"They're trying to guide you," says Nim, her voice hushed.

Gabby straightens as she spins to face her mother's grave. She was kneeling there, so freaking lost, when the symbol appeared. "Was it...Mom? Is she trying to tell me something?"

There's a pause. "I'm not sensing Shell. But the spirits are definitely trying to help."

Turning, Gabby peers at the symbol. It's already starting to fade. "I think I've seen it before, but I'm not sure. And I have no idea what it means."

Nim sighs. "The spirits sense trouble." The frown in her voice is unmistakable.

A gust of wind has Gabby looking up as the leaves rustle above her. She gasps as she focuses beyond them. The sky that was so pretty and soft only minutes before has changed.

Dark clouds are storming in, heavy and low. But it's not the sudden shift in weather that has Gabby's hand flying to her throat.

It's the flesh-colored stain that is now the sky. As if the whole thing's been dipped in watery blood.

Lust is back much sooner than they expected.

MAC

"I really don't feel like a maple bacon muffin, no matter how much you wax lyrical over it," grumbles Reign.

But Mac doesn't release his hand. He's coming to this meeting, no matter what.

"You need to keep your energy up if you're going to keep sucking face with Lizzie like that," she says playfully, even though her stomach rolls in disgust.

She wants to punch Lizzie's lips right off her face.

Reign stops tugging and lets her lead him to the front door of the university cafe. "You're right." He grins. "We're meeting again later today."

Like hell they will.

Inside the cafe, Mac scans the room and finds Arielle sitting at a table tucked in the corner. She turns to Reign. "There's someone I'd like you to mee—"

But Reign's gaze has already found the blonde girl. And hasn't let go. He blinks once. Twice. But still doesn't move.

"Do you know her?" Mac asks.

Reign drags his gaze away, looking a little dazed. "No. Well, I don't think so."

"Her name's Arielle and she wants to speak to you."

He frowns, as if he's not sure how he feels about that, but Mac already has his hand and is dragging him over.

Arielle smiles as Reign approaches, looking as if her gaze is devouring him. "Hi, Reign."

He sits across from her, looking tense. "Hey."

Mac sits, watching the strange play between these two. There's chemistry here, the deep, primal kind. And yet Reign is looking confused. The same way she's felt as things have unfolded she had no recollection of.

Arielle leans forward a little. "You don't remember me, do you?"

He shakes his head. "Sorry, no." His lips twist up. "And I'm pretty sure I'd remember meeting you."

Arielle nods sadly. "People often go to great lengths to deny the truth. But you and I dated." Her hands tighten on the table. "Before Lizzie came along."

Guilt flushes through Mac. Apparently she's the one who introduced Lizzie to Reign.

Reign shakes his head again, this time with more force. He stops, glancing around suspiciously. "Is this one of those shows? Are there secret cameras around, waiting to see whether I'd cheat on Lizzie?"

Mac huffs in annoyance. "No. Reign, you need to listen to Arielle. Lizzie's trouble."

"And I think she may have tricked you," adds Arielle, looking at Reign closely. "How has she got you under her spell so quickly?"

He stiffens. "I don't do drugs, if that's what you mean."

As Reign says the final word, images fly through Mac's mind. Reign walking toward her through a door. Her sitting in a dingy room on a dingy mattress.

He holds something out, scowling. "Someone left their bowl of weed in my room, still burning."

She's reading a newspaper, seeming unperturbed.

"Dammit, Mackenzie! It's your bowl!"

Reign pushing to his feet has Mac snapping out of the memory or vision or brain glitch or whatever it was. "Look, you seem nice, but I can't imagine us ever having something going on between us." His gaze turns angrily to Mac. "And you're going to some disturbing lengths to get between me and Lizzie."

Mac stands too, her hands fisted by her sides. "That's because—"

"No," Reign snaps, slicing his hand through the air. "Enough. I'm with Lizzie, and that's that."

He spins on his heel and strides out of the cafe. Mac watches him storm away through the large windows, his spine stiff. He doesn't glance back once.

"Urgh," she growls. "He's so stubborn!"

Arielle sighs. "Like I said, people often go to great lengths to deny the truth. It holds them prisoner."

Mac crosses her arms, watching Reign make his way to the parking lot. He's probably off to brush his teeth before seeing Lizzie again. "What do we do?"

"We keep pushing. He needs to accept the truth, no matter how hard that is."

"Dufus," Mac mutters. "His life is on the line."

A white van drives into the parking lot, pulling up right in front of Reign. She watches in horror as the sliding door jolts open, two men jump out with hats pulled low over their faces, and haul Reign inside.

The door's barely shut before the van roars away.

Mac runs out of the cafe, knowing it's useless, but unable to help herself. "Reign!" she shouts.

But the van's gone.

Taking him with it.

SIERRA

Sierra stands in the hospital waiting room, grimacing as she takes a sip from her cheap coffee. Reign's been out of surgery for almost twelve hours now, but apart from waking and wanting to make sure Arielle and Rachel are okay, he's slept the sleep of the healing.

She'd sat there and watched his steady breathing. She'd sat there and watched her daughter watch his steady breathing.

Which is why she's out here now. The bond between Reign and her daughter is undeniable.

And yet, neither of them know...

Blaise appears around the corner, today dressed in flowing emerald green. Sierra's been friends with Blaise long enough to know it's the color associated with health and healing. She probably chanted a spell over the wooden box she holds out.

"Arnica, grape seed extract and gotu kola. They'll all help him heal."

Sierra takes it. "Thanks. We might need to hide it in a burger to get him to eat it."

Blaise smiles. "With strategies like that, it's obvious you're a mother."

Sierra sits on one of the nearby plastic chairs. "Possibly not a very good one," she mutters.

"Hey," says Blaise, taking a seat next to her. "You love Arielle with every fiber of your being. Unconditionally. You raising your daughter has been beautiful to watch."

Sierra smiles weakly. "And yet, she won't listen to me."

"She's reeling from everything she's learned and she's grieving after losing Shell. She just needs time," Blaise points out.

"She's making impulsive choices."

"She has a good heart," says Blaise firmly. "That's what counts."

"And she's falling for Reign."

"Oh."

Sierra sighs, wishing that hadn't stalled the conversation as well as it had. She wonders if Blaise realizes that Arielle will probably love as fiercely and completely as she has.

Blaise turns to her. "You need to tell him. You need to tell him everything."

That Reign is the Grail Keeper. The last one. That so much hinges on him.

"I know," she says resignedly. "I've been trying to find the right time."

Blaise glances down the hall to Reign's room. "Well, you have a captive audience for the next few days."

Sierra nods. She's already thought of that. "I'm going to give him a day or two get some strength back, then we'll talk."

"Good," says Blaise, patting her knee. "We'll protect him, just like the Archivists are supposed to."

"Yes, we will," Sierra promises, just as much to herself as to Blaise. She failed Reign once, she won't do it again.

"And I think you should tell Ari about the Seeker," Blaise adds softly.

Sierra's spine snaps straight, the word Seeker instantly making her tense. But then her back bows again. "You're right. She should know." Especially if Nim has seen it in her destiny. "Once Lust is out of the way." She's already tried to kill Reign once. Who knows who will be next.

"Actually, I came across a banishing spell in one of my grimoires."

"That's good news," says Sierra, brightening.

"I'm not sure if it'll work on a demon as powerful as Lust, so I'm going to do some more research."

Sierra pushes to her feet, waving away the caveat. "You're the most powerful witch I know. If anyone can do it, it's you, Blaise."

Blaise stands, too. "Let's hope that's enough," she says, flexing her shoulders as if she's prepping for a fight.

With a quick hug, Blaise leaves. Clutching the wooden box, Sierra sits back down, not quite ready to return to the room. She hopes Reign drinks herbal tea. It would be good to give him some good news before she tells him the truth about his past.

And the part she played in it.

CHAPTER 23

ARIELLE

Arielle stands in the doorway of Reign's hospital room, watching as he sleeps. The morning light slips through the blinds, caressing the black lock of hair boyishly flopping over his forehead. His thick lashes rest on cheeks that finally have a little color and his lips are slightly parted, luscious and plump. He's shirtless, the sheets pulled up under his arms, with a white bandage peeking above it.

There are so many layers to Reign. So many flavors.

The gruff, tough Reign.

The witty, unflappable Reign.

The courageous, almost self-sacrificing Reign.

She grips the doorframe. This sweet, sleeping Reign.

And she's drawn to every single one of them.

As she stands there, after coming so close to losing him, the truth's no longer willing to be ignored or denied or pushed away. She stops fighting it.

What she feels for Reign is far more than friendship. Deeper. Far more electrifying. Breathtakingly stunning.

Now, she has to decide what to do with that.

He stirs, no doubt vigilant even when resting. He always

seems to sleep with some part of his brain still engaged. His eyes flutter open, the beautiful green unerringly locking on her. He smiles, his lush lips tipping up. "Hey."

She enters, clutching the takeaway coffee cup far too tightly. "I just spoke to the doctor. The surgery went great and as long as the healing goes well, you'll be out of here in a few days."

His mouth twists. "Yeah, that's what he said to me, too. He won't let me go home before that."

Arielle takes another step in, lifting the cup. "I brought coffee," she offers.

The smile returns, this time bigger and more luscious, making her pulse trip. "Thanks. I don't know what it is they have here, but it's an insult to anything caffeinated."

"That's what my mom said." She stops beside the bed. "Quite a few people were worried about you."

The faintest tinge of pink graces his cheeks and if everything didn't feel so heightened right now, she probably wouldn't have registered it. "I noticed. The nurses said something about winning a popularity contest."

She sits on the edge of the bed, smiling. "It's like they care or something."

Reign glances down, picking at some nonexistent lint on his sheet. "Who would've thought."

She passes him the takeaway cup. "My guess is that the only person who's surprised is you."

Reign takes it and their fingers brush. Electricity zings up Arielle's arm but she doesn't pull away. Now that she's admitted how she feels, she doesn't want to.

It feels too good.

Reign pulls back, looking like he's chewing on the inside of his lip. He brings the cup to his lips and takes a sip, his bare bicep flexing. Arielle swallows. Holy heck, his shoulders are a map of valleys and ridges she has to snap her gaze away from.

He leans back, letting out a low groan. "You're a lifesaver."

The trickling warmth that had been dancing through her awareness fizzles out. "Actually, I'm quite the opposite."

He lowers the cup, frowning. "Don't say that."

"What? The truth?" She's the one who landed him in hospital, with a stab wound that could've been fatal.

Reign takes her hand and grips it. "No. It's nowhere near the truth. You were trying to save people."

And yet she hurt those closest to her. She knows she should pull her hand away, that she doesn't deserve his reassurance, but she stays where she is. "We should never have gone to City Hall. It was stupid."

"Lust wanted Rachel. She would've swooped in not long after she left the hangout, no matter where she went."

"But we might have been better prepared." They might've had Gabby and Colt, who are supernatural and actually know how to defend themselves. They wouldn't have stood there with a stupid letter opener...

Nor would she have been solely responsible.

He shakes his head. "We don't know that. It could've happened anytime, anywhere." He grins. "And like you said, I'm going to be fine, so no harm done."

His words shock her for a long second. Does he really think so little of himself? That what happened can be brushed away because he was lucky enough to survive?

His hand tightens around hers, the movement making him wince so she shuffles forward a little. "Nothing's changed with Mac?"

She shakes her head, her chest tightening. "No."

And Colt believes they're progressively running out of time. That soon, Mac will be trapped, but she's not mentioning that now. He'd jump out of bed, recent surgery be damned.

His shoulders sag. "I didn't think so."

"Colt and Gabby are still on Dumah's trail," she says encouragingly. "And she could find a way to break out of this herself."

Reign chews his lip again. "If anyone can do it, Mac can."

"And Blaise thinks she may have found a banishing spell to deal with Lust."

"Good," he mutters, wincing again as if just the mention of the demon tugs at his wound. "That bitch needs a serious ass kicking."

Arielle rubs her thumb over Reign's knuckles, mulling over the rest of the information she needs to share. It's only when she sees a wave of goosebumps climb up his arm that she realizes what she's doing. "Are you cold?"

Reign frowns. "No, I'm fine."

She blinks. That means the goosebumps were caused by something else… Arielle mentally shakes herself. She has things to say. "I'm going to start training at a local dojo."

His eyebrows brush the stray lock on his forehead as they leap in surprise. "You are?"

"Yeah. I need to stop being a liability."

Reign's brows slam back down. "You're not a liability. You're an important part of this team."

Arielle looks away. That's what she wants to be. So much.

He tugs on her hand, waiting. She slowly returns her gaze to his, her breath catching as the blaze of green traps her.

"You can't give up, Ari. There aren't many things I know, but I do know this is your destiny."

"How, Reign? There's no way you can be sure."

The jungle green of his eyes clears, becoming emerald pools of sincerity. "I can feel it. And I've got as far as I have trusting my instincts."

Trust her instincts. He's right. She would've quit by now if it weren't for some inexplicable drive she can't ignore. She's a part of this, even if she doesn't know how.

The very same drive that pulls her toward Reign. Her gaze drops to his lips. The very same drive that wants to touch him. To see those goosebumps again. To taste him.

She shifts forward, careful not to bump him, her pulse suddenly feeling heavy and rapid. Reign's breath seems to stop, his mouth parting as his tongue darts out to moisten his bottom lip.

She's never seen anything so sexy in her life.

Leaning in, Arielle pauses a breath away, but Reign doesn't move. Has she read this wrong? Have her own overwhelming feelings clouded her judgment?

"Arielle," he says softly.

Her name is said with reverence.

In surrender.

It's all she needs.

She kisses him, pressing her lips to his. Finally doing something right. And sweet heavens, it's beautiful. So achingly sweet. Reign's lips are supple and soft, a delicious, perfect fit. Their mouths move intuitively, discovering that they're creating something unforgettable.

And yet, it's not enough. Arielle instinctively knows she wants more. She melts and molds, increasing the pressure. Reign's hand spears into her hair, cupping the back of her head and angling as a groan rumbles through his chest. She instinctively opens her mouth, knowing what he wants. What she needs.

His tongue sweeps in, finding her own and tangling. Branding. The heat that explodes disintegrates her breath. Her ability to think.

Her desire to be anywhere but here.

Her hands come up to clutch his shoulders, and she gasps as

her palms connect with burning skin. She never knew a kiss could be like this. As if it's everything.

And yet, it's a taste, a window, of something so much more.

Arielle moves closer, the need for more an insatiable drive, when Reign draws in a sharp hiss. She instantly pulls back, horrified she's forgotten about his injury.

"Sorry," she breathes, letting her forehead drop to his. She goes to pull away but his hand draws down to cup her chin, keeping her there.

He wordlessly shakes his head. "Why, Ari?" he asks in a whisper. "Why would you do that?"

"I was tired of fighting how I feel for you, Reign. Friends was never going to be enough."

Just like one, sweet kiss wasn't.

His lashes flutter closed, his thumb stroking her cheek as his breath puffs over her. "Ari..."

He says her name heavily, as if it hurts, and she's not sure what that means. She carefully, gently brushes her own fingers over his lips, almost smiling when she sees a spray of goosebumps down his throat. "Yeah?"

"I'm sorry, did you say room four-oh-six?" comes a strident voice from down the hall.

Arielle and Reign pull apart and she quickly shuffles away. Reign's face twists with pain as he leans back against the pillows and closes his eyes. Rachel enters a moment later.

"Sorry I'm late," she says cheerily. "I assumed they'd put you in the pediatric ward."

Reign snorts. "I tried. Do you know they have a PlayStation there?"

Arielle tries to pull her scattered senses together as she rises to her feet. She smiles weakly as Rachel walks past and drops the laden plastic bag she was holding next to Reign.

"I brought all the things you'll need to get better. Cheerios. Soda. Hershey's bars."

"Thanks, Rach," Reign says, not quite meeting her eye.

He glances at Arielle then quickly looks away. Awkwardness steadily weighs down the air. Whatever he was going to say will have to wait.

Rachel's brow hikes up as she crosses her arms.

Arielle glances at the clock on the wall. "Oh gosh, I have to get going. I have an appointment soon."

"You do?" Reign asks, finally looking at her for longer than a second.

"Yeah, I have to go home and get changed." She retreats to the door. "Sorry, Rachel. I'll see you around."

Ducking out before there's a chance for goodbyes, Arielle hurries down the corridor. It's only when she reaches the lift, that she finally acknowledges everything that just happened.

So many things just became clear. Her feelings for Reign. And what she should do next.

There aren't many things I know, but I do know this is your destiny.

Reign believes in her. She's seen that something amazing can rise from the ashes of defeat.

She's not giving up.

And doing what the Mayor asks so she can catch Cain is exactly what she needs to do.

GABBY

Gabby slams the large tome shut, frustrated that it makes little more than a soft thud. "How can there be so many books at Veritas, and none of them have the symbol I saw?" she wails.

"Well, it could be here," Nim points out, flexing her shoulders and twisting a little in her wheelchair. "But there are a lot of books. Which is part of what makes it so awesome."

Blaise indicates to the stack of books in the center of the desk. "And these were the first ones my locator spell detected. There could be more."

"You people really need to think of going digital," Gabby huffs.

Nim grins. "Where anyone can access it? I don't think so."

Feeling dejected, Gabby opens the book again, absentmindedly noting that it magically opens to the last page she was at. "I know this symbol is significant. I can feel it. Which just makes it weird that I can't remember where I saw it."

Blaise glances at Nim. "The spirits haven't given you any other hints?"

Nim shakes her head, her dark bob flicking her chin. "The spirits can only help the living so much. They can drop hints, but don't interfere with this realm directly. It's why only seers or psychics can hear and understand them." She wrinkles her nose. "Or maybe reapers and necromancers."

"I think we have enough going on without adding them to the mix," says Gabby tartly. Their plate isn't full, it's freaking under Mt. Vesuvius.

Nim straightens, her bright gaze returning to Blaise. "Maybe you could help her."

"Me?"

"Yeah! If this memory is buried deep, why don't you perform a spell to help Gabby access it?"

Blaise twirls a strand of black hair in thought. "I suppose I could..."

Gabby leans forward, excited. "Yes! Do it! That's a flocking great idea."

Blaise's gaze turns calculated. "I think I know just the spell."

"Yes!" Gabby jolts to her feet. "To the couch!"

She hurries over to one of the large brocade couches that seem to sit in all the right places in Veritas, just where you need them. She lies down, making herself comfortable. "Symbol, here I come."

Nim wheels over while Blaise brings a chair. "It should be fairly straightforward," she says. "You'll need to keep the symbol in mind as we sort through your memories."

Gabby closes her eyes, pulling up the three interlinked crosses within a pentagram. "Got it."

"Just take a few deep breaths," Blaise says soothingly. "And let's see what we can find."

Gabby hears her move closer, then senses hands hovering somewhere near her head. "Misty sky meets burning sun," Blaise intones.

Images appear almost straight away, flashing through in a quick-paced montage. Colt last night, hesitantly proposing that she move in with him.

"Smoky air meets gale spun."

Her mom bustling in the kitchen, singing and clueless to the tendrils of smoke creeping out of the oven.

"Forgotten, remembering, remembered."

They go all the way back to her first memory at her two-year birthday party. The fun and laughter. The strange vision that terrified her to tears.

"Let the memories be found."

And the symbol doesn't appear anywhere.

"Hm," Blaise muses, a frown in her voice.

The memories flit again, images working forward through

Gabby's life like index cards. All the people and places who have molded her are there. Home and her mom and Sierra and Ari. Mercy Academy and the moment she met her father. Colt.

Still no symbol.

"Gabby," Blaise says quietly. "A part of your memory, a very small part, has been wiped."

Gabby's eyes shoot open as she sits up. "My memory has been what?"

"Wiped. I'd say only a handful of seconds, but that moment of time is blank." The frown Gabby heard appears. "I detected witchcraft."

"That would have to be some pretty strong magic to wipe the memory of an angel," says Nim.

Not liking the sound of that one bit, and annoyed that finding out who will have to wait for another time, Gabby scowls. "Can you undo it?"

Blaise's frown deepens. "I can probably reverse the spell, but magic that powerful comes with risks. It could—"

Gabby raises her hand. "Don't tell me. I don't want to know. We need to find out what's been hidden from me." She lies back down and closes her eyes resolutely. "Do it."

The symbol could help her find her mother's Grace. It's too freaking important.

Blaise sighs. "Very well."

Gabby closes her eyes again, settling into the couch as she feels it mold to her body. They have to find that memory.

"Misty sky meets burning sun," says Blaise again. "Smoky air meets gale spun."

The memories start flashing again and Gabby pulls the symbol to mind. She's seen it before. She knows it.

"Forgotten, erased, lost," intones Blaise, her voice singsong soft, yet firm and unyielding. "Let the memories appear."

The flashing stops, a crystal clear image appearing, almost

as if Gabby's there again. She's with Colt. And they're waltzing.

Her breath catches as she relives those beautiful moments. Colt in a tuxedo, looking desperately uncomfortable and heart-breakingly handsome. Her in a dress that he kept gazing at with blazing heat. They'd danced and danced, lost in each other and never wanting to be found.

He'd spun her, and her heart had twirled its own merry dance in her chest. The walls had zipped past and she almost missed it. The symbol. Etched into the wall paneling.

The vision fades as Gabby sits up, gasping.

"I know where the symbol is," she says, wondering what that building has to do with her mother's Grace. "It's at Mercy City Hall."

CHAPTER 24

REIGN

"So," says Rachel, drawing out the one syllable for far too long. "What's the dealio with you two?"

Reign wishes he could pretend he's asleep, just like he does whenever Sierra's checked in. But he has no doubt that Rachel saw more than just the aftermath of the kiss. He suspects she arrived earlier then caused the commotion to alert them.

"There's no dealio," he mutters.

Rachel sits on the edge of the bed. "Not according to what I just saw."

Which confirms his suspicions. His hands clench, even that movement causing the wound in his chest to flare with pain. Or is that his heart screaming for Arielle to come back?

Even as his mind knows it's a good thing she left.

He lets his head fall back against the pillow as he stares at the ceiling. "What you just saw was a...mistake."

Even though, in all the wrongs that have made up Reign's life, that's the first and only thing that felt right.

Ari deserves more. So much more.

Rachel pouts. "How come my mistakes don't look as fun as that?"

It was more than just fun. Reign's kissed fun. And just like a blast, it's short-lived. Kissing Arielle felt...eternal. He shakes his head, trying to get himself to snap out of it. "I'd rather not talk about it."

"That is such a Taurus thing to say," Rachel huffs. "But I don't have time to be an annoying Sagittarius. I also have an appointment shortly."

Reign's relieved there isn't going to be a cross-examination. He's seen a little of Rachel's determination at City Hall, and it was impressive. With painkillers blissfully taking the edge off his pain, but also numbing his reactions, he'd never stand a chance.

She pushes to her feet, grinning broadly. "But I know where to find you, Reigny-Boy."

"That's a terrible name," he snaps as she half-walks, half-skips to the door.

She glances back, her red hair brushing her shoulder. "You'll get used to it," she says cheerily.

And with that, she's gone. A low level tropical cyclone, taking what little energy he has with her. Reign closes his eyes, letting himself sink into the mattress and pillows.

What has he done? Of all the stupid, screwed up, shit-for-brains things he could've done, giving into his feelings for Arielle tops the list.

In the privacy of his own personal darkness, the memory of the kiss returns. Actually, it never left. It's forever branded on his soul.

Arielle's soft mouth. Her passionate responses. The way she ignited in his hands.

Her scent, the way she felt, plays through his senses. If they weren't interrupted, what would have happened? He likes to think he'd have some sort of principles and he would've pulled away. Told Arielle they can't do this.

But he's not that strong. He would've tugged her back. Kissed her some more, discovered every delicious crevice of her mouth. His hands wouldn't, couldn't, have stayed still. The silky skin of her throat, the curve of her collarbone, the dip in her cleavage that he's forever trying to pretend doesn't exist.

When he feels lips press against his own, he jolts with awareness. For the briefest of seconds, he revels in the fact that Arielle's come back.

But then he realizes it feels wrong. Good, but most definitely wrong.

His eyes fly open, then widen exponentially when he finds Lust hovering above him. Her fiery red hair slips over her shoulder, caressing his chest.

"I could make myself look like her, if you like," she purrs.

"Get off me, bitch."

He goes to lift his arms, only to find they're clamped to the bed with invisible bonds. He struggles against them, gasping when pain tears through his chest. He arches his back, making it hurt worse, but not caring. He needs to get off this bed.

"I know who you are," Lust croons, ignoring his struggles. "Grail Keeper."

Reign falls still. "You're delusional as well as ugly," he spits.

Her crimson eyes flare as her hovering body twitches. But she quickly calms as her gaze roams over him. "Hmm, no shirt."

Disgust crawls over his skin and he tugs on the bonds again, knowing it's useless, but unwilling to give up.

Lust lifts her hand and draws a red-nailed finger down his throat. "Do you know what the fun part of doing this is?" she purrs, her nail raking over his skin down to his chest. "Making people want it. Enjoy it. Revel in their own death. It's so satisfying."

"I can't say I'm enjoying it so far," he grinds through clenched teeth.

She bares her teeth as her hand comes up to wrap around his throat. "Other times, I just focus on my own pleasure."

Her face twists in a sick mix of sensuality and cruelty as her hand tightens. As the other comes to join it. As both hands grip hard.

He tries to scream, but it's too late. His air is cut off along with any chance of rescue. He thrashes, the need for oxygen outweighing the need to keep his stitches together. But a weight is progressively pushing down on him, the bonds steadily tighten. He can't move his arms, his legs, his torso is being crushed onto the bed.

His vision narrows, and all he can see is Lust's evil, smiling face. "That's it, Grail Keeper," she croons, looking like she's panting with excitement. "Fight it. Make the end come sooner. It always makes my climax more powerful."

Black spots dance across his vision as his lungs convulse uselessly. At least he got to taste Arielle before he died...

There's a blast of white light and Lust shrieks so loud, Reign wishes he could cover his ears. She rears back, arching like she was just shot in the back. With a flash, she dissolves into black smoke and slips out the window.

Reign lays in the hospital, drawing in great big gulps of sweet air. He's been saved. Again. He turns to look at who arrived in the nick of time, half expecting to see the Mayor again.

Except it's not Virginia. It's not even a her.

Gabby's father stands in the doorway, his arms crossing over his too-broad chest. "Seems I visited at just the right time."

MAC

Panicked, Mac runs out of the cafe and to the parking lot. The white van is long gone as she stands at the curb, wondering what the fuck just happened.

Arielle appears beside her, dialing on her cell phone. She lifts it to her ear. "Reign's been kidnapped. He was just pushed into a van."

"We'll be there in five," says a female voice Mac recognizes as Gabby.

"We have to do something!" Mac says, wanting to shout the words. For a brief moment, she considers running after the van, but she'd never catch it. Not unless she could sprout wings and fly after it.

"We will," Arielle assures her. "We'll get him back."

The five minutes it takes Gabby to get there feel like five lifetimes. Mac paces, wishing she'd got the license plate. That she'd followed Reign, insisting he'd listen. That there's something she could do to end all this.

When a black muscle car pulls up, Mac tenses until she sees Gabby in the passenger side. She exits, the driver doing the same, revealing a tall, well-muscled guy with mahogany red hair. "Mac, this is my boyfriend, Colt."

"Hello," he says, the one word almost sounding formal enough to have him bow at the waist. He stares at Mac intensely, as if he's expecting some sort of profound response.

Creepy, much?

"Hey," she says, her gaze sliding back to Gabby. "We have to find Reign."

Before it's too late.

Colt nods curtly. "I have an idea of where he might be. Get in."

Arielle moves without hesitation, and Mac figures she doesn't have much choice. They climb into the back seat and the car roars out of the parking lot.

"Where are we going?"

Colt's gaze dances from the rearview mirror, to his side mirrors, to the road. "Not long after we found out about the Mayor's illegal dealings, we also discovered that Reign's father is the head of an underground movement, intent on thwarting her plans."

Thwarting? Is that even a word anymore?

But Gabby doesn't seem to notice. She turns to look at Mac. "He's discovered that even the Mayor's slum redevelopment plan is full of financial swiss holes."

Mac frowns, trying to remember Reign's dad. But no image comes to mind. Surely she would've met her best-friend's father...

"So I think the logical place to start is City Hall," Colt finishes.

Mac sits back against the leather seat, everything feeling out of control. These people stormed into her life, just before Reign was forcefully taken from it. And they're telling her this goes as high as their city's political leader. That she's corrupt, with some sort of nefarious agenda of her own.

And they're going to take that on.

Except, what choice does Mac have? They have Reign. And Reign is all she has. Somehow, despite all the confusion over the past few days, he's been her one truth. Just like he's always been. She can't turn her back on him.

They reach City Hall, a large, ornate, multi-story building that would be impressive if it wasn't so intimidating. They have to look for clues in that monstrous thing?

Colt pulls into the parking lot and they climb out. He and Gabby look resolute as they link hands and walk toward it. Arielle seems determined but worried. Mac's just plain anxious. She was supposed to find out her results for the advanced program today. She would've rung her parents, and they would've been either ecstatic or over-flowing with support. She's messing with a perfect life, and she would've thought she was above self-sabotage.

Despite the uneasiness clawing at her gut, Mac follows the

others. Turning her back on this means turning her back on Reign, and she's not going to do that.

They enter through large, carved doors, finding themselves in a well-lit, marble foyer. A woman dressed in a too-neat navy outfit with her hair in a too-neat chignon approaches them with a smile. "Welcome to Mercy City Hall. We're open until four o'clock, so you have plenty of time to enjoy the history of our beautiful city." She holds out a brochure. "All the areas open to the public are marked in yellow."

Gabby takes it and thanks her while the woman waves her arm toward two open doors like some game show hostess. Gabby and Colt pass through first, Mac and Arielle right behind. They find themselves in a large ballroom, the city's coat of arms shining up from the marble floor. The ceiling soars high above, white and arched, while two ornate staircases curve to a landing on the second floor.

The place is amazeballs, but perfectly polished and pristine and unlikely to have any clues as to Reign's whereabouts.

Gabby frowns as she studies the brochure. "There are a few rooms beyond this that are open to the public, but most of the building is secured for administration purposes."

Mac moves to the nearest wall, running her fingers over the panels running along the bottom half. A pale tan with rich bronze marbled through the stone, they're almost as tall as Colt. "You do know this is the proverbial haystack, don't you?"

"I didn't think you were one to back down from a challenge," says Colt, watching her closely.

She stiffens. What does he know about her? She frowns. Even if it's true. She looks away, focusing on her slow walk down the wall. "Maybe I'm not like that anymore. Maybe the status quo is just fine."

"That's what we're here to find out," Gabby says under her breath, obviously not realizing Mac has always had super-sensitive hearing.

She's about to call her out when she stops and retraces her steps.

"Hang on a sec," she mutters. She runs her fingers over the panel she just passed, her fingers bumping as they hit the edge. She peers closer.

A small symbol has been etched into the side, what looks like three interlinked crosses enclosed in a pentagram.

Arielle's quickly by her side. "What have you found?"

"I'm not sure, but there's something engraved in here."

Colt arrives with Gabby and they all study it. Gabby takes a step back. "Actually, I think I can see the symbol in the marbling."

Mac does the same along with Arielle and Colt, her eyes widening when she sees Gabby's right. It's faint, almost lost in the variegations of the stone itself, but it's there. Three crosses inside a pentagram. Almost as big as the slab of marble itself.

Stepping back Mac raps on it, her breath catching when there's a light, echoing sound instead of the sharp, solid sound it should've been. "It's hollow."

Gabby's eyes widen. "There's something behind it."

"And we need to find out what," Mac states flatly.

CHAPTER 25

ARIELLE

The sky is bruised and dark even though it's morning as Arielle pulls into a parking lot a few suburbs over. The newsreader over the radio reports of more murders happening through the city, baffling police as the serial killer seems to appear and disappear without a trace. With the same somber tone they announce that a meteorologist will be on next with their opinion on the weather change.

Arielle turns the car off, not needing to hear any more theories. The murders and the sky are due to one thing. Lust.

Cain has triggered a chain of events none of them could have fathomed. While Gabby searches for her mother's Grace, Arielle finally has a chance to do something about it. And she gets to help Mac at the same time.

Glancing at the card the Mayor gave her, she tucks it in her pocket. The same name is typed on it as on the building she's standing in front of—Rising Phoenix Dojo. And she's just in time for her eleven o'clock training session.

She enters, finding herself in what looks to be a large gym. Punching bags hang along the wall on the left, while large squares of padded matting make a chequerboard across the floor. On one, an elderly woman wearing a white martial arts uniform is circling a nice-looking, well-built man, both their fists raised. The woman lets out a "kyai" before swinging her leg at his head.

The man ducks, lifting his hand in a smooth block, almost as if he didn't have to think about the instinctive movement. The woman's leg collides with his forearm and he seamlessly leaps away before she has a chance to consider a second strike.

He straightens and smiles. "Nice one, Gladys. You didn't wait for me to strike first."

"I would've swept her," says a voice and Arielle realizes there's someone to her right, also watching the fight.

She stifles a gasp as she sees who it is.

"That's because you're a hard ass," the man says affectionately.

Rachel plants her hands on her hips, tilting her head at the man. "And you're a marshmallow with a seventh dan black belt, Dad."

The man—Rachel's father—chuckles, then realizes Arielle's standing near the entrance. He excuses himself to Gladys then walks over. "Hi, I'm Paul. You must be Arielle."

"Ari?" Rachel says, shocked. She overtakes her father. "What are you doing here?" She leans forward, speaking in a hushed tone. "Did you follow me to see what Reign said after you kissed?"

"What? No!" Arielle says, indignant and wishing she wasn't flushing so brightly. "I have an appointment."

Paul nods. "She's right. Arielle's booked our intensive package."

Rachel draws back, looking surprised but impressed. "The intensive package, huh?"

"All paid up," says Arielle. She'd swallowed hard when she

saw the cost, but had clicked to sign up anyway. What little savings she has is going into learning how to fight.

"Smart girl," says Rachel. She turns to her father. "Can I train her?"

It's Paul's turn to look surprised. "Because you know her?"

Rachel grins. "In part." She sobers as she looks back at Arielle. "But also because I know why she's gone with the package that's going to give her the best fighting skills in the shortest amount of time."

Paul seems to note the look of understanding between the two girls, because he nods again. "I was going to assign you to her anyway. Poor Gladys isn't ready for you, yet." He presses a kiss to her forehead before making his way back to Gladys, clearly a doting father. "Be nice," he says under his breath.

Rachel beams. "Always."

Once Paul's gone, Arielle fiddles with the edge of her t-shirt, not really sure why she's nervous. "So, your dad owns a dojo?"

"Yup, I grew up here. Earned my blackbelt when I was nine." Rachel makes her way to the nearest square of mats. "Now I help him teach."

No wonder Rachel could hold her own against the demons. "I want to fight like you," Arielle blurts.

Rachel grimaces. "I doubt you'll ever be able to fight like me."

"What? Why?"

Rachel snaps out a kick, her foot cracking against Arielle's thigh, making her gasp. "Because I'm heartless," she says cheerily. "You, on the other hand, have a great big, beautiful heart, Ari."

Arielle frowns, rubbing her leg. She takes a quick note of Rachel's stance—feet spaced apart, facing forward—and mirrors it. She raises her fists in the same way she saw Paul do. "I can have a heart and fight."

"Yeah?" taunts Rachel. "Then hit me."

"What?"

"You heard me," she says, eyes gleaming. "Take a swing."

Bracing herself, Arielle shoots out a fist, expecting Rachel to block the strike in the same way her father did. But her knuckles connect with Rachel's nose and she drops to the mats, clutching it. "Ow! I didn't mean hard!"

Arielle falls to her knees beside her. "Ohmigod, I'm so sorry, Rachel. I thought—"

The world flips and the air is thrust out of her lungs as her back hits the mat. Rachel appears above, pinning Arielle's arms as she grins. "See? Told you."

Arielle huffs, pushing her off. "Not fair."

Rachel bounces to her feet, still looking cocky. "And you think demons play fair? Will Lust?"

Frowning, Arielle dusts herself off, more to give herself some time than anything. Rachel's right. The forces they're up against don't care about fair.

She runs at Rachel, head down like a battering ram, knowing she has no finesse, but wanting to make a point. A jolt of satisfaction shoots through her when she sees Rachel's eyes widen.

Right before she lands on her back again with a grunt. And in an armlock. "Not bad, grasshopper," says Rachel, admiration in her voice. "There's hope for you yet."

They stand, and Arielle shakes off her shoulders. "Let's do this."

Rachel grins. "Looking forward to it."

The next hour, Arielle discovers several things. There's a particular way to hold your fist when punching. Blocking hurts almost as much as striking. And Rachel is definitely heartless— Arielle has the bruises to prove it.

Panting, Arielle steps away, wiping the sweat from her

temple. She's looking forward to going home and having a shower. Then she'll call Reign, hoping to heck it's not awkward.

Hoping to heck they can talk about where their relationship goes next.

As if she wished it, her cell phone rings. Sending an apologetic glance Rachel's way, she steps to the edge of the mat to answer it, turning her back. A robotic, pre recorded message sends a chill down her spine.

"The location of the target has been confirmed in Damascus. The office has taken care of all necessary travel arrangements. A car will arrive shortly to pick you up from your location."

The line goes dead and Arielle looks at her cell in shock. Damascus? So soon? How is she going to explain this to her mom? Gabby? Reign...

"What target?" Rachel's voice behind her has her leaping and almost dropping the phone.

Arielle spins around, almost crashing into her. "You were listening in?"

She shrugs. "Eavesdropping is kinda fun. You should try it someday." Her gaze narrows. "Now spill. What was that all about?"

Arielle glances around even though they're the only ones here now, unsure how much she should disclose.

Rachel lifts a hand to her hip. "Does this have to do with getting inside the Mayor's limo at the hospital?"

Arielle's jaw drops. "Do you have any integrity at all?"

"I prefer to think of it as a fluid concept," Rachel says breezily. "Kind of like what gender a person might be attracted to."

Realizing Rachel knows too much, Arielle sighs. "The Mayor has learned where Cain is. Damascus, Syria."

"And you're going there? What do the others think about that?"

Arielle's jaw tightens. "There's an unspoken agreement I don't tell them. I have to go alone."

Rachel crosses her arms. "I'm coming with you."

"Not happening," Arielle responds instantly. "This is dangerous."

Rachel rolls her eyes. "And now that you know how to fight, you can protect yourself?"

Arielle chews on her lip, acknowledging Rachel's point. "Don't you need to work?"

"I'll tell my dad I'm staying with friends. Besides, my biggest client would've just left town." She looks at Arielle with an arched brow.

"I've already paid, okay?"

Rachel flips her hair. "I've always wanted to see the middle east." She takes two steps away, glancing back at a gobsmacked Arielle. "Well? Are you coming?"

Arielle rushes to catch up, unsure how this has happened. She's still trying to process going to Damascus, let alone Rachel coming with her. They're both in workout gear, for crap's sake!

They reach the glass doors of the dojo and Arielle stops. A black limo is parked at the curb, a young woman stepping out in a black coat, despite the warm air.

"You know her?" Rachel asks under her breath.

"No." She thought the Mayor would be here to give her instructions.

Rachel steps through the door, Arielle right behind. The woman turns around, her dyed black hair layered to flick over her face, intelligent eyes rimmed in dark-eyeliner watching from behind.

She steps forward. "My name's Daria." She opens her jacket

and pulls out a large, thick envelope. "Everything you need is here. Passport. Visa. Tickets."

Arielle takes it. "Ah, thanks."

Daria steps back, indicating to the limo. "Are you ready?"

Now? Arielle's heart hammers against her ribs, noting her reflection in the tinted window. She looks the least prepared she ever has in her life. Did she really think she could do this?

Rachel shakes her head. "She can't go alone."

"I'll be going," says Daria. "And I'm a witch."

Surprised, Arielle looks at Daria more closely. She's going to have company. From a witch...

Rachel raises a brow. "I'm also going, and I'm a Sagittarius."

Daria stares at Rachel for long seconds, but when she doesn't back down, Daria sighs. She turns away and pulls out her cell phone. Pressing the screen with sharp jabs of her shiny black-nailed finger, she speaks into it curtly. "We'll need more documents. Rachel Donovan."

Rachel and Arielle glance at each other. Daria knew Rachel's name.

"Yes, all the usual. Deliver to the airport." Daria hangs up, looking like she's not someone used to practicing patience. "Can we go now?"

"What was the tattoo on your wrist?" Arielle asks, conscious she's buying time, but also curious as she fingers the pendant hanging from a chain beneath her shirt.

Daria glances at the inside of her arm. Three crosses sit within a pentagram, the same pentagram hanging from Arielle's necklace. "It's the symbol of the organization I work for," she says, her face tight. "A powerful organization."

Which means the Mayor must be associated with it.

"What sort of organization?" Rachel asks.

"An old one, one involved in the rise and fall of many kingdoms and countries," Daria says enigmatically. "But that's not why we're here."

Arielle frowns. She was right to hesitate. This isn't seeming like such a good idea right now.

Daria flicks at the ebony hair almost covering one eye. "We're here for Cain. He's been a slippery bastard, but with your help, we're confident we can catch him. You've come the closest to him than anyone else has in decades. And we believe we know why he's in Syria."

"Why?" Arielle asks, knowing the answer is going to decide whether she climbs in that limo. Whether she follows him halfway across the globe without telling those she loves. Rachel seems to sense it too, because she shifts closer to Arielle, crossing her arms.

"Cain's there looking for the Holy Grail."

GABBY

Gabby watches as Colt unfolds from his car, appreciating the lean, sensual grace. He approaches, his own eyes darkening when he sees the glint in her eye. He knows exactly what she's thinking...

Except there's no time to spark the passion that's only grown with time. Not when they're standing outside City Hall.

"Thanks for coming," she tells him, weaving her fingers with his. "Ari's okay?"

"She went into the dojo almost an hour ago," he says, nodding. "Looks like she's decided to learn how to defend herself."

Gabby blinks, impressed. "Good on her." It means she hasn't given up.

Nim smiles. "She's fulfilling her destiny."

The words make Gabby a little uneasy. Destiny speaks of a foretold outcome, one where Ari's future is already mapped out. That's she's barreling head first into whatever the universe has in store for her.

Nim turns her wheelchair to face City Hall. "Shall we?"

Gabby squares her shoulders and tightens her hand around Colt's. "Let's do this."

They walk up the stone steps that stretch across much of the old building, making their way up to the ornate front doors. A sense of nostalgia sweeps through her.

"Do you remember?" she whispers to Colt.

"Yes, I remember," he says gruffly. "I'll never forget."

She never thought she would either... It had been a magical night.

And significant in ways they hadn't realized.

Gabby suppresses a frown. Has anything else been wiped from her memory? And by who?

Inside, a man in a dark suit passes them a brochure with a pleasant smile. He says something about a tour just having left and if they hurry, they might be able to catch up, but Gabby only nods politely. They're not here to sightsee.

They're here for answers.

They pass through the foyer, the majestic beauty of the place muffling their footsteps. On the other side is the ballroom. They enter, finding an older couple standing near one of the curved staircases, reading through the brochure.

"It was designed by a man called Sir Jeremy Mercy Davenport," the woman says to her husband. "He was a very famous architect."

"Quite a talented man," rumbles the husband.

To Gabby's right, she sees the symbol hidden among the marbling of one of the panels. A symbol someone went to great lengths to wipe from her memory. She chafes, knowing they need this couple out of here. Why couldn't they go on the tour?

She sees Colt staring at them intensely and she leans over. "Not the stomach ache spell."

He huffs. "Spoil sport." His eyebrows drop down as he lasers his focus as his lips move silently.

A moment later, the woman's spine stiffens. "Oh goodness. I need to find the bathroom."

The husband glances around. "Right now?"

"Right now," she snaps back. "My pelvic floor muscles aren't what they used to be, you know."

The couple rush out the door at the other end of the ballroom, and Gabby suppresses a giggle. "You gave her the need to pee?"

Colt's lips twitch. "I was unaware of the pelvic floor...challenges."

Nim wheels past them. "Good work, Colt. Now, we need to be quick."

They need to find what this symbol means before someone else enters the ballroom.

Colt glances over his shoulder, his lips working once again. "We'll have time. I've put a repellant spell on the door."

"That's my demon," Gabby beams.

She spins around and hurries to the panel. The septagram is there, camouflaged by the mocha lines of marble, but there, nonetheless. The three crosses reminiscent of a tic tac toe board.

Now what?

Wishing she knew what the symbol stands for, Gabby reaches out and runs her hand over it. The surface beneath it instantly heats. She presses harder, feeling the warmth grow.

Suddenly, lines of light shoot from the point of contact, streaking along the line of the pentagram and crosses. She watches in fascination as the panel morphs into a door.

"Cool," she breathes.

A quick glance over her shoulder reveals Nim's excited face and Colt's cautious one. Gabby flashes them a quick smile then turns back and pushes. The door opens inward, revealing a room.

"Double cool," she murmurs.

She enters, marveling at the space they find themselves in. They're surrounded by floor to ceiling, wall to wall wood paneled cupboards. The honey color of the wood gleams in the soft light, the scent of antiquity in the air.

A few more steps and they're inside. Gabby draws in a sharp breath. "My mother's Grace could be in one of those cupboards."

Colt's by her side in an instant. "We need to go slow."

Gabby swallows as she nods. He's right, but that doesn't make it easy. There's magic in this room. She can feel it.

Nim wheels close to them as they walk further into the large space. The floor beneath them tiled with a large square in the center. Gabby walks toward it, slowly circling. So many cupboards, and who knows what's inside them.

And whether one holds her mother's Grace.

Colt is beside her, looking tense and alert as they reach the center. Nim joins them, looking thoughtful. "How long will your repelling spell last, Colt?"

He never has a chance to answer because a soft *click* has them all freezing. The door they just stepped through slams shut. And thick, black bars shoot from the ground to the ceiling, surrounding them.

"No!" Colt shouts, throwing himself against them. He grips two and shakes them, but they don't move, don't rattle.

Shit. It was a trap.

There's a soft whoosh behind them and they spin around to find another door on the other side of the room opening. Gabby and Colt close in around Nim, coiled and ready to fight despite the cell they're now standing in.

A woman in a chocolate-colored suit walks through the door, her heels clacking on the pale tiles. Her black hair is in a tight, perfect ponytail and she studies them from behind a pair of dark-rimmed glasses.

She angles her head. "Why, hello. My name's Bess. Can I ask what you're doing here?"

CHAPTER 26
REIGN

R eign lays gasping in the bed, the memory of any painkillers feeling like a very long time ago. The dressings on his chest have become damp and sticky. He's torn his wound open.

Gabriel walks over, eyes bright and assessing, making Reign's jaw tighten. There's an arrogance about the archangel that screams 'I'm immortal, you're not, and I won't ever forget that.'

Without a word, Gabriel lifts his hand and extends it toward Reign. Fighting the crippling pain, Reign tries to push it away, hating how weak he feels. Gabriel easily avoids his lame-ass attempt and presses his palm to Reign's chest.

The warmth and relief are instantaneous as a white glow radiates between their point of contact.

Gabriel straightens. "I've healed you enough to stop the medical personnel from becoming suspicious. That is the most I can do."

"Ah, thanks," says Reign, wincing as the dull throb returns to his chest.

"You're welcome," Gabriel intones, his arrogance shifting to pompousness. Reign wonders if angels can have strong veins of narcissism.

"What are you doing here, Gabriel? If you wanted an update on my health, couldn't one of your minions have peeked over the edge of a cloud or something?"

"I want to talk to you," the archangel says, crossing his arms. "Grail Keeper."

Reign tries to hide his reaction to the second time someone's called him that today, but the pain, the healing, Lust getting off on trying to kill him all take their toll. He draws in a sharp intake of breath. His hands clench the sheets. He flinches.

And Gabriel notices every movement.

Dammit.

Gabriel lowers his chin, his eyes turning into lasers that feel like they pierce right down to Reign's soul. "You should have accepted your destiny by now."

"I've been fighting my destiny since kindergarten," Reign snaps. He decided when his first foster care placement broke down that if he was going to be a loser, he was going to be a loser on his terms. No one else would plan his trajectory for him.

"Did you know that one of my angels had a big part in shaping the Grail Keepers?"

"I wouldn't put that on his or her resume, if I were them. The Grail doesn't exist."

Gabriel stiffens. "Although all traces of the Holy Grail have been lost, it exists," he snaps. "Angels and demons can feel its power. They have been searching for it for centuries. Fighting for what it promises."

Reign's jaw tightens. "That's not my problem."

"It is. The Grail Keepers were created to protect not only the Grail, but humans from being collateral damage in the supernatural war that's going on in the shadows."

Reign doesn't answer, in part because it feels like his jaw is steadily being wired together, in part because there are no words to be said. He doesn't want to have this conversation.

"All these murders by Lust are just a distraction," Gabriel continues.

Reign's gaze snaps to his. "People's lives being brutally taken is just a distraction?"

Gabriel glares at him, his features molded with intensity. "Yes, if another Innocent is found, another Gate of Hell is opened, and more demons will be set free on Earth. But the Grail can stop all of this. Close every Gate forever." He holds up a clenched fist. "It must be protected."

For a short, foolish second, Reign considers accepting the mantle that's being offered him. There's a flash in time where he naively believes he can be the person an archangel is saying he is.

But then the harsh weight of reality snuffs out the stupid idea. He's a liar. A thief. Someone who was rejected by those who were supposed to love him, those who were paid to love him, and a society that's supposed to give a shit.

He looks away from Gabriel's piercing gaze. "Then you're going to have to find the right person for the job."

"There is no one else," Gabriel grinds out. "You are the last one."

Pressure, much?

Reign rubs his hands down his face, wishing he took more painkillers. He hears Gabriel move and he drags his hands down to see the archangel is walking toward the door.

He's leaving. Thank fuck.

Gabriel stops in the doorway. "If you accept your destiny, you'll likely be able to protect Arielle better," he says, eyes glinting knowingly. "The lost lore of the Grail Keepers could save the world."

Reign's struck silent. Protecting Arielle is the only thing he wants to do. And yet he kissed her. Getting involved with Ari will mean hurting her, letting her down like he has everyone else.

How does he protect her without doing that?

"You are a leader, Reign, the Keeper of the Grail. And the sooner you accept that, the better it will be for the ones you love, let alone the rest of humanity."

Gabriel turns and leaves, but there's no reprieve for Reign. Joseph of Arimathea appears in the doorway the archangel just vacated. "It is time," he says solemnly.

Reign rests his head back against the pillows, closing his eyes only to find it does nothing to block out the raging wildfire Gabriel's words ignited. That Joseph is waiting to fuel.

Mostly because the inferno is *in* him.

Shit just got complicated.

MAC

Mac runs her finger around the edge of the panel, a sense of urgency clawing at her throat. She quickly realizes it's far more than a decorative slab of marble.

"It's a door," she says in disbelief.

"We have to get in," says Arielle, the same urgency vibrating through her words.

Mac glances at the two girls. "Do either of you have a credit card of some sort?"

Gabby reaches into her pocket and pulls one out. "Here."

Mac quickly sets about jiggling it in the narrow gap between the door and wall. She soon finds the hidden latch of the door and sets about trying to get it at just the right angle to trip it.

Gabby peers over her shoulder. "How do you know how to do this?"

Mac frowns but doesn't answer, pretending to be focused on the task. The truth is, she has no idea how she knows how to break in using a credit card. And she's pretty sure someone who lives the life she does, wouldn't usually know.

Click.

The door jolts open a crack as the mechanism unlocks.

"Yes!" Arielle hisses.

They quickly slip through, Mac wired tight as she scans the room they find themselves in. Apart from about a thousand cupboard doors lining the walls, the place is empty.

"Quick," Mac whispers. "Let's see if we can find anything."

They disperse, opening and closing the wooden doors as quickly and quietly as possible. Each cupboard is its own cubicle, housing some sort of artifact. As Mac registers each one she sees, she shuts the door again. Knives. Jewelry. Scrolls. Small chests. Bowls. A crown. Several goblets and plates.

The relics are interesting, but they're not Reign.

Suddenly, the faint sound of voices wafts into the large room. Mac freezes, noting that Arielle and Gabby do the same. They heard it, too. They carefully gravitate towards its origins—the door on the other side of the room.

Someone else is here.

Reaching the door, Mac discovers it's cracked slightly open, the crack revealing nothing but a sliver of wall and the edge of a desk. It looks like an office of some sort.

"You're enjoying this, aren't you?" says a female voice with glee.

Lizzie.

There's a male chuckle, one that's certainly not Reign. "I've been waiting a long time for this."

Ice trickles down Mac's spine and she suppresses a shudder. She doesn't recognize the voice, but the venom in it is universally understood. Whoever it is, they have a deep hatred for whatever it is they're talking about.

"He's all yours," says Lizzie.

Mac jolts. He?

There's a pause, then a thud and groan. "Why, Reign?" the guy screeches. "Why did you have me sent away?"

The scream that fills the air is so full of agony and suffering that it has Mac moving without conscious thought. She pushes through the door, barreling into the room. She sees Reign in the center, bloodied and tied to a chair, a dark-haired guy standing over him with a crimson-stained knife held aloft.

"No!" roars Mac, running at them, only for a blonde bitch to barrel into her.

Lizzie shrieks as she attacks Mac, clawing at her face. They fall to the ground, a tangle of hatred and determination to inflict pain. Mac manages to grip Lizzie's wrists, her manicured nails curled like claws as they try to get to her eyes.

A brief glance reveals Colt and Gabby attacking the dark-haired guy and getting him away from Reign. Arielle's on her knees, desperately working to undo his bonds.

They outnumber these two. It's only a matter of time before Reign's safe.

Mac lifts a leg and slams her knees into Lizzie's back. She arches in pain and it's the reprieve Mac needs. She bucks and twists, launching the blonde tramp off her and she leaps to her feet. A few well aimed punches and Lizzie will be out of the game.

Except the door they entered through is shoved open, men in bullet-proof vests and guns streaming in. They spread out across the wall with military precision, and it feels like they're being surrounded by black ops.

Mercenaries. No doubt hired by the Mayor.

As a circle of guns is pointed at them, Colt and Gabby release the dark-haired guy and step close together as Arielle curls around a barely conscious Reign.

Fear ices Mac's veins, freezing her to the spot. It feels like she might shatter if she moves. They've lost.

Lizzie's back on her feet, and she flicks her straw-colored hair over her shoulder with smug arrogance. "Well, well, well. Here we are at our inevitable conclusion." Her mouth curves into a victorious grin. "Once you three are taken care of, we'll be getting all the answers we need out of Reign. And all it took was you setting up one blind date, Mackenzie. Thank y—"

It could be Lizzie using her full name. It's probably the need to wipe that self-satisfied smile off the bitch's face.

It's definitely the fury, the decision that no one is touching Reign, that propels Mac forward. She closes her eyes for the briefest instant.

She calls on her wings.

And with one massive pulse of their powerful span, she launches forward, knocking over Lizzie, and wiping out several mercenaries and the dark-haired bastard who was torturing Reign. A handful more are toppled over by the mighty pulse of air. Mac takes great satisfaction in kicking and striking any others she can reach using her fists, feet. And her black, silver-tipped wings.

Energy is thrumming through her as she hovers beside Reign and Arielle, finally something feeling right. The mercenaries flee the room, Colt and Gabby running after them as Lizzie and the dark-haired guy lie unconscious on the floor.

She feels her wings flex behind her, notes the way her feet aren't touching the ground. Even without a mirror, she knows her eyes are glowing red. Potent dark magic is thrumming through her veins.

In the still silence that follows, Mac has no choice but to face the truth.

She's a demon.

CHAPTER 27
GABBY

"Well?" the woman who just introduced herself as Bess says archly. "What are you doing here?"

Gabby narrows her eyes at her. "The more pressing question is, who are you?"

Bess arches a brow behind her glasses, her gaze flitting from Gabby to Colt to Nim, and back to Gabby again. "I am the Mayor's second in charge." She smiles a little. "And responsible for the security for this building. Which brings me back to my first question. Why are you three here? In this room."

"Look," says Colt, holding his hands out in a placating gesture. "We saw something weird, next thing we know, we're in this room. This whole thing is one big mistake. All we wanted to do was see the Mayor."

"You expect me to believe that?" Bess asks incredulously.

Gabby subtly shifts, finding her center of balance. They're trapped in a cell, but that doesn't mean she's not going to fight whatever's coming. Maybe with her and Colt's combined magic, they can incapacitate this woman and find a way out.

The door opens behind Bess and a man in a suit enters,

passes her a sheath of papers, and exits again. Gabby watches, tense, as Bess scans them.

Then looks at them, her eyes once again narrowed and calculating. It's obvious whatever's written there just sealed their fates.

"Gabrielle Hartley. Colt Grayson. And Nimrodel Dubois," she says, revealing she knows their identities. "Do you know Arielle Hartley?"

Gabby stiffens, feeling the invisible jolt of surprise that also passes through Colt. She clenches her hands as she decides how to answer this, knowing it could make all the difference. "Yes, we know her."

Bess instantly relaxes, chuckling as she shakes her head. She flicks her fingers and the bars surrounding Gabby and the others retract into the ground in a blink.

Meaning Bess is also supernatural.

What the flock have they stumbled upon?

Trying to understand these sudden changes of events, Gabby frowns. "You know Arielle, too?"

Bess smiles. "I only know of her, but I've met her mother, Sierra."

Colt is glancing around the room, clearly still suspicious. "What is this place?"

"A very special place," Bess says warmly, all signs of hostility gone. She walks to the nearest wall and opens a small, square cupboard. "We're in a secret wing, one under my protection." She pulls out an ancient-looking dagger. "I'm a collector, you see. And this is where I store all my relics."

She moves to another cupboard a few feet down, opening it to reveal a goblet and plate. "Sorry about the trap, but we need to be careful. This room is designed to ensure the artifacts don't fall into the wrong hands."

Gabby glances around the room, her gaze flitting back to

Bess periodically. They've stepped into a goldmine, but at the same time, she's not sure whether they can trust the Mayor's right hand woman yet.

Bess turns to face them. "Interestingly, only supernaturals can enter this room."

And Gabby, Colt, and Nim are all in here. Gabby's gut tightens, conscious the time for chit chat is over.

"So," Bess angles her head. "I'm going to return to my original question. Why are you here? And I'd appreciate the truth."

Gabby's not sure if there's a threat implicit in that statement, but they're definitely at a disadvantage right now. And they came here for a reason...

She lifts her chin. "We've tracked angelic Grace here."

To her surprise, Bess nods. "Well done."

She turns and walks to the other side of the room, and opens a cupboard much smaller than many of the others. Gabby gasps when she sees what Bess withdraws.

A vial containing bright white essence.

She holds it up, the luminescent matter inside looking like a liquid and a gas all at once. "I collected this from a crime scene not long ago."

It takes everything Gabby has not to run over and snatch the vial. It's her mother's Grace. She can feel it. It calls to her, wanting to go home.

And her heart wants nothing more than to give her mother her last wish.

Colt reaches down, gently taking her hand and offering his strength. She clutches it tightly, waiting to see what Bess is going to say next. Whether there's going to be a fight after all, because Gabby's not leaving this room without that vial.

"I'll give it to you," says Bess, her gaze sharp. "In return for something."

"What?" Colt asks quietly, no doubt knowing Gabby is willing to sell her soul.

"I want Cain," says Bess, a hard edge to her voice. "He's looking for the Holy Grail. If he destroys it, no power can stop the Gates of Hell from opening. I want him captured and delivered to the Mayor, alive."

Gabby blinks, unsure whether this is a stroke of good luck or not. She was already searching for Cain. It seems Bess wants him out of the picture as much as she does.

But Gabby's father asked her to return Cain to him.

The presence of her mother's Grace makes the decision for her. Surely her father would understand she can't let this opportunity pass.

She nods, trying to keep the movement short and sharp. She might be eager for this deal, but she knows she can't let Bess know that.

Bess smiles, slowly and widely. "Excellent."

She walks to Gabby, the softly pulsing glow coming closer and closer. Bess holds it out, then quickly withdraws it again. "I will hold you to your word, Gabrielle."

Gabby's palms are itching. They've never felt so empty. The need to hold her mother's angelic essence has her hands quivering.

She nods. "I'd expect you to. I will uphold my end of the bargain."

Her smile returning, Bess passes the Grace to Gabby. She takes it, her eyes stinging when her fingers wrap around the warm vial.

She pulls it close, opening her hand to stare at it, not quite believing it's happened.

She's holding her mother's Grace.

SIERRA

Sierra strides into Reign's room, knowing she's avoided this too long, and almost crashes into the doctor who was just leaving.

"Whoa," he says, his hands shooting out to grasp her arms. "Sorry about that."

"No need to apologize," Sierra says, flushing a little as she steps back so his hands slide away. "It was my fault."

The doctor grins, and she realizes he's a little younger than her, and good-looking in a clean-cut, I-could-be-on-a-medical-romance-cover kind of way. And that he's looking her up and down. "If you're after a full physical, you'll need to make an appointment."

Sierra almost does a double-take as she registers what the guy said. He's busting a move on her!

She steps around him, smiling politely. "If I were single, I'd appreciate you being so proactive about my health." She shrugs. "But I'm not."

The doctor snaps his fingers good-naturedly. "That's too bad," he says, his gaze giving her another quick once-over. He's gone before she can point out the cuteness is fast wearing off.

Entering, she finds Reign sitting up in bed looking at her, one eyebrow raised. "Wow. He didn't offer me a full physical."

Sierra flushes again. She'd rather not attract the attention of other men. "Maybe you should try making an appointment."

"If it would get me out of here, I'd consider it," he mutters.

She stops beside the bed. "It shouldn't be much longer?"

The fact Reign should be discharged soon is the reason she's here.

"That's what the doc was here for," says Reign. "Said he just needs to talk to the surgeon to confirm a few things."

"That's great news," Sierra says with a smile. She doesn't know Reign well, but she suspects he'd be chafing at being stuck in here all day.

"Yeah," he says, his gaze sliding away as he picks at the sheet.

Sierra realizes he's uncomfortable with her being here. She can't blame him. She's not comfortable being here, either. But she's not going to back out. There are things that need to be said.

"So," Reign says, filling in the silence. "Is that how you get guys off your back? By telling them you're not single?"

"Yes." Because it's the truth. "I'm not single."

In fact, running into the doctor also happened with Arielle's father. She was on her way somewhere, not looking where she was going, and they crashed.

But the attraction as his hands gripped her arms had been instantaneous. Electric. They fought it, they really did. And they lost the battle. It had been a beautiful, life-changing surrender.

One where Arielle was conceived.

Reign frowns. "Arielle's dad's been...gone a long time."

"Some loves last a lifetime, Reign. Even after the other person's taken away."

She will love Ryder forever. No one else will ever come close.

Reign nods, looking back down at the sheet. "If you say so."

Sierra's heart constricts at his response. Reign should know love exists. That it can be depended on, no matter how many years pass.

And part of that is her fault.

She sighs. "I have something I need to tell you."

Although he's wearing a shirt unlike much of his time spent in hospital, Sierra sees him tense. "Can it wait?"

"No. It can't."

His lips thin. "I had a feeling you'd say that."

Sierra sits on the edge of the bed, only to quickly stand again. Her muscles twitch with agitation, unable to remain still.

"I met Arielle's father, Ryder, when I first became an Archivist. He was working for Cain—"

Reign sits up, wincing. "He was what?"

"I didn't know who Cain was at the time. Neither of us did. That's when I first learned how important it was that we find the Grail before him. And it's also when I met the Grail Keepers."

Reign's gaze darts to Sierra. "There was more than one?"

She nods. "Three of them. They'd been systematically hunted and killed." She shifts her weight. "They were desperately protecting a fourth Grail Keeper. A baby whose parents had been murdered."

Reign stills, and she's not sure, but she thinks he pales a little.

Sierra clears her throat as it tightens around the next words waiting to be said. "But Cain manipulated us and they were killed. Blaise, Nim and I managed to save the baby, knowing he was the last Keeper."

Reign's fallen silent, his entire focus lasered on Sierra. Listening to her every word.

"I knew the baby needed a family. Someone who would take him away, keep him safe, and raise him until it was time to fulfil his destiny." The words start tumbling out faster, a painful wound that's now bleeding freely. "David was my best friend, we grew up together. He and his girlfriend, Mikki, were about to move away. They planned on getting married."

"Mikki?" Reign whispers, frowning as he tries to place the name. Recognition dawns a second later. Shell was at Mikki's house when she was abducted. It means although it was brief, Reign met her.

It means Sierra was able to visit her and find out what happened after her own part in this story.

"David would have been a wonderful father," she chokes, knowing that possibly makes this even less okay. She never expected him to—

"David died," Reign bites out, finishing her thought for her. "Mikki told us."

Sierra winces, feeling those two words pierce her soul. "He did. Two years later in a tragic car accident. And Mikki felt she couldn't care for the young child alone. She gave him up to the authorities."

Reign blinks. Then blinks again. It's the only part of him that moves.

Sierra draws in a shuddering breath. There's one last piece of the story to tell. "Before he left, I named the baby." Her face twists as the bitter-sweet memory, something in her chest also contorting as it echoes the pain. The baby was so beautiful, so precious. So calm in the face of the destiny that now weighed on his fragile shoulders. "I named him Reign."

That child, now a man, draws in a sharp breath as his eyes widen. "You..." he breathes.

Sierra stays where she is, holding his pained gaze, her own eyes stinging. This is her moment of reckoning. Her karma, as Blaise would call it. She tried to do the right thing.

And she let him down. In the worst possible way. He grew up alone and unloved. Clueless about his destiny. Unaware of how important he is to the world.

Color flushes Reign's cheeks a florid, furious red. He swallows, the process looking difficult and painful. His hands clench the sheets so hard his knuckles turn ghostly white.

"Get. Out."

Sierra nods, unsurprised but wishing they could have discussed it more. "I just want you to know, the Archivists will do everything we can to help you." Her lashes flutter as she says the next words. "And protect you."

He snorts derisively, green fire flashing in his blazing eyes. "Get. The fuck. Out."

Her heart cracking all over again, Sierra turns and walks to the door. There, she stops, glancing over her shoulder but not looking at him. "And Reign, I'm sorry."

CHAPTER 28
REIGN

Reign swings his feet off the bed, only to stop. He thought his chest hurt before. But being stabbed by a demon is nothing compared to what Sierra's words have done to him.

They carved away at his heart.

Shredded him.

Changed everything.

He glances down, half expecting to see fresh blood seeping through to his shirt. He never let himself dwell on could-have-beens. There was no point.

But now, he finds out they literally could have.

And that's so much worse. Unbidden and unwanted, flashes of an alternate history assault his mind.

Sierra kept him. He called her Mom. He would have had a home, a bedroom, a family.

He groans, pain twisting through his insides like acid. He would have grown up with Arielle. They would've been best-friends like Sierra and David were. Gabby would have been their annoying older cousin-sister. Shell would've been his aunt.

Life would've followed a completely different trajectory.

Maybe Arielle would've known about the supernatural all along, being raised alongside a Grail Keeper.

But fate snatched it away from him. Deciding he didn't deserve it.

Reign's head drops into his hands, his breath coming out in gasps. He swipes at his eyes, hating that there's moisture there. He never cries. Never.

"Is everything okay?" comes a concerned voice from the door.

Reign looks up to find the doctor from earlier entering, his face scrunched with concern. If Reign didn't feel like his chest had just been excavated, he'd make some comment about needing a full body examination.

But Sierra's words are too fresh. Mikki's betrayal too raw.

And the doctor looks like he's wondering whether his earlier, jovial "looks like you'll be right to leave today" was premature.

Reign straightens. "Yep, feeling great."

"You're a little pale," the doctor murmurs, looking worried. "You didn't move too quickly? Have you opened your wound?"

The torn flesh and muscle where the blade impaled him is fine. That one missed his heart.

Sierra's words, on the other hand, were a direct freaking hit.

He shakes his head. "No, I just realized that my favorite Thai place won't be open until later. I've been hanging for their pad thai."

The doctor grins. "A good pad see ew can certainly work wonders."

Reign nods, having no idea what the guy is talking about. "So, the surgeon gave the green light?"

The doctor lifts the paperwork he brought in. "You've been

discharged," he announces. "Once you've got yourself organized, you're free to go. Is there someone to pick you up?"

"Yep," Reign blatantly lies for the second time. Mac's in a coma. He can't confuse Arielle any more than he already has by asking her to come and get him. Sierra...well, Sierra just turned him inside out. And Colt and Gabby have better things to do.

"Excellent," beams the doctor. He places the paperwork on the bed. "No more hanging around dark alleys, okay?"

"I've learned my lesson," he says, straight faced. He figures why stop at two lies, he may as well go for the trifecta.

The doctor leaves, and Reign glances around the room. The walls are probably used to absorbing pain. Used to ignoring the pleas for mercy.

"Story of my life," he mutters.

He's about to reach for the paperwork when a body appears between them, solidifying enough that his hand bumps into it. Reign yanks his hand back. "Shit, Joseph!"

The old man crosses his arms. "It is time to talk."

"Of course it is." Reign sits back down on the bed, sighing loudly. The fact that Joseph's gained substance suggests he plans on staying for a bit.

Joseph comes around to stand in front of him. "It is time."

Which is exactly what he said after Gabriel left. But now the evidence is mounting.

Lust.

Gabriel.

Then Sierra's painful confession was the glistening cherry on top.

He can't deny it any longer. He's the last freaking Keeper of the Grail.

"What exactly do the Grail Keepers do?" he asks heavily.

"They protect the Grail and all its lore," Joseph says gravely.

"They are an important part of keeping the balance in this world."

Reign nods. He already knew this, but for once, he's actually listening. "And the Grail? Where is it?"

"No one knows."

"When was it last seen?"

"There is no record of such a time."

"So no one even knows what it looks like?" Reign asks, incredulous.

Joseph nods, looking unworried. "It is buried deep. Hidden. As it should be."

Reign rubs his temples. He's being given an impossible task. And no one seems to realize he hasn't even done what most kids his age manage to achieve. Graduate. Stay on the right side of the law. Become a functioning part of society.

"And there's no one else?" he asks heavily.

Joseph shakes his head. "Just you."

Of course there fucking isn't.

"And if I agree—"

"You have already been chosen," Joseph points out.

Reign ignores him. "And if I agree, this will help protect people?"

People like Arielle.

"Yes." Joseph frowns as if he just thought of something. "Although you cannot take unnecessary risks. You are too important."

Reign suppresses a snort. He can't guarantee the first, and he disagrees with the second. He looks up, holding the old man's gaze, seeing the calm faith in their gray depths and wondering if he'll ever experience that.

"What would I need to do?"

"Find the Grail."

Joseph says the words simply. As if the task is easy. Possible. Realistic.

Shaking his head, Reign pushes to his feet. He steps past Joseph, heading to the door. "I'll let you know," he says, exiting the room.

He's going to go back to the cottage. He'll visit Mac. He'll check in on Arielle. He'll do everything he can to avoid seeing Sierra.

And then he has a decision to make.

CHAPTER 29
ARIELLE

Arielle wishes she could appreciate the fact she's in another country. That she's now in one of the places her mother has visited. She dreamed of seeing what she did. Of trying to understand the magic that drew her mom to the middle east so regularly.

Little did she realize it was literally magic drawing her here.

But Arielle barely registers the rich reds boldly featured in the hotel room they just entered, just like she hardly noticed the sun setting on the bustling markets defined by startling white robes and rich, earthy shades and congested, modern streets. She's exhausted after the flight. Her body clock is reeling from the jetlag. And her stomach hasn't stopped churning with anxiety since the moment she climbed into the limo with Rachel and Daria.

They're here to find Cain. To capture him.

To do what no one else has managed to do through the ages.

Daria drops her suitcase on one of the beds in the large space, her thick eyeliner starting to smudge. "I suggest we rest. Tomorrow we begin the search."

Arielle sits heavily on another of the beds. "You do have some idea where that is, don't you?"

Daria nods. "There's a site that Cain will go to. A site where the Grail is rumored to be buried."

The Holy Grail. Cain getting his hands on that is even worse than Cain finding the next Innocent. It was that piece of information that cemented Arielle's decision to leave. The threat is just too great.

"But first, we sleep," Rachel says grouchily. "I can't kick ass with bags under my eyes."

Daria nods. "Yes. We need to be well rested." She sits on her bed cross legged. "I just have a few things I need to check," she says as she pulls her tote toward her and tugs out the laptop she spent much of the flight focused on.

Arielle and Rachel glance at each other. Daria's committed, that's for sure. Although it makes her serious and unsmiling, Arielle decides she's comforted by the fact she's so intense. What they're taking on is the poster child for intense.

She curls up on the bed, uncaring that she's still wearing the leggings and top she wore on the plane. Pulling up the blanket at the end of the bed seems to take the last of her energy. She'll find out what Daria's been studying with such focus in the morning.

Sleep comes quickly, along with the dreams that have been invading it for the past couple of weeks. This time, Reign's sitting on the edge of the hospital bed. He smiles when he sees her approach, and relief courses through her. He looks well. She's been worried about how he's been.

"Hey," he says softly in that rich, sexy way of his.

Her heart flutters as if it comprises of a million butterflies. "Hey."

They gravitate toward each other, neither fighting the pull that's stronger than the tide. She stops in front of him, her breath catching at the tender fire in his eyes. They reach for each other simultaneously, her hands on his shoulders, his on her waist.

And just like the other dreams, she's confident in what she wants. Certain that he wants this too. She watches the fire in his eyes blaze so hot that she almost feels the heat as she places her knees on the bed and straddles him. Chaste kisses aren't enough. A sweet embrace won't cut it.

She craves far more than that.

And then they're kissing again, but this time, his hands don't stay still. They spear up her back, leaving a scorching trail of heat, then down again as if he's learning all her lines and curves. His thumbs brush the side of her breasts and she shudders in need.

"Arielle."

She jolts. That wasn't Reign's voice.

"Arielle," it comes again, more urgently.

She opens her eyes reluctantly, sad to see Reign's beautiful face fade away.

Daria's face is hovering above her, Rachel's beside it. "Wake up," she hisses. "It's tonight."

Arielle sits up, shock waking her like a dousing of cold water. "Tonight?"

"Yes, tonight," says Daria. "We've been tracking Cain. He's going to the site."

Arielle scrambles off the bed, her sleep-heavy brain trying to catch up. "But...we haven't talked about it. We need a plan."

Daria is shoving items into her tote bag. "We will all have a role to play. I will be casting the spell to trap Cain. Rachel, your fighting skills will come in handy if he has men with him." She picks up a jar and passes it to Arielle. "And your job is to hold this."

She takes it, glancing at it. The clear glass is thick and

sturdy, the silver lid made of metal. If she was going to make jam, it's exactly what she needs. "You brought me to Damascus to hold this?"

Daria's already heading to the door, slinging her backpack over her shoulder. "Your role is vital. I need to focus on the spell, while Rachel needs to focus on protecting us. And we have to wait until Cain completes his own spell before we can trap him. That is when he'll be at his weakest."

Rachel frowns. "That must be one heck of a spell to weaken someone as strong as him."

Daria steps through, glancing over her shoulder. "Necromancy usually is."

Arielle blanches and Rachel's frown deepens. Necromancy is the magic of the dead. Usually communicating with them. Sometimes raising them.

She's about to ask what that has to do with the Grail, but Daria's already left the hotel room. She and Rachel rush to catch up, meeting her at the lift where she's tapping her foot impatiently and glancing at her watch. Everything about her is next-level intense, so Arielle decides not to say anything. Right now, they need to focus on catching Cain.

They exit the hotel, a warm, night breeze pushing Arielle's hair out of her face. She draws in a deep breath, noting the hint of earth and exhaust. She can't afford to fail.

Not again.

The limousine that drove them from the airport is waiting out the front and they climb in, silent and tense. Daria passes the driver a slip of paper and they pull out. She sits back, staring straight ahead, clearly communicating she has no interest in talking.

Arielle's kind of glad. Her mouth is dry and her throat tight. She grips the jar, feeling the smooth glass press against her palm. She's not entirely sure how her role is vital, but it's too late for questions.

The lights of the city quickly fade away, and the world beyond the car becomes nothing but blackness. Rachel starts to fiddle with the ends of her hair, suggesting she's feeling as nervous as Arielle.

What if the Mayor's motives aren't what she said they are. What if she's working with Cain.

What if Arielle just ensured she and Rachel are going to be sacrificial lambs...

Without warning, or a landform to be seen, the driver pulls over, staring straight ahead as if he doesn't want to witness them exiting to whatever fate Arielle's signed them up to. She glances out her window, seeing that the black landscape hasn't changed. They're most definitely in the middle of nowhere.

"The jar must be opened, Arielle," says Daria. "No matter what, do not close it until it is time."

"And how the poppycock am I supposed to know when that is?" she hisses.

Daria opens her door. "There can be no more talking," she says in a low voice, her gaze barely meeting theirs. "We must be silent."

She slips out of the limo and Arielle knows she has little choice but to follow. She's just stood up when Rachel's hand reaches out to grip hers and squeeze. Arielle squeezes back, wondering if her new friend's giving or receiving comfort. A small part of her is hoping she's not the only terrified one.

Within a few breaths, Arielle realizes there's a crescent moon high above, casting the world in a pale, ghostly white. She quickly discovers that's a good thing, because Daria soundlessly breaks into a jog.

Arielle and Rachel jolt into action and catch up. The sand beneath their feet absorbs their movements, confirming

Arielle's suspicion—they're in the desert somewhere. They haven't run long with Daria stops, raising her hand as she looks around.

At first, Arielle can't tell how this part of the desert is different to any other, but then she sees it. A grave. And seven ashen scorch marks creating a circle around it.

And nowhere to hide.

Holy crap. And several men approaching from the other side, Cain at the forefront.

Ice spears through Arielle, freezing her veins. They're out in the open. She's had one martial arts lesson. And she can't fight even if she wants to—her job is to hold an open jar.

She has most definitely screwed up again.

The need to run is thumping through Arielle. She has to get Rachel away from here. She can't be responsible for her getting hurt, too. Or worse.

Daria reaches out and grips her arm as if she senses Arielle's need to flee. She shakes her head, the whites of her eyes blazing with intensity within her kohl-rimmed gaze.

Arielle remains where she is, trembling as Cain and his men reach the grave. He surveys the area, his gaze sweeping straight past the three girls. No, straight through the three girls. As if they're not even here.

Daria's rendered them invisible.

"It's here. I know it is," Cain growls. "Spread out and guard the area. Nothing can interrupt me."

The men do as instructed, blending into the darkness. With a sharp nod, Rachel does the same. Daria nudges Arielle, her gaze flicking to the jar. Slowly and silently, Arielle twists it open. There's no possibility of asking any more questions. They have to be silent.

Cain moves slowly, glancing around as if he's looking for something. He stops, standing next to the grave but seemingly unaware of it. "This will have to do," he mutters. He reaches into his pocket and removes a pouch. Tipping it upside down, he shakes it, watching as the flakes flutter to the ground.

"Mullein," he intones. "Wolfsbane and mandrake. The herbs of summoning."

Arielle's glad she's not breathing, otherwise she would've gasped. Cain's casting a necromancy spell. Is the Holy Grail still being held by one of the Grail Keepers? Is a soul about to rise, carrying the ancient relic? She grips the jar even tighter. Whatever her role is, she's going to see it through, no matter what.

Cain can't get his evil hands on the Grail.

He extends his arms and fills his chest. "Dark as night and bright as white," he calls to the night. "The time of loss has ended."

Arielle has to lock her knees as fear starts her legs shivering. She's never been more scared...and determined. Daria is watching Cain closely, practically bouncing on the edge of her toes. She's waiting for the right moment to enact her own spell.

"Break the spell and end our plight," Cain continues, his voice climbing, each word trembling with emotion. "What's taken will be surrendered."

He booms the last words, making the spell a demand, a strange edge of desperation weaving through it. Cain holds himself there, body vibrating with energy, waiting. Waiting to raise the dead.

But nothing happens.

A gentle breeze plays with the ends of Arielle's hair, flicking a few strands over her face. She ignores the need to brush them away. Maybe there's a delay...

Cain lets out a soul-wrenching cry and falls to his knees. "No! Not again!" He throws his head back, pleading to the sky. "Please! It's all I want!"

Daria starts muttering her own spell, her hands weaving

intricate shapes in front of her. Cain's head snaps up. He's heard them.

His gaze unerringly finds them, flaring when he sees Arielle and Daria. He pushes to his feet. "Get them!" her roars.

But no one emerges from the darkness. Rachel's done her part. The men are incapacitated.

Daria continues to murmur words and sounds Arielle's never heard before. Surely she should be done by now.

Cain lifts his arm, pointing at Arielle. "You! You ruined this, just like your mother!" He breaks into a run, the need to kill twisting his features.

Arielle's rooted to the ground in fear, watching the first murderer running at her, her terrified mind unsure what to do. Her job is to keep the jar open, but Daria can't do hers if Cain reaches them. Her decision made, Arielle breaks into a sprint, running directly away from Daria. Cain swerves, not losing sight of his target.

Injecting everything she has, Arielle runs blindly into the night, clutching the jar. Daria said Cain would be weak, but a panicked glance over her shoulder reveals he's chasing her with all the predatory speed of a lion. A furious one.

The spell had no effect on him.

A frantic second later, his body crashes into hers, knocking her to the ground with such ferocity that Arielle cries out. She curls around the jar, trying to protect it from the fall like a fragile newborn.

Her body ploughs into the sand, Cain's right on top of her. Before they've come to a stop, he's rolled her onto her back and wrapped his hands around her neck. His face above her is purple with rage.

"You bitch!" he roars. "You'll die for this!"

Arielle struggles, twisting and jerking as she tries to push him off, but Cain's too heavy. Too driven to kill. His hands tighten their chokehold, crushing her throat. If she released the jar, she might stand a chance. Fight him off long enough for Rachel to help.

But holding it, keeping it safe, is her one job. Her only way to play a part.

Her lungs spasm as a scream is trapped in her throat. Bright lights dance across her vision as pain starts to swallow her whole. Her mouth works, but she has no idea what for. She can't breathe. Can't talk. And there's nothing to say.

She's failed. Again.

"Die, you Archivist whore."

But Cain never closes his mouth after the last, awful word. His head snaps back and his jaw drops low. Red-black smoke pours past his lips and into the night sky.

"The jar!" Daria calls.

Summoning the last shreds of her strength, Arielle lifts it. The smoke the color of night and Hell pours into it, coiling and accumulating in the bottom. The moment the last stream of mist is in, she slams the lid back on, screwing it tight.

Cain collapses, his body crumpling to the side.

Arielle crawls to her knees, clutching the jar as Daria and Rachel run over. Rachel crouches beside her. "Are you okay?"

She nods, although her throat feels like there's an inferno inside it. "Is he…is he dead?" she chokes, her gaze still on Cain.

Daria shakes her head. "He's very much alive. He's immortal thanks to his Mark. But his demonic energy is what you now hold. His magic is gone."

Arielle glances at the jar and its ominous red-black contents. "We did it."

Rachel falls back on her haunches. "Wow, we really did." She arches a brow at Arielle. "And boy, do you take your jobs seriously."

Daria reaches into the satchel hanging over her shoulder.

"The Mayor wanted you to have this if we were successful. As a token of thanks." She holds out a large silver dagger. "This can kill Lust."

Arielle takes it, hefting its weight in one hand as she cradles the jar to her chest.

She did something right.

They can save Mac.

And they can end Lust.

CHAPTER 30
REIGN

Reign wakes the following morning, grimacing as he rolls over, acknowledging that sleeping on the floor, even carpeted floor, isn't great for a healing stab wound. Then again, he's done a lot of things doctors wouldn't recommend. He doesn't intend on following their instructions now.

Not when Mac is still in a coma.

He sits up, glancing at his best friend on the bed just a couple of feet above. Her face is serenely at peace, the blankets tucked neatly around her. He's not sure if anyone's noticed, but being away for a few days, he certainly has. Mac's breathing has slowed.

They're slowly losing her.

Reign pushes to his feet, grimacing at the twinge of pain but ignoring it. There are more important things to worry about right now. He exits the room and heads to the kitchen, looking forward to a strong cup of coffee. He has decisions to make. After he's had some serious caffeine.

He stops the moment he enters the open plan living room,

sensing a change. Although nothing's out of place, his instincts are on high alert. Someone's here.

Sierra appears in the kitchen doorway, holding a steaming mug. "Good morning," she says warmly, if a little cautiously.

Reign allows himself the space of breath to respond, unsure of how he feels about Sierra being here. The stab of betrayal had flared the moment he saw her, and although he logically knows she thought she was doing the right thing when she gave him away, the part of him that lived every day as a reject is having difficulty coming to terms with what she did.

Sierra's brows twitch. "Is Ari still asleep?"

He frowns. "I have no idea." Is she fishing as to whether they fell asleep in the same room again?

She glances down the hall. "Wasn't she with you last night?"

Reign takes a step further into the living room, suddenly feeling uneasy. He hasn't seen Arielle since she left the hospital after they kissed. He was kinda glad she was avoiding him.

"She's not with you?" he asks, working to keep the worry out of his voice.

Sierra shakes her head, her face twisting. "She didn't come home the last two nights. She said she was staying with Rachel, then I assumed she was with you last night."

"And you didn't check?"

She flinches at the accusation in his tone. "I've been trying to give her some space. To show I believe in her."

Reign jams his fingers through his hair. Of all the days to start giving Arielle space, she had to do it now? His flash of anger dies as quickly as it flared. He's not annoyed with Sierra. He's annoyed with himself, and it's for the exact reason he shouldn't have kissed Arielle. How he feels about her is getting in the way. Because he's avoided her for two days, he has no idea how long she's been missing.

Sierra strides to the dining table and puts down her coffee. She quickly pulls out her phone and dials. Reign holds his breath as she brings it to her ear, her other hand at her throat. The soft, rhythmic sounds of the dial tone count out the long seconds, then Ari chirps out her voicemail message.

Shit.

"Maybe Gabby's heard from her," says Sierra, the hint of a tremble in her voice.

Reign walks closer, having just thought the same thing and wanting to hear what Gabby has to say. A painful clamp has tightened around his chest and it has nothing to do with his wound.

He's taken two steps when there's a sharp rap on the door. It opens a moment later, and Gabby enters, Colt behind her. She smiles brightly, holding up a paper bag. "I brought bagels. Ari's favorite."

"Gabby!" Sierra rushes toward her. "Have you seen her?"

She stops, her own frown already creasing her brow. "No, I thought she was with you."

The clamp tightens another notch around Reign's ribs. "We haven't seen her for a couple of days."

Colt stills, like he always seems to in an emergency. "We've been busy."

"Doing what?" Reign asks, once more annoyed that none of them seem to have realized Arielle's disappeared.

"That's not important right now," Colt growls. "When did you last see her?"

Reign manages to hold his gaze even as the memory of the kiss scorches through his mind. "At the hospital." He draws in a sharp breath. "She said she had an appointment."

"She did," says Gabby. "She booked in to take martial arts lessons."

Surprise jolts through Reign, quickly followed by admiration. Arielle's decided to learn how to kick ass.

"It turns out the dojo's owned by Rachel's father," Colt adds.

Reign's hands tighten into fists. "We need to have a word with him." If that bastard has touched her—

Gabby shakes her head. "He checks out. He raised Rachel single-handedly, runs the dojo, including offering classes for kids on the street, and volunteers at a soup kitchen every weekend."

"He's practically a priest," says Reign, one eyebrow raised. Even those men in the most sacred of roles have abused others' trust.

She rolls her eyes. "I would sense if he's evil."

"After that, we don't know where she went," says Colt.

Sierra clasps her hands. "You've been following her?"

Gabby flushes as Colt nods, not bothering to look apologetic. Reign grits his teeth. With her mother deliberately trying *not* to check up on her, and her cousin keeping tabs on her, no wonder Arielle's so desperate to prove herself. Everyone's either watching her or consciously ignoring her as they pretend she's not the focus of attention.

"So we have no idea where she's gone," Sierra says, her face pale.

"Arielle's tough," Reign points out. "She's a fighter, through and through."

One who tends to make snap decisions, but a fighter nonetheless.

Gabby smiles. "She really is."

Sierra nods, but the color doesn't return to her cheeks. "We have to find her."

"We definitely do," says Colt. "Have you heard the morning news?"

Gabby shifts, slipping a hand on his arm as she shakes her head. Colt presses his lips together, but it's too late. The question has been asked.

Reign braces himself. "What news?"

Colt rubs the back of his head. "The murders are escalating. Multiple sites last night." His jaw twitches. "They're even calling them the lust murders now."

Sierra's hand flies to her mouth and Reign realizes why Gabby didn't want Colt to mention this. His own stomach just bottomed out.

What if Arielle went looking for Lust. What if she found her...

Reign strides for the door, panic starting to make him feel twitchy. "I'm going to the dojo. Rachel may even be there."

"I'm coming with you," says Sierra.

Reign yanks open the door, freezing when he discovers there's someone else on the other side.

Arielle draws the hand back that was reaching for the door-knob. "Reign," she says, surprised.

Her hair is a mess. Her clothes are rumpled. She looks like she's barely slept.

And yet, he's never seen anything more beautiful.

Before he can stop himself, Reign draws her into a tight embrace. "Thank fuck you're okay."

GABBY

Relief has Gabby sitting heavily on the nearest chair. Colt comes to stand behind her, placing her hands on her shoulders and squeezing. She places her own hand over one of his, acknowledging his wordless support.

Arielle's safe. She's back.

She and Reign disentangle themselves from one of the tightest hugs Gabby's ever seen, even flushing a little as they step back. And then Sierra's there, clutching her daughter and stroking her hair.

"Ari, we were so worried!"

"I'm fine, Mom." Arielle pulls back, shaking her head as she smiles. "Really."

They enter and Arielle sits at the dining table, looking exhausted. "Sorry, I didn't mean to worry anyone." She looks at her mom. "I told you I was with Rachel."

Reign arches a brow. "That's quite the training session."

A two day training session, Gabby thinks to herself. She looks closely at her cousin, noting the weariness dragging at her shoulders. But beneath the tiredness, there's an energy buzzing. Arielle's...happy about something.

She shakes her head. "You have no idea."

Her mom frowns. "Where have you been, Ari?" There's an edge in Sierra's voice. Now that the relief is wearing off, she looks like she's thinking of getting mad.

"It's a long story," Arielle says, not quite meeting her mom's gaze. She reaches into the backpack she rested by her feet. "But I got this."

Gabby shoots to her feet as Arielle places something on the table. A jar. Red-black smoke coiling like a serpent within.

Colt strides past her and picks it up. "Where did you find this?"

"Another long story," says Arielle. She smiles. "Do you know whose it is?"

Colt lifts the jar to eye-level, glaring at the contents as if he hates them. "I can sense its origins." He returns his gaze to Arielle, shocked. "It's Cain's demonic essence."

Arielle beams as Gabby tries to process that her suspicions were right. She knew it was demonic essence, but couldn't begin to comprehend that it could be from such a powerful one. That it could be...Cain's.

Arielle turns to Reign. "We can use it to save Mac."

Reign's eyes widen. "You're amazing."

Arielle flushes, pleasure creeping up her cheeks.

Reign turns to Sierra. "We need Blaise. Stat."

Sierra hesitates, but then nods. She knows they're running out of time. "I'll call her now." She takes a few steps away, pulling out her phone. Blaise answers almost straight away and Sierra ducks into the kitchen so they can talk uninterrupted, taking the jar with her.

"Thanks, Ari," Reign says softly.

Arielle ducks her head. "That's not all I got." She reaches into her bag again and Gabby stills. She even feels Colt tense beside her.

It seems Ari has more to show and tell.

Gabby instantly recognizes the dagger that Arielle reveals. Long and silver with a black hilt, it glints softly in the morning light. It's the dagger she used to kill Pothos.

She strides forward. "Where did you get that?"

"There's no time for that right now," says Arielle. "The important thing is that this dagger can kill Lust."

"Kill Lust?" asks Reign, astounded. And possibly a little excited.

"Yes." Arielle shoots to her feet, bringing it closer to show him. "The person who gave it to me assured me it could kill her."

"Whoa, Mac *and* Lust. That was most definitely one heck of a training session."

Arielle's smile seems to bloom under Reign's adoring sunshine. It breaks Gabby's heart to be the one to end it.

"We can't focus on Lust right now."

The two of them spin to face her, insta-frowns compressing their faces. Arielle shakes her head. "I heard the news this morning. More and more people are dying. We have to take care of the Sin wreaking havoc in our city."

Gabby tries to keep her voice gentle. "We need to focus on finding the next Innocent. We have to stop the next Gate of Hell from opening."

Arielle sets her jaw. "Lust is looking for the next Innocent. We kill her," she lifts the dagger, "now that we know we can and the Innocent is safe."

"The dagger might not work," Gabby points out.

Although it killed Pothos, a winged god of love and desire, Lust is a next level demon. She's one of the seven Sins. They need to make sure the dagger has been prepared.

Not to mention Arielle hasn't told them how she got it...

"Even this isn't enough?" Arielle asks, her eyes moist and blazing all at once. "I bring Cain's essence to save Mac and a dagger to kill Lust, and you still won't listen?"

"That's not what this is about, Ari," Gabby bites out. "We have to find the Innocent—"

Arielle jams the dagger back in her backpack and slings it over her shoulder. "I don't know why I even bothered," she mutters. When she straightens, she glares at Gabby. "I'll always be your clueless, human cousin."

Before Gabby can say anything, Arielle storms back out the door, her body vibrating with anger.

Gabby stares at the door, blinking. She's never thought Arielle is clueless. And yes, she's human, but a tough, brave one.

"You two really need to work on your communication," Reign mutters, following Arielle out the door.

"You tried to tell her," Colt says quietly.

Gabby leans against him, sighing. When did things get so complicated between her and Ari?

Sierra reappears from the kitchen. "Blaise is on her way. She says Cain's demonic essence will be more than enough to wake Mac."

Gabby nods, relieved that something's going right. But the feeling is short-lived as Sierra glances around.

"Where's Arielle?" She stills. "And Reign?"

"They're fine," Colt assures. "There was a disagreement about what we should do next and Arielle left. Reign went with her."

Sierra glances at the door, her eyebrows pinched. "Arielle would want to go after Lust. She'd be conscious of all the deaths that could be prevented by killing the demon."

Arielle has always had a strong compassionate streak. A sense of social responsibility, as if she's bound to protect every soul on Earth. And Gabby gets it. Hearing about more lives lost hurts her, too.

But she also knows that they can find the next Innocent.

She reaches into the pocket of her shorts, pulling out the vial that's tucked in there. Her mother's Grace glows in her palm, illuminating it.

Sierra walks toward it, her eyes wide with wonder. "Is that..."

Gabby nods, her throat tight. "Yes. And with it, we can stop the next Sin releasing."

Ultimately, she wants the same as Arielle.

To stop more people dying.

CHAPTER 31

ARIELLE

Arielle realizes there are tears tracking down her cheeks when she reaches the curb outside her house. Frustrated, she wipes them away. She's not sad. She's angry.

She's downright pissed.

Except more tears creep down the tracks created by the first ones, catching at the edge of her mouth. Even that slight weight is enough to pull the edges down. She claps her hand over her mouth, trying to stop the sob that escapes. And fails.

"Ari," comes a soft voice behind her. A warm voice. A comforting voice.

She spins around, finding Reign a few feet away, face soft with tenderness. Arielle doesn't think, right now it hurts too much to do that. She stumbles toward him, another sob climbing up her throat as he opens his arms.

She throws herself into the offered embrace, wrapping her arms tightly around his waist as she buries her face in his chest. When Reign's arms close around her, she clutches him even tighter. There's nowhere she's felt so safe. So...wanted.

It was the same when she returned from Syria. She wasn't home until she was in Reign's arms.

Reign holds her as the sobs tumble over each other, the tears washing down her face unabated. He strokes her hair. He murmurs her name. And he lets her cry.

The breakdown doesn't last long, the tears quickly running dry and the sobs dissolving into hiccups. As she stands there, enclosed by Reign's sweet scent and steady strength, Arielle realizes this was all brought on by exhaustion.

She peeks up at Reign. "Sorry."

He shakes his head, pushing her hair back from her face. "I get the feeling you went to hell and back to get that stuff."

Her throat clogs at his words. "I try so hard," she whispers, knowing she sounds pathetic.

She thought she'd done well. She went to the Middle East, for poppycock's sake, practically on her own. And yet, Gabby still won't take her seriously.

Reign's eyes soften to an achingly beautiful moss green. "And look at what you've managed to do. You're determined. You're brave. And you care, Ari." He smiles. "Those qualities are what will save Mac."

Her breath comes to a halt. The sincerity in Reign's gaze is one of the most beautiful things she's ever seen. He's not paying her lip service. He really means it.

And the Arielle he paints is everything she wants to be.

Her hands move up his chest to rest on his shoulders, finding her breath once again. "Reign," she says, wondering if that name is the sole reason her lungs work. The memory of their kiss rises in her mind, scorching away the moisture of her tears.

His eyes widen a fraction, his hands tensing around her waist. He almost looks like he's hesitating. Is it because she was just crying and he doesn't want to take advantage of her? Or is it because—

His lips crash down on hers, claiming her with explosive passion. The way Reign hauls her up against him and deepens the kiss burns away any worries that were trying to germinate. She meets his ardor with her own, her every sense yearning to taste him again. She angles her head, he delves deeper with his tongue. Simultaneously, they moan.

Arielle's melting. Combusting. Dissolving. Detonating.

She can barely feel the ground beneath her. The world is slipping away. Her eyes flicker open and she gasps, recoiling she sees her front yard has disappeared. Everything has become night.

Six obelisks surround her, towering and overwhelming. The one to her right cracks, the lightning sound making her flinch. Golden light pours from the fractures, blinding and painful. It curls together, becoming a figure. The demon reaches out, long spindly fingers clawing the air, trying to get to her. A scream crawls up from deep in her chest.

"Arielle!" says Reign, sounding far closer than she would've expected. "Arielle!"

She jolts back to reality, seeing his concerned face and the familiar surroundings. She steps away, pressing her fingers to her temples. "Sorry. I saw..."

"It was another vision, wasn't it?"

"Yeah." Arielle swallows the fear that's still lodged in her throat. "I saw the obelisk cracking again. A demon, the next Sin, was coming out." Reaching for her.

Reign frowns. "That's why you're so worried about the next Innocent."

Because, for some inexplicable reason, she's tied to the obelisks. She's cursed with seeing their fate.

Their possible fate, she thinks determinedly.

"I have to stop it," she says. Why else would she be seeing it? "Especially now that I have the dagger."

Reign's lips thin as he thinks this over. The very same lips that were lush against her own only moments ago. It seems there won't be a chance to talk about the amazing evolution of their relationship.

Unless he agrees with Gabby, and thinks they should focus on finding the Innocent...

"You're right. It's what you need to do," he says resolutely. His eyes twinkle in a way that's starting to become familiar. "But you're not doing it alone."

KEEPER
CHRONICLES

SIERRA

Sierra looks up from where she's sitting on the edge of Mac's bed, smiling tiredly when she sees Blaise enter. "Hey. Thanks for coming so quickly."

Blaise, all in black today, as is often the case when she's going to wield powerful magic, nods. "Of course." She glances at Mac, then frowns. "I think we're doing this just in time."

Sierra follows her line of sight, taking in the sleeping girl. There are times she wonders if Mac's even breathing. "Yeah. She's gone in pretty deep."

Blaise sits in a nearby chair. "You still think she'd make a good Archivist?"

"You mean, even though she's a demon?" Sierra asks, raising a brow.

"More so because she's a demon that the angels have shown an interest in."

Sierra picks up Mac's hand, realizing how cool it is. "I

haven't changed my mind. She'd make a wonderful Archivist. She has a thirst for the truth."

Blaise nods, her face pensive. "She's certainly tough to have lasted this long." She glances around the room. "And where is this demonic essence?"

Sierra unwraps the jar that was sitting in her lap. She'd rolled it up in tea towel, knowing it's silly, but the slithering smoke made her uncomfortable. It seems very unhappy to be trapped in there.

Blaise lets out a low whistle as she takes it. "Where did you get this?"

Shifting a little on the bed, Sierra frowns. "Arielle brought it. It's Cain's essence."

"How in the ghost did she do that?"

"I don't know," Sierra says quietly, gripping Mac's hand a little tighter as if the unconscious girl can give her comfort. "She wouldn't say."

"You're worried about her," Blaise observes.

"Aren't you?" Sierra demands, noting the way Blaise's lashes flicker. "My daughter is throwing herself into this with everything she has."

"She's surrounded by people who love her. A team who look out for each other."

Except she's determined to work alone. Thank goodness Reign is with her. Sierra sighs, acknowledging that Mac needs her focus right now. She indicates toward the jar. "Do you think it will work?"

Blaise lifts it, looking at the red-black smoke with keen intensity. "I do believe it will." She reaches for her satchel. "And I have just the spell."

Relief that Mac will be safe again has Sierra sagging. She watches as Blaise opens her grimoire and scans the page, sitting the jar on the bedside table beside her. The contents swirl in agitation, a serpent angry at being caged.

Sierra wraps her arms around her middle. She's not sure what's unsettling her more. Knowing Cain's demonic essence is in the same room as her.

Or that her daughter obtained it, and she has no idea how.

CHAPTER 32
GABBY

Gabby sits on the couch in her childhood home, memories and grief crowding around her. She looks at the vial containing her mother's Grace sitting in her palm, and her throat clogs with emotion.

"Are you sure you want to do this alone?" Colt asks from beside her.

She sighs, patting his knee with her free hand. "I'm sure." She smiles at him. "Plus, you'll be on the other side of the door."

He nods. "Yes, I will be."

Colt's never apologized for his protectiveness and it makes Gabby's smile grow. It's his love language and she wouldn't have it any other way. Not when she'd do the same for him. "Thanks."

He presses a kiss to her temple before rising and exiting the front door. With a last long look in her direction, he closes it quietly.

Gabby sighs. He knows this is going to hurt. And yet, she's never wanted to do anything more. How many people get a second chance to talk to a loved one they've lost?

Lifting the vial and pressing it to her chest, Gabby closes her eyes. She pictures her mom, her blonde hair always up in a clip, her soft, smiling face. The aching sadness hits her with the same power as the sweet gratitude that she was part of her life. Like oil and water, the two feelings don't mix. They clash and war, fighting to rise to the top. It depends on the split second as to which one wins.

"Gabby."

Her eyes fly open. She never thought she'd hear her name said in that voice again.

Her mom is standing before her, wearing the apron shaped like a strawberry she always did when in the kitchen, her blonde hair up in a clip, wisps floating around her face. Gabby's heart fractures and heals all at once.

"Mom," she chokes.

"Hi, honey. It's so good to see you."

Gabby goes to stand up only to find her legs aren't working. It's probably a good thing. She can't touch her mom, she's here only in spirit. "I'm so sorry," she whispers. "I didn't protect you."

Her mom shakes her head, her face soft with understanding. "There's nothing you could have done, Gabby. No one knew. Not even me." She smooths her apron, tugging on the frilled edge. "And I'm at peace now, honey. I'm okay, really."

Tears track down Gabby's cheeks, feeling warm against her cold skin. "I miss you so much."

Her mother smiles. "Angel tears," she says fondly. "Remember how I used to call them that?"

Gabby's smile is bittersweet. That's exactly what her mom used to call them. Little did they know... Not only is her father an angel, her mother's one, too. It reminds her why she's here, holding her mother's Grace. "We need to find the next Innocent, Mom. They're in danger."

She nods, understanding heavy in her gaze. "Yes. I sense it, too."

"Who is it?"

Her mother closes her eyes, concentrating. "It's a man," she says. She winces. "A father."

Gabby shoots to her feet, the mention of someone else losing their loved one jolting through her. "Who?"

"It's Paul," her mother says, opening her eyes in astonishment. An image of a fit-looking man flashes in Gabby's mind, as if her mother planted it there. "He runs a martial arts training center on the other end of town."

The moment her mother says the words, she starts to fade. "No!" cries Gabby, instinctively reaching out.

Her hand passes through air, her mother already transparent. "I love you, Gabby. Thank you for finding my Grace."

"Mom!" More tears are scorching her cheeks. "I love you so much!"

"I know, honey. Your love was always the most precious of gifts."

Gabby blinks and she's gone. She's glad she got to tell her mother one last time. And yet, she fights the pain of losing her all over again and the anger at wishing this had ended differently.

It's that simmering, searing emotion that has Gabby straightening. She wouldn't wish this agony on anyone.

"Colt," she calls out, heading toward the door.

They have the name of the next Innocent.

They need to warn him.

THEY'VE JUST PULLED into the parking lot outside of the Rising Phoenix Dojo when the front door opens. A man exits, wiping his face with a towel.

"That's him," Gabby gasps. The Innocent.

Colt leans forward, staring intently through the windshield. "Have you thought about how we're going to tell him?"

Gabby chews her lip. "I've thought about it." And come up with nothing. If a stranger walked up to her mother and told her she's actually an angel on a demons' most wanted list because their death will open a Gate of Hell, her mom would've *tsked* in sympathy because they'd lost their marbles then walked away. Real quick.

"So you're winging it," Colt observes, his hand on the door handle. "Just the usual, huh?"

Gabby shrugs. "Hey, it worked against the Grigori."

Colt's about to exit, Gabby following, when the front door of the dojo opens again.

"Dad!" calls a red-haired girl as she runs after him. "You forgot your drink bottle."

Gabby and Colt freeze as they watch Rachel pass him one of the largest drink bottles Gabby's ever seen.

"She just said Dad," Gabby breathes. The Innocent is Rachel's father.

Except Rachel never reaches her father. A blast of light hits her in the chest and she's knocked back, the drink bottle flying out of her hand. Colt and Gabby leap out of the car, running toward her.

Demons stream in, converging on Paul like a swarm.

"No!" Gabby shouts.

They can't have been too late.

Colt powers forward, his head down like a vengeful battering-ram. He knocks one demon over, but a large, black wing bowls him out of the way. He's thrown through the air, landing several feet away and gouging through the gravel of the parking lot.

Lust swoops in, grabs Paul, and soars into the air. Several strokes of her powerful wings and she's gone. The demons scatter like the cowards they are, disappearing almost as quickly as they appeared.

Gabby reaches Rachel and helps her up. "Dad!" Rachel wails. "No! Where did they take him?"

Colt stands, dusting the gravel from his arm as the graze begins to fade, his demon healing taking care of it. He strides over, his face grim. "Lust took him."

Rachel goes pale as she twists her hands together. "Why? He hasn't been with anyone. I know he hasn't."

Gabby shakes her head. "That's not why," she says, realizing they're going to have to explain what's going on. "But we'll do everything we can to get him back," she vows.

She won't fail Rachel's father in the same way she failed her mother.

MAC

As Mac's feet touch the ground, everything and nothing makes sense.

She's a demon. A creature of Hell. A wielder of dark magic.

But as her wings tuck back in, ready to be called on again, she's not sure what she's supposed to do with that. She realizes she hasn't from the moment she knew.

Is she good? Is she evil?

What is she supposed to fight for?

Reign groans beside her as Arielle unties his bonds. "Ari?" he whispers.

She smiles softly. "I knew you'd realize who I was eventually."

He looks around. "Mac. You two saved me?"

"It was mostly Mac," Arielle says. "She had quite the surprise tucked up her sleeve."

Actually, it was tucked in her back. And it's been in her blood all along.

The ropes fall to the floor and Reign pushes to his feet, then promptly stumbles. Arielle and Mac both move to help, but Arielle's closer. She tucks under his arm, smiling up at him. "It's okay. I'm here."

Reign's face softens. "I'm glad you are." He presses a kiss to her temple.

Mac watches the interaction, glad that Reign's found someone he can lean on in more ways than one. She was worried he was going to be a lone wolf for the rest of his life. The Reign she knows would've told Arielle that she might be here for now, but he's learned that no one sticks around.

There's a groan from the other side of the room, and Mac sees that the dark-haired guy is coming to. She turns to Arielle. "Get Reign out of here. I'll tie these two up and then we can call the cops."

Arielle nods, encouraging Reign to lean on her as she leads him out of the room. He limps beside her, face bruised and eyes closed against the pain. The torture he was put through has taken its toll.

Once they're gone, Mac walks over to the guy, grabs his black hair and yanks it up. "Why did you hurt Reign?" she demands.

The guy's eyes flutter open as he grins up at her. "Because the bastard betrayed me."

Mac narrows her eyes, hearing the venom in his voice. "Who are you?"

"No one," he spits. "Only Reign's brother."

Mac almost reels back on her heels. "Brother?" she asks incredulously. She only has faint memories of Reign mentioning a foster *brother from his younger years, Lance. He said it didn't end well and he'd rather not talk about it.*

"Of course you wouldn't know I exist," Lance says bitterly. "Something else I'll make him pay for."

Mac tightens her grip on his hair, making him wince. "You won't be going anywhere near Reign again."

Lance slides her a dark look. "I got out of the asylum once, I can do it again."

Asylum? No wonder this guy seems like he was born on the wrong side of whacky. Except she's not here to discuss this guy's issues. "Why did the Mayor want Reign?"

Lance looks at Mac as if she's the one who's crazy. "Because he knows where the Grail is."

Mac's hand goes slack and Lance's head thumps to the floor, knocking him unconscious again. She winces, but can't bring herself to feel bad. Lance tortured Reign, and has said he wants to do it again. A small part of her wishes she'd knocked him out with her fist.

She stands, frowning. The Mayor is looking for the Holy Grail. Strangely, the knowledge doesn't surprise her. With everything that's happened, the Mayor has to be supernatural. And Mac knows the Holy Grail exists. She doesn't know how, but she does.

A sound behind Mac alerts her to the fact she's not alone in this room with Lance. She turns around in time to see Lizzie running at her, face twisted in a snarl. A quick spin and unfurling of her wings, and Mac knocks her to the ground. By the time she's done the full turn and is facing Lizzie again, the wings are gone. Mac almost wants to pat herself on the back. That was one cool move.

She strides over and lifts Lizzie by her shirt, shaking her. Lizzie whimpers, the lioness gone, leaving a trembling lamb behind. "Please don't hurt me."

Mac's lip curls with disgust. "But that would ruin all my fun."

Lizzie's head curls into her shoulders. "No, please. I can show you something."

"Show me what?" she growls. Lizzie's trying to buy mercy, and Mac's willing to humor her.

"The cupboard behind the desk. There's paperwork in there that the Mayor stole from Reign's father. She went to some extreme lengths to get it."

Dread trickles down Mac's spine. "What sort of paperwork?"

Lizzie shakes her head, her hair, now limp and lank, catching on her false eyelashes. "I don't know. Just that it's important."

Mac grinds her teeth. She's getting tired of all these cryptic pieces of information.

"But I can help you," Lizzie cajoles, her voice almost a whine. "I've always had feelings for Reign—"

A quick fist to the jaw and Lizzie's unconscious again. Mac lowers her to the ground beside Lance. The authorities will take care of the two of them.

Walking quickly, she circles the desk, seeing a small crack along the wall behind it, as if a cupboard door has been left ajar. She pries her fingers in and opens it, seeing that Lizzie was telling the truth. A small compartment lies behind, a stack of papers sitting inside. A folded note sits on top.

Mac reaches in and grabs it, seeing there's a symbol scrawled on the front. It's not entirely legible, but it looks like a septagram with some sort of crossed lines in the center. A strange feeling weighs down in Mac's chest, as if this is significant. She unfolds the slip of paper, reading the single line scribbled inside.

Find it or—

"Mackenzie."

Mac looks up, surprised to hear her name said with such joy. The apparitions she saw in her room are back, hovering in the middle of the room. But this time she recognizes them. It's Sierra and Blaise.

Sierra smiles and extends her hand. "It's time to come back."

CHAPTER 33

ARIELLE

Arielle watches as Reign paces the length of the living room, doing a wonderful impersonation of a caged panther. His moves are lithe yet full of restless energy that feels like he could do this for as long as it takes.

Until Mac is awake.

"How long does it take?" he mutters.

"Blaise said she might have to go in deep," Arielle reminds him. "She's a powerful witch. She knows what she's doing."

Reign stalks over to where she's sitting at the table, a map of Mercy City spread out before her. "Any ideas of where we should start looking for Lust?"

Realizing he's looking for a distraction, Arielle points to the dots she's marked. "These are all the places Lust has been." All the places Lust has killed. "I figure we go to the most recent one and do what we did last time." Although they had Gabby to help with glamoring them then.

He nods, leaning over her so he can look more closely. "It could still take a while, but it's the best we've got."

Arielle suppresses a sigh, knowing he's right. Lust is thirsting for blood and as it feeds her it makes her stronger. The longer they leave it, the harder it will be to defeat her. But she's not going to point that out while Reign's worried about Mac.

Her cell phone rings and she sees it's Rachel. They haven't spoken since they got back from Damascus, and Arielle hopes she's recovered from the trip. She almost doesn't answer, figuring Rachel's just checking in, but she picks up. They've been through a lot in the short time they've known each other, and a deep friendship has been forged. Rachel deserves a quick hello and a promise she'll talk to her later.

Arielle never gets a chance to say a word before Rachel speaks. "Hey, can you come and pick me up from the dojo?"

Arielle stills, noting the tremor in Rachel's voice. Reign must notice because he sits across from her, watching intently. "Yeah, sure. Why?" she asks.

"Something's happened and I can't stay here. Gabby and Colt said they'd come and get me when I finished packing, but I'd prefer to travel with you."

"Of course," Arielle says, concern tightening her shoulders. Tough, sassy Rachel sounds like a scared, vulnerable Rachel. Something's definitely happened. "Are you okay, Rach?"

"You need to hurry. Lust has taken my dad," she chokes. "Ari, he's the next Innocent."

ARIELLE TAKES in Rachel's pale face as she climbs into the car and gives her an awkward hug over the center console. "Hey."

"Thanks for coming," Rachel says, drawing in a shuddering breath. "I could really use a friend right now."

"We're going to find him," Reign says determinedly from the back seat he just climbed into.

Arielle looks back at him, sending him a grateful glance.

Reign came even though he's waiting for news of Mac. He'd be desperate to see her when she wakes. Or to be the first to know if Blaise is unable to reach her, even with Cain's demonic essence.

He'd insisted, saying Rachel helped them, it was only right they were there for her. Arielle had almost kissed him again.

"We most definitely are," agrees Rachel, a hint of her strength creeping back into her voice. "And I'm going to kill that bitch."

"You'll have to get in line," says Reign wryly.

Arielle removes the dagger from the satchel on her lap. "And now we have a way to do it."

"Gabby and Colt have gone back to her house to get her mother's Grace so they can track Dad again," says Rachel, staring out the windshield. "I hope it doesn't take too long."

The pink-stained sky above them is a testament that they're running out of time.

Rachel gasps, pulling her phone out of her pocket. "I know how we can find him!"

Reign pushes between the two front seats, his face intense. "How?"

Rachel taps on the screen of her cell. "I gave Dad a watch for his birthday. It has a tracking chip in it." She flushes. "I've always needed to know where he is since I lost my mom."

"Reign, you drive," she says, unbuckling her belt.

He jolts in surprise. "I don't actually have my license."

"Don't start with the law abiding talk again," Arielle says as she opens his door. Reign's driven at speed before—which was obvious when he almost ran over her the first day they met. "We've lost enough time as it is."

Reign jumps out and into the driver's seat. "Make sure you buckle up, then."

"I don't think they've got very far," Rachel says, staring at her screen. "He's on the outskirts of town."

They roar out of the parking lot, gravel spraying behind them. Arielle grips her seat belt as Reign expertly, but very, very quickly, navigates them through the city. But despite their speed, she notes the way he stops at red lights, is always checking his surroundings. It makes her realize that if anyone else was driving the car that day, she probably wouldn't be here. And yet, would any of it happened if he wasn't involved in the first place...

Reign is definitely someone who dances on the line between good and bad. Someone her fate is interwoven with.

They've just passed a farmhouse when Rachel tells him to turn right. They have to slow as they make their way down a dirt road, green pastures on either side. Arielle looks around, surprised that Lust would take Rachel's father to somewhere so open.

"Stop," Rachel says tightly.

She exits the car and Arielle and Reign quickly follow. Barely glancing up from her phone, she climbs through the fence and makes her way onto the field.

"Rachel?" Arielle asks. "Are you sure this is the right place?"

Rachel stops, green shoots reaching to her ankles. "This is where it registers he is," she says in a small voice.

"Rachel," Reign says, his voice low. He squats down and picks something up.

A man's watch.

Rachel grabs it, the look on her face telling them what they already suspected—it's her father's.

Lust's demons must have realized he could be tracked with it.

Rachel clutches the watch to her chest as she throws her

head back. "No!" she screams, the one word drawn out with pain.

Arielle engulfs her in a hug, her heart aching. "We'll go back and find Gabby. She'll be able to track him."

They'll just have to hope it's not too late.

Rachel nods, sniffing a little, and they separate. "Let's hurry."

Reign has just taken a step toward the car when the sky darkens to a deep, bloody maroon. Lightning strikes so close that it has them all shielding their eyes.

As Arielle lowers her arm, she sees they're no longer the only ones in the field.

Lust lowers from the sky, her onyx wings expanded to their full width. She smiles maliciously. "You'll see your father again," she purrs. "When he's dead and the next Gate of Hell has opened."

"You Hell-faced bitch," Rachel spits.

Lust waves away the insult. "And there's little point trying to find him. I've cloaked him."

"Please," Rachel pleads, making Arielle's eyes sting at this proud, strong girl resorting to begging. "He's everything to me."

But her words only seem to amuse Lust. Maybe even arouse her a little. "I'm not here to talk. I'm here to end you. You three are becoming quite the nuisance."

Arielle reaches into her satchel and withdraws the dagger. "It will be a little more even this time."

Her aunt lost her life so this demon could be free. She's not going to let that happen again.

Lust pauses for a brief moment as she sees the weapon, her lip curling. But before Arielle can blink, she attacks anyway, tucking in her wings and coming at them like a missile.

Reign and Rachel leap in front of Arielle, fists raised. Lust's eyes blaze with excitement that she'll have two opponents. She spins, her black-clad leg shooting out, narrowly missing the two of them as they duck back.

Rachel doesn't waste a second, leaping with a volley of strikes that instantly puts Lust on the defensive. Reign launches forward, but rather than aiming for the demon, he slides under her as she leaps to kick again, slipping over the moist grass. He comes to his feet on the other side, ready to attack.

But Lust's leg changes trajectory as she kicks backward, simultaneously reaching out to grab Rachel by her top. Her foot connects with Reign's chest, making him cry out as he's launched backward.

"No," Arielle whispers even though the word screams through her. Reign's still healing from the first time Lust wounded him, and she knows that.

With Reign groaning on the ground several feet away, Lust focuses on Rachel. She holds her shirt as she unleashes a barrage of punches to Rachel's face. "Yes," she hisses in pleasure.

But her thirst to inflict pain is just the focus Arielle needs. She surges forward, gripping the dagger with all her strength. She doesn't flinch as it slices through Lust's side, impaling right up to the hilt.

Lust screeches as she rears back, arching backward. Rachel drops to the ground, face bleeding and barely conscious. Arielle rushes to her, watching in horror as blood pours down Lust's leg. She lands on the ground on one knee, glaring at the weapon impaled in her flesh.

Arielle holds her breath, hoping Lust's death is a quick one. The adrenalin is wearing off, and the gravity of what she's done is hitting her. It's over, Lust is finished. But she also killed a living being.

Lust reaches down and yanks out the dagger, hissing with pain. The slice in her leather top reveals a jagged gash with blood steadily trickling out, making Arielle's stomach roll. But as she watches, the cut steadily closes and the flow of blood stops.

She's healing!

Before Arielle can understand what's going on, Lust leaps, her hand spearing around Arielle's throat. She lifts her so her toes are just brushing the tips of the grass.

"There will be no slow strangulation for you," she spits. "Just one, delicious snap of the neck."

She lifts Arielle higher, so her feet are dangling along with the rest of her body. The strain on her neck has Arielle gasping, the last of her breath escaping and her lungs unable to draw any more back in. Pain radiates down her arms and back, lancing up her skull. She grips Lust's hand, even though it's futile, feeling the power thrumming through the demon's veins.

Lust smiles. "First you, then your two irritating friends."

Her fingers loosen as a bolt of white light hits her in the back. Lust drops Arielle, screeching with pain. She spins around, and Arielle sees what attacked the demon.

Gabby is flying toward them, her magnificent wings glowing in the sunlight, her face tight with fury. She looks every bit the avenging angel.

Lust hisses in frustration then disappears, leaving Arielle lying in the field, gasping. Gabby lands lightly, and Arielle sees Colt is with her, his midnight wings a stark contrast to her pearl ones.

Gabby looks around, seeing that everyone's still alive. She turns back to Arielle, the fury still very much blazing. "When the fuck will you learn, Ari?"

GABBY

Arielle winces, but Gabby's too angry to feel sorry for her. She almost died! If Gabby had been a few seconds later, she would've lost another person she loves with everything she has.

Her heart hasn't healed from losing her mother, she can't lose Arielle, too.

Colt steps in, helping Arielle to her feet. "She was worried about you," he says softly.

Gabby frowns at him, not really appreciating his calm, steady, rational presence right now. "And now I'm pissed with you," she snaps, keeping her gaze on her cousin.

Arielle rubs her throat. "But I thought the dagger..."

"Has it been dipped in Cupid's ashes?" Gabby demands.

"I...I don't know."

"Well, if you had asked, I could've told you it needs to be. Otherwise it's useless against Lust."

Reign stumbles to Arielle's side, frowning protectively. "She was told it would work," he grinds out.

Even Rachel limps to her other side, her face puffy and bruised. "And as a Sagittarius, I'm not known for patience. I wanted to go after him there and then."

The fury dies, quickly replaced by the real emotion that was driving it. "And you couldn't have called me? Like Reign did?"

Arielle gasps, turning to him. "You called her?"

He ducks his head. "Technically I texted her. I just thought she should know. I didn't know she'd come."

Although it's darned lucky she did. They'd all be dead right now.

Gabby's about to say that when Colt's hand brushes her. The caress is subtle, but they're so in tune with each other, she feels it. And she knows what he's trying to tell her.

That she needs to calm her farm.

She draws in a deep breath, tucking her wings away. "We need to work together, Ari." It's the only way they'll win.

Arielle flushes. "You're right. I'm sorry."

Gabby blinks, surprised at the apology, and not entirely sure what it means. Are they going to work together now? Like she'd secretly dreamed they would?

But there's no time to have that conversation. It'll have to wait. "Then you need to tell me what's going on."

Arielle nods, her heavy gaze meeting Gabby's. Slowly, but with steady strength, she tells Gabby how she came across the dagger and Cain's demonic essence. Gabby listens, astounded, as she learns that Arielle went to Damascus and faced Cain as he tried to cast a spell. That she was attacked but saved just in time.

That the Mayor had been behind the whole thing.

"I knew there was something off about that woman," Colt mutters.

"And we made a deal with her right hand woman to return Cain to her," Gabby muses. She frowns. "Why did she want Cain so badly that she orchestrated two of us to bring him in?"

Rachel clears her throat. "Can we try and figure that out after we find my dad?"

"You're right," says Gabby, everything feeling like it's closing in on her. "To do that, we're going to need Cupid's ashes."

The sound of a car on the dirt road has them all turning around. A black limousine pulls up behind Colt's car.

"What's the Mayor doing here?" Rachel asks suspiciously.

"Speak of the manipulative mamzer," mutters Colt.

"Mamzer?" Reign asks.

"It's Hebrew, and you probably don't want to know what it means," Gabby explains, breaking into a jog. Whatever the Mayor wants, it'll have to wait.

Colt joins her, and she realizes the other three are, too. It seems they all want to greet the Mayor. But the woman who steps out of the car isn't Virginia Goodstone. Or Bess.

"Daria?" Arielle says incredulously.

The dark-haired, dark-eyed woman glances at Arielle then Gabby. "I have something for you."

She reaches into the car and Gabby braces herself, ready to fight and protect once more. But it's a man's body that tumbles out of the car and onto the ground.

Cain.

And a not very well Cain, at that. He lolls on the ground, looking battered and semi-conscious.

"He's yours," says Daria. "This way, you uphold your part of the deal with the Mayor."

She knows about that? Gabby narrows her eyes. "Why are you doing this?"

Daria shrugs. "It's nice to do the right thing for a change."

Gabby frowns, confused. Then she sees the tattoo on the inside of the woman's wrist. It's the symbol she's been researching. "Hey! Where did you get that?"

But Daria doesn't say anything, just pulls her sleeve down over it.

It's Arielle who answers. "It belongs to the organization she works for."

"Who? Who do you work for?"

"You don't have time for this," Daria snaps. "You need to locate the Innocent before Lust kills him. You do not want another Gate of Hell opened."

Gabby chafes with frustration, knowing this mysterious girl is right.

Daria steps around Cain. "But first, bring Cain to the Mayor. She's not someone you want to trifle with."

She climbs back in the limo and it reverses away, leaving the half-dead Cain with them.

"Well, that complicates things," Reign says drolly.

Gabby clenches her hands. They don't have time for this. She turns to Colt. "You take Ari and Rachel to get Cupid's ashes," she instructs.

He nods. Just like she does, he knows exactly where they are.

She settles her gaze on Reign. "We'll return Cain." It will honor her deal with the Mayor, and take care of the powerful demon who had her mother killed.

Reign glances at Arielle, but she angles her face away. His own features tighten. "Sure. It's not like I have anything else to do."

Unsure what just passed between the two, but not having an opportunity to find out, Gabby nods. "Good. We need to be quick."

Lust has the next Innocent.

Time is running out.

CHAPTER 34
REIGN

Reign sits in the backseat of Arielle's car as Gabby drives, wondering if it's okay to punch a barely-conscious demon. He's always had a rule about not hitting someone when they're incapacitated, no matter how much Rico said he was passing up an easy shot, but this is different.

Cain was the one who had Shell killed.

Cain unleashed Lust on the world, sparking all these murders.

And Arielle is angry after Reign called in backup so they could fight Lust.

In his mind, that's Cain's fault.

He groans beside him, mumbling incoherently. Seeing Cain so...undone is almost karma. Almost.

But Reign's hand still clenches. Too much frustration is pounding through him. Arielle believes he betrayed her by texting Gabby. But all he was doing was trying to keep her safe. Alive.

And Cain would be a great outlet for that frustration. Plus, he could see if that pain power that appeared the last time they fought still exists...

Gabby glances in the rear vision mirror. "It won't help."

Reign frowns. "Now you're a mind reader?"

She shakes her head, taking a turn onto the street that will take them to City Hall. "No. Just an empath of sorts. I can sense your emotions, and you're low grade pissed."

"Cain has hurt a lot of people."

"He has." Her hands tighten on the steering wheel, almost as if she wouldn't mind taking a shot at him herself. "But he's a blubbering mess. Hitting him won't give you the satisfaction you're looking for."

Reign looks out the window. "If I punched him, I'd figure that out myself."

Gabby smiles a little. "And is this really about Cain?"

That shuts Reign up. He has no desire to find out where that thread of conversation will go.

Actually, he knows. A great big, messy knot. One he doesn't have time to disentangle.

Gabby pulls into the parking lot, seeming happy to let it go. Her lips thin. "Let's get this over and done with. We have more important stuff going on."

And yet Gabby's ensuring she upholds her word. Reign respects that.

He glances at Cain. "Do we have to carry him in?" he asks, not looking forward to the task. People will ask questions. And he'll have to resist the temptation to not walk the bastard into every pole and column they pass. Self-control isn't his strong suit.

The fact he kissed Arielle a second time is proof of that.

Gabby glances at her watch. "Bess agreed to—"

A woman in a sharp suit and tightly pulled back hair appears beside their car. "You're a woman of her word, Gabrielle."

Gabby exits the car and Reign does the same, coming to stand beside her. "He's all yours, Bess," Gabby says tightly.

Bess bends at the knees, her eyes lighting up with something Reign would rather not name when she sees Cain slumped in the back seat. "Finally," she murmurs.

She flicks her fingers, and a man climbs out of a nearby car with tinted windows. He manhandles Cain from Gabby's car to Bess's, not bothering to be gentle as he shoves him onto the back seat.

When the door is slammed shut, Bess lets out a satisfied breath. She turns back to Gabby. "Now, you have a demon to kill. The dagger Arielle has should take care of that.

"How do you know about the dagger?" Reign asks, uneasy about whatever the heck is going on here. That agreement was with the Mayor.

Bess chuckles, her features slowly, steadily morphing. Until the Mayor is standing before them.

Gabby's hands clench, as much on high alert as Reign is. "You're a witch!" he says, not knowing why he's surprised.

Virginia rolls her eyes. "Just because I wield magic doesn't make me a witch. I'm something far more ancient than that." Before either of them can ask what, she continues. "Lust is wreaking havoc on my city. I'm under a lot of pressure to end these murders. She must be stopped."

Great. A supernatural who-knows-what with political pressure. Just what they need.

"We're working on it," Reign says through gritted teeth.

Virginia gives them a tight-lipped smile. "Excellent." She spins on her heel and climbs into the passenger side of the dark car and it pulls away.

Gabby watches it leave with narrowed eyes. "I don't trust her."

"And yet we just gave her Cain."

She flashes him a glare. "You want to keep him at your house?"

Grinning, Reign puts his hands up in surrender. "No way. He drools too much."

Gabby shakes her head, an unwilling smile pulling at the edges of her lips. "Come on. The Mayor spoke the truth when she said we need to take care of Lust."

Reign sobers and they climb back in the car. That depends on Arielle and Colt finding Cupid's ashes.

And so far, nothing has been easy or straightforward.

MAC

Mac's eyes flutter open as she draws in a sudden breath like she just broke above water. She sits up and the room she's in spins. A room she doesn't recognize.

Has it happened again?

"Mac! Thank goodness!" Warm, feminine arms engulf her and Mac instinctively returns the hug, frowning.

Slowly, her surroundings come into focus. They progressively look familiar. She knows this room. This bed. She knows the woman holding her.

"Sierra?" she asks, finding her voice hoarse like it's been unused.

She pulls back, smiling and misty eyed. "Are you okay?"

"I...I think so." Mac looks around seeing Blaise sitting nearby. She jolts. "Where's Reign?"

"He wanted to be here," Blaise assures. "But things have been a little...hectic."

Mac glances back at the bed. "I've been asleep, haven't I? I was dreaming."

That's why everything was so real, yet so surreal.

"Kind of," says Sierra. "The angels trapped you in a sort of artificial universe. An alternate reality they concocted."

"The bastards," Mac says, steadily getting angry. Everything she just went through was all fake? Some sort of awful play? "Why the fu—" she quickly stops herself, conscious of the two women in the room. "Why would they do that?"

"My guess is they wanted you to learn something," says Blaise, watching Mac closely. "Maybe show you something."

Mac frowns, remembering everything she went through. Lizzie. The Mayor. Discovering her demon powers all over again. The secret room. Some note she didn't get to read.

She rubs her temples. "That could take some time to unpack."

"Which we don't have right now," Sierra says gently. "Another Innocent has been taken. We have to stop him from being sacrificed at the next holy site."

Mac shuffles on to the edge of the bed. "What are we waiting for?" she says urgently.

"Are you okay to do this?" Sierra asks, looking concerned.

Mac pushes to her feet, energy thrumming through her veins. Energy she now knows is demonic in origin. Energy that gives her power to fight for what's right.

She hoists her hands on her hips. "I just had the longest nap ever, I'm definitely okay to do this."

Sierra smiles, something warm glinting in her eyes. "I had a feeling you'd say that."

Mac nods. It's time to forge her own destiny.

CHAPTER 35
ARIELLE

olt drives through a set of large ornate gates and slows the car as they rumble up a gravel driveway. Arielle looks around, curious as to what they're doing here. Although she's never been to Mercy Academy, she certainly knows of it.

This is where Gabby went to college. Where she met Colt.

As they approach what's left of the old building, she also remembers that it burned down several months ago.

Arielle leans forward, taking in the black, skeletal hulk. Gabby spoke about the place with such excitement, describing how grand and impressive it was. All that's left is charred earth and two lonely chimneys.

"What happened?" she asks Colt as the car comes to a stop.

"The blaze must have been one heck of a fire to have razed such a large building to the ground," observes Rachel as she also studies their surroundings.

"Gabby fought her final battle against the Grigori here," he says solemnly. "She saved the world, but couldn't save the Academy."

Arielle frowns, wondering how she hasn't heard of this. "I would've thought it was in the news more."

"The angels and demons who survived wiped people's memories of the event. It wasn't something humans could know of."

Colt exits the car and she follows, chewing her lip. He's right. Knowing what went down here would terrify people. Send them into a panic. It's best if they don't know.

She's just about to shut the door when she stills. Is this what her mother was thinking when she didn't tell her about the supernatural?

"You okay?" asks Rachel. She angles her head, watching Arielle closely. "Are you still upset because Reign texted Gabby to help us?"

Arielle resists slamming the door. Hearing Reign betrayed her hurt. A lot. She thought he was the one person who understood that she needed to do this.

Except he was right. They'd all be dead if he hadn't texted Gabby.

And she knows what to do with that as much as she does the revelation about her mother.

"It's this way," says Colt, either unaware of their conversation, or acting as if it's not happening. "We must hurry."

"Does he always talk as if he's a hundred?" Rachel asks under her breath.

"I'm pretty sure he's older," Arielle whispers back.

Colt ignores them again, leading the way around the burned building. The scorched lawn that once surrounded it crunches underfoot. They're almost at the end of the massive rectangle of ruin when he turns suddenly, picking his way through the debris. Arielle and Rachel follow, stepping around objects that have melted and burned beyond recognition.

He stops several feet in. "Gabby's secret cache is here," he says, although it's impossible to tell what part of the Academy they're standing in. Everywhere is nothing but coal and ash and broken bricks. "It's protected by a spell and deep underground."

Rachel's hands twist together. "How deep? We don't have a lot of time to be digging."

Colt reaches into his pocket and pulls out a vial. They'd stopped off at his apartment on the way here, and he'd ducked in and out, his hands seemingly empty, but it turns out this is what he picked up.

Arielle's stomach clenches. It looks like a vial of blood.

"We won't be digging," says Colt. "Although you may want to prepare yourself."

Arielle and Rachel glance at each other. Prepare themselves for what?

Colt squats down and brushes away the ash, revealing a stone with a symbol etched into it. "It can only be opened with Gabby's blood," he says quietly.

He opens the vial and tips it, a drop of crimson liquid tumbling over the lip and onto the stone.

The moment it hits, the stone drops away, creating a narrow hole.

Rachel peers closer. "Well, we can't fit—"

The world goes black, only for reality to return a split-second later. Arielle's eyes widen as Rachel appears next to her. They're in a stone room of some sort. They were just transported into Gabby's secret cache.

The stone-lined room isn't very big, and is musty with the smell of abandonment. Arielle does a slow turn, the light from the hold above illuminating the contents.

Shelves line the walls, the metal sort that would be found in a garage. But that's where any reference to modern times stop. One length of shelves holds books, old and leather bound, large and small. Another shelf holds jars and clay pots.

Many of the shelves hold weapons. Knives. Daggers. Spears. Shields.

"What is all this stuff?" Rachel asks in awe.

But Colt barely glances at the armory they're surrounded by. "Some of these weapons could end the world as we know it. It's why Gabby buried them where no one could find them. They're deadly in the wrong hands."

Rachel curls her fingers into her hand, as if she's just decided she won't be touching anything. "Intense."

"When we're done here, I'll seal it in such a way that both my blood and Gabby's will be needed to open it." He frowns. "Then I'll cloak it."

"I'm thinking that might be a good idea," Rachel squeaks.

Arielle looks around again. "So where are the ashes?"

Colt walks the few steps to the shelf with the jars and picks up a flat, wide-mouthed one. He removes the cork lid. "Do you have the dagger?"

She withdraws it from her satchel, nodding. She approaches Colt, glancing inside and seeing the gray dust.

Rachel does the same. "I feel kinda sorry that Cupid's dead," she says forlornly. "It's hard enough to find love as it is." She sighs as she steps back, her shoulders sagging. "I'm going to be single forever."

Colt shakes his head. "There's more than one Cupid. This is the ashes of just one of them."

She brightens a little. "I suppose that's something." She glances at the dagger. "Let's do this."

Unsure of what she's supposed to do, Arielle dips the tip in the ashes. The blade flares a bright red, then returns to its usual silver.

"It's done," says Colt.

Arielle lets out a breath.

Rachel straightens her shoulders. "Let's go get my dad."

Arielle glances around. "What about all this stuff?" Colt just said he was going to disappear it even deeper than it was before.

Colt glances at the books. "You're right. They may come in use." He flicks his hand and the books disappear. "Everything else stays."

Arielle doesn't argue. Gabby was right to keep this stuff down here. For a brief second, she marvels at what her cousin has achieved. She never knew, because she never told her, but for the first time, the thought doesn't sting. She's starting to understand what they're up against.

"Come," says Colt, standing beneath the small hole they somehow entered through. A second later, he's gone.

Rachel quickly follows him, no doubt keen to get moving now that the blade is ready. "Ready," she calls. Just like Colt, she disappears.

Arielle's taken one step to follow them out when she pauses. Something on a shelf to her left catches her eye. In fact, despite its small size, it's the only thing on that particular shelf.

A small, black gem of some sort, about the size of a golf ball. Although it's smooth, it's not round, instead a strange mix of angles and lines, never quite symmetrical on any one side. It's fascinating yet unsettling.

Obsidian, says a voice in her mind, making her freeze. That wasn't the voice of Trinity. It was something deeper. Darker.

As she stares at it, seven lines, jagged and irregular, flash over its surface like cracks. They fade as quickly as they appeared, leaving the stone whole once more.

"Arielle?" comes Colt's voice, jolting her out of the strange trance.

"Coming," she calls back, moving toward the square of light as she shakes her head. She's not sure what just happened, but she's going to ignore it. There's more important things to focus on right now.

They need to end Lust and save Rachel's father.

This time she feels the pull of the magic that Colt must be weaving to draw them back to the surface. And the moment she's gone, this place will be lost to humans and supernaturals, alike. Everything within it buried, almost impossible to be found.

Without conscious thought, Arielle's hand darts out, snatches the obsidian, and buries it in her pocket.

She finds herself once more standing among the ashes of Mercy Academy.

Rachel's face hardens. "Let's go own this bitch."

CHAPTER 36
REIGN

Reign stands at the barricade across the road, staring at the large flour mill factory in the distance. "You're sure they're on their way?"

Gabby huffs, no doubt because he's asked the question for the fifth time. "I'm not answering that because you clearly don't trust the answers I've been giving you."

"Fair call," he acknowledges. He's not going to relax until he sees them.

Mac has woken up.

And Arielle has prepared the dagger.

Both are on their way here, now.

Gabby comes to stand beside him, staring at the mill with narrowed eyes. "Angel Dust Flour Mill," she muses. "I wonder if all the Innocents are taken to somewhere connected to angels."

Reign studies it, too. According to the research they did when they traced Rachel's father here, it's been closed down for several years. "Possibly." Shell was killed at the base of an angel fountain. "There's going to be a lot of demons inside, isn't there?"

Gabby nods. "Lust will have an army of them, protecting

295

her. She knows we can trace Paul, and she doesn't want us stopping her."

"I'm going to pretend you answered no," he says dryly. The thought of facing a horde of demons isn't a pleasant one.

The sound of a car approaching has him spinning around, heart jolting to his throat. He recognizes Sierra in the driver's seat, Blaise in the passenger. And a mop of dark curly hair in the back.

Joy is singing through his veins as he runs toward the car. Mac's opened the door before Sierra's completely stopped, and she barrels toward him. He catches her, the jolt of their bodies colliding ricocheting through his chest. It hurts, but he doesn't care. A part of him was terrified he'd never see her again.

They clutch each other tightly. Silently. Theirs is a bond that never needed words. Their friendship is so much deeper than that. He squeezes tighter, letting her know how much she means to him, and Mac does the same. Pain slices through his chest, the wound that Lust inflicted then kicked when they were out in the field objecting to the pressure.

He winces and Mac instantly pulls back, frowning. "You're hurt?"

Reign loosens his arms. "Long story, with an outcome you'll approve of—I'm fine."

Her frown doesn't budge. "You don't look fine."

"Ouch! I've been stressed while my best friend was having the world's longest nana nap, okay? It takes its toll."

Mac's lips thin, but the sound of another car approaching has them turning to face it. Colt's Mustang pulls up beside Sierra's car. Colt, Sierra, Blaise, and Arielle step out, and this time, Reign's heart stutters.

Arielle's okay. Gabby told him that, but he had to see it to believe it.

Her gaze finds his and their eyes lock and he instantly

knows something's changed. She's not angry with him. She doesn't even look hurt. He's relieved. A little unsettled. And dammit, he wants to hold her and find out everything that's happened in the time they were apart.

Mac clears her throat, snapping him out of whatever the hell that just was. "You know, in my alternate universe, you two actually got it on."

He spins to face her. "What are you talking about?"

She shrugs. "Another long story. Also with an outcome I approve of."

Colt comes to stand beside Gabby as she rolls her eyes. "These two need to have a long talk after this." She sobers, glancing over her shoulder. "Once we deal with our little issue."

Colt turns to face the flour mill and Gabby joins him. One by one, everyone does the same, standing in a line so they can take in the location.

"That's where he is?" Rachel asks, her voice strained.

"Yep," replies Gabby. "This is where my mother's Grace traced him to. Our job is to get him out of there."

"And I'm going in with you," says Rachel determinedly.

Gabby nods. "I figured you'd say that."

"Her fighting skills are the best I've ever seen," says Reign. "She'll kick demon ass."

"That's why she'll be coming with Colt and me." Gabby glances at Blaise. "I propose that you stay outside the mill and work some spells to keep the demons inside. We need this contained."

Blaise pats the satchel by her side. "I already have some ideas."

"And Mac, are you right to join us?"

Mac nods sharply. "I'm pissed that I'm the same supernatural being as them. They need to be reminded they chose the wrong side."

Surprise lurches through Reign. That's the first time he's heard Mac talk so openly about being a demon. He's glad. She's realizing exactly how powerful she is.

"I've been giving Arielle pointers," volunteers Rachel. "And she's the one who got us the dagger."

Reign isn't sure who stiffens more, Gabby or Sierra. To be honest, a part of him goes very still. Arielle deserves to be in there.

And yet, if he was one of the winged-ones like almost half of them are, he'd pick her up and get her the flock right out of here.

"Ari?" asks Gabby. "What do you want to do?"

Arielle glances from her cousin to her mother. Her gaze settles on Reign for a breathless second, before returning to her family. "I want to fight, but I'll do what you think is best for everyone."

Gabby's lashes flutter as if her brain is working overdrive as she's left speechless for long seconds. It seems now that Arielle's letting her make the decision, she's realizing how hard it is.

Sierra steps up beside her daughter. "I think we should both go."

Arielle goes as still as Gabby and Sierra just did. "You do?"

"Rachel's right. This is your fight, too." Sierra smiles a little. "And I get to fight beside my daughter."

Arielle glances at the factory then back at her mother. It's the first time Reign's seen her really consider her next move. "Let's end this," she says tightly. "Together."

The one word triggers an inhale in the group, as if everyone just gained strength from it. A warm feeling expands in Reign's chest. He never imagined that he'd be part of something like this.

Gabby straightens. "Damn fine idea." She glances at Reign. "You should stay here with Blaise."

The warm feeling is instantly doused, leaving behind the ache of a healing wound. "You're kidding, aren't you?"

She shakes her head. "Someone with fighting skills needs to stay with her. And you're injured."

Reign's hands are hot fists at his side. "I told you, I'm fine. There's no way you guys are going in and I'm standing outside, not doing my bit."

"This is doing your bit," Colt points out. "Blaise needs to be protected."

Reign opens his mouth to speak but Sierra cuts him off. "And you need to realize that your role comes with responsibility. We can't afford for you to be seriously hurt."

He clamps his jaw shut. He'd really rather not do this right now.

Arielle looks between them. "What role?"

Mac arches a brow. "Yeah. What role?"

Gabby and Colt glance at each other, neither looking surprised. Blaise turns her calm, expectant gaze on Reign.

Fuck.

Joseph materializes beside Arielle, looking just as intent as everyone else.

For a moment, Reign considers denying it. Rejecting it and everything that goes with it. Especially if it means he has to start being careful. Protecting is what he does. The only thing that resembles anything good within him. He won't let some ancient organization take that away from him.

But, it turns out the truth doesn't care about any of that. It wants air time. It's downright demanding it. And it tumbles out of its own volition.

"I'm the Keeper of the Grail," Reign says, almost like it's a confession. As if he's resigned to it.

Arielle gasps. Rachel looks confused. Mac nods, as unsurprised as the rest of them.

Joseph smiles then disappears.

"You knew?" Arielle says in almost a whisper, a question implied at the end. *Why didn't you tell me?*

"Kind of," he replies, hoping she'll understand. "I was dealing with one heck of a case of denial."

Sierra moves closer to him. "He's never admitted it," she explains. "Until now."

"It doesn't change anything," says Reign angrily.

"It kinda does," says Mac.

Reign glares at her. "Worst best friend ever."

"Because I want you alive?"

He sets his jaw. Now he knows how Arielle felt—everyone's determined to wrap him up in cotton wool. All because of some prophecy no one knows is even true.

Arielle's frowning slightly as she stares at the ground, processing this. "You're the Grail Keeper."

"Not by choice," he snaps.

"And the Grail could end all of this. Close the Gates forever."

Reign doesn't answer that. He doesn't need to be reminded of exactly how big this is. Or that he'll no doubt mess it up.

"Which is why you need to stay back," says Sierra. "Lust has already tried to kill you twice."

Blaise nods. "You're the last one, Reign."

"And someone needs to back up Blaise," adds Gabby, just in case he'd forgotten what they're trying to use as emotional blackmail.

He turns to Mac. "You can't agree with them."

"Lust tried to kill you two times?" she asks, horrified.

Reign looks away. He's not going to get any support from her. His gaze falls on Arielle. Her lashes flicker. "Do what you think is right."

Damn straight he will. He turns to Sierra. "Sure, I'll stay with Blaise."

Mac glances at his quick assent, her eyes narrow suspiciously. He shrugs. "It makes sense."

Gabby nods. "Good. It's decided."

Silence weighs heavily as one by one, they turn to face the mill again.

It's time.

They start the trudge toward the factory. Reign allows himself to fall back a little, remaining beside Blaise. He estimates it will take them about four minutes to get there.

He notes the determined tension spearing down Arielle's spine. The dagger is tucked into the back of her jeans. She looks kick ass.

But looks can be deceiving. They round a bend and the metal hulk looms ahead, shiny silos lined beside it. They'll split up shortly. He'll watch the others enter, knowing there's an army of demons in there and one powerful, pissed off Lust. And every molecule of his body will be screaming to be by Arielle's side.

Except he'll stay by Blaise's, just like he said he would. For about five minutes. Maybe six.

Just because he admitted he's the Grail Keeper doesn't mean he's going to start telling the truth.

He has no intention of remaining outside.

CHAPTER 37

ARIELLE

The closer they get, the bigger the factory becomes. The more monstrous this feels.

Arielle stops herself from glancing over her shoulder at Reign. Him staying behind is the right decision, she tells herself. Over and over. If she says it enough times, maybe she'll believe it.

She pulls her shoulders down and back. It had felt so right to make the decision to come with Gabby and her mother. She worked with them, they believed in her. She now realizes that's how it should be.

And yet, it doesn't feel right. Not without Reign.

You're strong, hisses a voice in her mind. *You can end them all.*

A chill spills down her spine as she feels the stone lodged in her pocket. The obsidian.

"The plan is we end demons, we find Lust, we end Lust," says Gabby, her voice low and tight. Her wings snap out, the pearl feathers glistening in the sun.

The memory of the avenging angel who arrived at the field flashes through Arielle's mind. She's glad the might of her cousin is on her side.

"Lust will know we're here," says Colt, his own onyx wings exploding out. "There's no element of surprise."

Mac's own wings appear and she flexes them, arching her neck from her side to side.

"I wouldn't mind a set of those right now," says Rachel under her breath. She bounces on her toes and shakes out her hands, loosening her muscles in preparation.

Arielle's heart rate accelerates with each tense word. She flexes her hands by her side. Like Rachel, she's never felt more human.

"I love you, Ari," her mother whispers beside her. "And I'm proud of the woman you've become."

Arielle's eyes sting. How did they not figure out that they just need to work together? "I love you, Mom." Their hands brush, affirming the deep bond that transcended pride and self-interest.

She finally gives into the need to glance back at Reign. He's standing beside Blaise, his stormy green gaze already on her. Suddenly, all the unsaid words she should've given life to choke her throat.

I'm not in the least surprised you're the Grail Keeper.

I like you. Like, a lot.

I want you with me.

Reign's lips part, as if he heard her. As if he has his own words to say.

"Go!" calls Gabby.

And they're running. Bursting through a door.

And facing more demons than Arielle ever knew existed.

The interior of the mill is large and with silos two stories high squatting rows, large pipes transecting and splicing between them, and poles as thick as an arm interlaced to support it all. Everywhere, there are demons. Wings shivering with anticipation. Eyes glowing with bloodlust.

Gabby lets out a cry, charging at the fray, Colt right beside her—day and night, light and dark coming together against a common foe. Working together as one. They're each other's shadow, each other's protection. When one blocks, the other strikes. When one defends, the other attacks.

Despite the number of demons coming at them, they mow them down like bowling pins. Uppercuts to the chin send several up in the air then sprawling on the ground as the others move out of the way, uncaring one of their comrades is down. Others fly up and rain down in a black deluge, but Gabby and Colt's wings are just as much a weapon as their fists and feet. One moment they're back to back, then side by side, then spinning so fast that they're a breathtaking, fearsome blend of yin and yang. They leap and twist, almost seeming untouchable.

"Stay close!" calls Gabby.

Because the more they move into the factory, the more they're encircled by the snarling beasts.

Mac launches into the air, her own eyes alive with crimson fire, then spears down on the demons coming from their right. Her own black wings blend with that of the beings just like her, tangling and clashing.

"Well, I'm not missing out on the action," says Rachel, launching a spinning kick to the left which connects with a demon's jaw.

"We need to get to the second floor," Arielle's mom calls out.

Arielle sees what she means. There's a metal staircase several yards away, going to a second floor and what looks like several offices. One door glows, runic symbols etched on it. That's where Paul is. That's where Lust is planning to sacrifice him.

Colt and Gabby change trajectory, steadily moving forward by finishing one demon after the other.

A demon breaks past Rachel, coming at Arielle.

"Ari!" her mother calls, launching toward her.

But Arielle's already running at it. The demon swings a meaty arm, and she ducks, slamming her elbow into his gut with a strength she didn't know she had. He grunts and she snaps her hand up, powering her fist into his face. Blood explodes as he roars, but a kick to his chest has him crashing into the demon behind him and crumpling to the ground.

Another quickly takes its place, but Arielle dispatches it almost as quickly as the first. She never knew she could fight like this. She can sense their moves before they make them. She doesn't care that she's hurting another being. In fact, there's a small jolt of satisfaction each time she inflicts pain.

Yes. End them all.

She lets the thrill of the voice ripple through her. They're outnumbered, but they're not out-powered. It's only a matter of time before they find Lust.

They reach the stairs made of thick metal mesh, and Gabby leads the way up. Mac takes the back, stopping any demons with their grabbing, grasping claws. They reach the first floor, and a wide landing built of more metal mesh stretches out.

"Look!" Gabby cries.

The runes on the door at the end of the landing are glowing even brighter.

"Dad," Rachel screams.

Except it remains closed and there's no way to hear if he calls back over the growling mass of demons. No way to know if they're too late.

"Aw crap," growls Mac, loud enough for them all to hear.

Arielle glances down. There are more demons emerging from the shadows of the abandoned mill. A second wave. Then a third. As if there are endless souls hiding and waiting. They pour up the stairs, countless others flying up to land on the metal landing. It creaks under their combined weight.

They're once more surrounded.

"We need to get to that door," Rachel screams desperately.

Except there's no way they can do that in time.

The demons in front of them charge, teeth bared and eyes blazing. The demons behind them launch into the air, ready to rain down on them. They're about to be enveloped by evil.

Fight. Take as many with you as you can.

Arielle locks every muscle, terrified and yet ready to battle. She's suddenly glad Reign's not here, and yet, selfishly, she wishes he was. His face would've been the last she saw.

There's a thundering crash above as metal tears and buckles. Colt instinctively covers Gabby while Arielle and her mother clutch each other. Mac and Rachel grip the railing of the landing. The roof of the factory is caving in.

More demons are coming.

Except it's not black winged creatures that descend into the mill. It's an army of angels.

"It's Dad!" Gabby cries.

Gabriel and his angels have arrived to help.

They dive down, alabaster wings glistening in the light pouring through the hole they just created. The angels swoop and plunge, striking the demons, picking them up, pummeling them with their angelic might.

Demons rise to meet them, taking the fight midair. Black and white clash, blurring and blending as grunts and cries fill the air.

Colt roars, taking advantage of the distraction, striking a demon and throwing it off the landing. Gabby joins him, fighting with renewed determination.

Arielle clenches her fist, her mother beside her, a fresh wave of strength washing through her.

Steadily, determinedly, they make their way along the landing toward the door.

CHAPTER 38

REIGN

Reign's about to run through the door Arielle and the others disappeared through a few minutes ago when a dark shadow falls over him and much of the factory. He glances up, and the dread that instantly bloomed is washed away by shock.

The sky is full of angels.

"Holy shit, is that Gabriel?"

Blaise is staring at the mighty sight, looking a little awed. "Yes. It is."

There's a screeching crash, like a steamroller just slammed into a freight train as they fall through the roof, joining the fray inside.

"Even less reason to endanger yourself," Blaise points out.

So much adrenaline is pumping through Reign's veins that he has to clench his hands. His jaw. Every fiber of his being.

"I can't do nothing," he grinds out. "And don't try the 'protecting Blaise' line, because there are no demons coming out."

Their focus is entirely on Lust's sacrifice of Paul. And stopping anyone who gets in the way.

Cries rise from inside, some short-lived, others drawn out

and infused with pain. Reign digs the balls of his feet into the ground, ready to run.

"No, you need to stay!" Blaise cries, her hand reaching out.

He almost doesn't stop, unwilling to humor the distraction it no doubt is. But he said he'd protect Blaise, and the need to make sure she's okay before he annihilates some demons has him looking over his shoulder, body poised to go.

Blaise is glancing around at the ground. "Remember how Cain's demonic energy was trapped when Arielle went to Damascus?"

"Yeah?" he asks, suspicious yet curious. The image of the mighty demon, half-comatose and glassy-eyed flashes through his mind.

"We can do the same!" She takes a few steps away from him. "We'll suck her essence right out of her."

And she'll no longer be a threat to Arielle and the others.

Reign turns. "What are you looking for? What do you need?"

"I haven't finished researching the banishing spell, but we have to try." She glances around. "We need something to trap the demonic energy in. A jar or a bottle of some sort."

Twisting, he walks in the opposite direction of Blaise, kicking at the long grass. They don't even know this is going to work, let alone whether they can find what they need. A few steps away he comes across a crisp packet, then a takeaway container.

"It has to be glass," Blaise says as she scours the ground. "It's the only thing strong enough to contain something like Lust's energy."

Of course it does.

But several steps away, Reign's foot connects with something hard and smooth. He bends down, picking up a beer bottle, the brown glass still intact.

He holds it aloft. "I'm more of a spirits guy myself, but will this do?"

Blaise's eyes light up. "Yes! Quick, bring it here."

He jogs over and Blaise takes it. She rolls her hand over the top of the bottle and a cork appears in the opening. "Power of night and day, I thee cast. Make this bottle ever last," she murmurs. She holds it up. "So it can't break."

Squaring her shoulders, she glances at Reign. "If this spell works, Lust's energy will be siphoned from her and into the bottle. It will leave her weak, enabling the others to finish her." Because Arielle has the dagger. "But the spell will take some time. Nothing can interrupt me."

Which traps Reign here with her, on protection duty again.

He glances at the door, seeing flashes of bloodied black and wounded white. This is what he's supposed to do? This is the part he'll play in all of this?

This is what being a Grail Keeper is all about? Doing something even when it feels wrong? When helplessness is burning through your veins like lava?

"Do it," he bites out through clenched teeth.

MAC

Mac growls as she throws another demon trying to make its way up the stairs back into the fray. She spins, using her wings to knock over two more, grinning with satisfaction when the blow splits open one of the bastard's cheeks.

No one is getting past her. Period.

One jumps, bearing down on her, but she leaps too, driving her heel into his solar plexus. The demon crumples, crimson gushing from his mouth. As he drops, Mac sees a pale-haired angel several feet away, surrounded by more Hell spawn. Two mount an assault while another somersaults over the angel, landing behind him and latching onto his wings.

The angel arches in pain as it looks like the demon is trying to tear them off. The other two make the most of the opening, raining a volley of blows over his face and body.

Mac moves instinctively, launching into the air. "Keep the stairs covered," she calls to Rachel. She lands on top of the demon tearing at the angel's wings, leaving streaks of blood across the alabaster feathers. The demon buckles, something snapping, and it falls lifeless.

The angel roars as his wings are freed again. He lashes out at the two demons still attacking him, striking so fast his hands are almost a blur. The demons instantly retreat, their own blood now a patchwork over their skin.

The angel spins around to face Mac. "I don't need help from one of you," he snarls. The revulsion in his voice is so full of vitriol it has Mac's stomach rolling in disgust as if it's contagious.

Except he's talking about her.

Not liking the way the words sting, she recoils. "I'm fighting on your side."

"You will never be on our side, daughter of Hell," he spits. With a pump of his blood stained wings, he launches into the air and careens away.

"Asshole," Mac mutters. She turns, seeing that Arielle and the others have made gains along the platform. Leaping, she flies back to them, landing beside Rachel.

They fight with everything they have, moving steadily toward the runic door. The closer they move, the more desperate the demons become, but it's too late. The team contracts together, forming a tight knit fighting machine.

"I need to be with Arielle," Rachel says between strikes.

Mac nods, understanding. It's Rachel's father on the other side of that door. She needs to be there.

Mac steps in front of Rachel, covering her spot. "Hurry."

The door's only a few feet away.

Suddenly, there's a blast of light and the door explodes. Gabby shoots another bolt of light from her hands, completely destroying it.

"Go, Ari!" she shouts. "We'll keep the entrance covered."

Arielle and Rachel burst into the office. A second later, the door reappears as if it had never been destroyed and slams shut behind them.

CHAPTER 39

ARIELLE

The room is full of demons, just like Arielle expected it to be. Their wings expand as Arielle and Rachel burst through, then contract as a new door slams behind them.

They're trapped, but that's fine by Arielle. Lust is in here. She can feel it.

Kill her.

Which is exactly what she intends on doing.

The office is a relatively large space. Apart from a couple of metal bookshelves and filing cabinets stacked against the wall, it looks devoid of furniture. The demons snarl, baring their teeth as a roomful of glowing eyes laser on the two girls.

Then Arielle sees the altar fashioned from a desk in the middle.

Rachel gasps. "Dad."

Paul is lying on his back, struggling against invisible bonds. "Rachel!" he screams.

The demons part, revealing Lust standing beside the desk. Languidly, she walks toward Arielle. Her crimson hair slides sinuously over her shoulders. "Your determination is quite a turn on," she purrs. "As useless as it is."

"It's over Lust," says Arielle. "Let him go."

Lust throws back her head, husky laughter rippling through her leather-clad body. "So naive. So clueless." She lifts an arm, indicating toward something in the air. "I crafted it myself in the bowels of Hell."

Ice slices through Arielle's veins as she sees the sword floating above Paul, the tip in line with his chest. It spins gently, looking like it's gaining momentum.

"There are a few minutes left," Lust coos mockingly. "Before the spell is complete and the sword drops, putting a nice little hole in the Innocent's chest."

Opening the next Gate of Hell and releasing another Sin on Earth.

Do it, the obsidian whispers, already knowing Arielle's intent.

"Rachel, get your father," she says, not taking her gaze off Lust.

Withdrawing the dagger, she runs at the demon, feeling the dark power coursing through her. Lust's eyes blaze with the fury of Hell as she launches forward, too.

Arielle slashes the dagger the moment she's close enough, but Lust easily sidesteps it. She lashes out with her own strike, eyes flashing with surprise when Arielle blocks it and counter-strikes. Lust blocks that too and they separate, circling each other. From the corner of her eye, Arielle sees Rachel take out a demon, moving one foot closer to her father.

"You fight as well as a demon," Lust observes.

"If that's what it takes to kill you, then I'm okay with that," Arielle spits, once more launching at her.

She hits faster and harder than she ever has, putting Lust on the defensive. Strike. Block. Strike. Strike. Block. Block. With every blow, they battle for the upper hand. Lust's claw-like nails slice Arielle's upper arm, sending stinging pain shooting down to her fingers. Arielle lands a punch in Lust's throat, making the demon gasp and choke.

It's the opening she was looking for.

Suddenly, Rachel cries out as she's thrown backward. She crashes into a filing cabinet with such force that she dents it. She falls to the ground, conscious, but in pain. She tries to get up, only for her legs to give out.

"Rachel!" Arielle cries.

Lust vaults forward. She grabs Arielle by the throat in what's obviously her signature move. Her fingers wrap around her neck, the nails biting into her flesh.

But she doesn't lift Arielle. Doesn't tighten her grip.

Arielle stills as something prickles her consciousness. She gasps when pleasure courses through her, warm and seductive. Reign's face appears before her, smiling and sexy.

Lust's voice purrs through her mind. "Ah, it is the Grail Keeper you hunger for." She lets out a low, sultry laugh. "And you thought it was love."

Arielle struggles against the invasion, but she's frozen, unable to even shake her head. Lust is inside her mind, and the worst part is, it feels good.

"You stupid, foolish girl. You didn't notice that those feelings grew with my arrival? You thought you were immune? Better than every other human who fell under my influence?" She laughs again, the sound rippling through Arielle in a sensual wave. "The desire was my influence. Anything you feel for him, or he feels for you, is nothing but me. Lust."

Anguish joins the pleasure, creating a hot, stinging mix. Arielle blinks, trying to fight it but it's like her muscles are frozen. Gripped by the unwanted, corrosive longing coursing under her skin.

You're stronger than her. End this. Then end her.

Yes. What she feels for Reign is real.

Arielle struggles with everything she has, physically and mentally. She pushes the demon from her mind. She lashes out with the knife.

Lust hisses as it slices her cheek and she releases her hold, the line of crimson on her cheek quickly becoming tears of blood trickling down her face. The rest of Arielle's muscles unlock and she pushes down on the balls of her feet. She catapults at Lust, gripping the knife tightly, seeing that behind her, the sword above Paul is now spinning so fast it's a silver blur.

Time's running out.

This strike has to count. It has to be the end.

Lust slams her arm down on Arielle's as the knife spears for her stomach, sending agony jolting through Arielle. She doesn't drop the dagger, but it also doesn't make its mark. She spins, carving the air as she tries to lodge it in the demon's neck. But Lust ducks and weaves, panting with the exertion as Arielle attacks again. She has Lust on the run. But it's not enough. She's still alive.

A hum sounds in the room. The sound of the sword spinning impossibly faster.

Rachel draws herself on to all fours, dragging herself toward Paul. Arielle has no doubt in her mind she'll try to sacrifice herself instead of her father.

Arielle thrusts one more time with desperate strength, and although she stabs nothing but air, Lust stumbles backward, clutching her stomach. Confused, Arielle glances down at the blade, but it's shiny and silver. There's no blood on it.

Lust throws her head back, screaming, black mist spewing from her mouth as she falls to her knees.

CHAPTER 40
REIGN

Blaise's chanting stops, the strange words rising into the air and doing who-knows-what. Reign holds his breath. Did the spell work?

When he hears an unholy scream, he almost drops the bottle and runs. The realization that it's not human a split-second later is what keeps him there.

"Now, Reign!" calls Blaise.

Although he has no idea what she wants him to do, he lifts the bottle high into the air. Thick, black smoke pours out of the mill and curves, tumbling into the bottle like oily fog. The moment the last wisp enters, he jams the cork into the top.

Blaise lets out a loud breath, her shoulders dropping. "We did it."

Reign lifts the bottle, looking through the dark glass to see the slithering, onyx smog. "We really did."

Has he finally done something right?

Have they actually won this time?

The next scream that echoes from the mill shoots ice straight down his spine.

"Reign, no!" Blaise calls out, alarmed. As if she already knows he's not going to sit around and wait to find out who that was.

Dropping the bottle is probably what gives it away. Thank fuck she made it unbreakable.

Reign goes from standing to sprinting in a split second.

He bursts through the door of the factory. "Arielle!"

GABBY

The demons all know the moment Lust has lost her essence. They all pause, eyes widening and the red glow within them dimming. Their leader has lost her mojo.

And the angels leap on the opportunity.

They become streaks of white, agents of fury. Their faces twist with the vow that no demon will be spared.

Gabby and Colt glance at each other, a silent understanding passing between them. They need to get to the door. Arielle may need help.

The Innocent actually stands a chance of surviving.

Simultaneously, they break into a run, leaving the fight to the angels. A fair-haired one runs at them, and they divide, giving him space. He can wreak his vengeance as much as he likes. They have an office to blast into.

Except the angel side steps as he's about to pass Colt, viciously slamming the arch of his wing into his face. Colt's head snaps to the side, the rest of his body following as he tumbles to the ground, already unconscious.

"No!" Gabby cries.

The angel flashes a smile, slamming a punch into Colt's chest before moving on. He ploughs into another demon, unleashing more violence, never once looking back.

Gabby falls to Colt's side, the fray around them dissolving into little more than background noise as she curls her wings around them, creating an alabaster curtain. "Colt," she whispers.

He doesn't answer, his head turned away, his face still twisted in pain. Gabby's hand flutters to his chest, resting over his heart. She focuses solely on one thing.

Healing the one who owns her soul.

SIERRA

Sierra's running along the landing when she sees Reign rocket through the doorway. The panic on his face echoes the same panic twisting through her insides.

"Reign! Up here!"

Never losing stride, he looks up, sees her, and changes trajectory. He takes the steps two at a time, the clang of his shoes ricocheting through her. "Where is she?"

Sierra's already running toward the door she's pointing at. "They're in there!" They fall into steps, side by side. "Was that what I thought it was?"

Reign nods. "Blaise siphoned Lust's demonic essence. And that scream wasn't human."

Sierra realizes he's right as her fear loosens its grip on her mind. The implications of that have hope rising through the panic. Rendering the demon weak is the advantage they need.

They reach the door. The same one Gabby had to blast through for Arielle to get in there. But it isn't glowing. In fact, when Reign grabs the handle, it swings open in welcome.

Lust has lost her power.

They've won!

CHAPTER 41

ARIELLE

Arielle recognizes what's happened as soon as Lust collapses to her knees.

Blaise has siphoned Lust's demonic essence, just like Daria did with Cain.

This is her chance!

Arielle hears the door creak open behind her as with one swift movement, she impales the dagger into Lust's chest. Victory floods her veins as Lust convulses, her head tipping up.

To Arielle's surprise, she smiles, even seeming to take pleasure in her own pain. In the end of her own life. "You're too late." The smile grows, revealing blood stained teeth as the thick fluid trickles over her lip and down her chin.

Horror robs Arielle of the ability to breathe. She looks up just in time to see the spinning sword drop. She hears the crack of bone and squelch of tearing flesh.

"No!" wails Rachel, echoing the scream that just exploded through Arielle.

She drops to her knees as a heartbreaking moment after Lust is pierced with a deadly, magical weapon, so is Rachel's father. He arches, face grimacing. Then falls limp. Lifeless.

Another Innocent is dead.

Luminous wisps curl up the sword and into the sky. The Grace now lost to them just as much as Paul is.

Rachel throws herself on her father, wrapping her arms around his head and pressing her cheek to his. "No, Dad. Please no."

Her sobs fill the air, staining it with grief. Tears slide down Arielle's cheek. Rachel's lost her father. They've lost against evil.

"Arielle?"

She turns to find her mother inside the office, Reign beside her.

"Oh, honey." Her mother falls to her knees beside her, taking her in her arms.

Arielle clings to her, still trying to understand how this could have happened. "What did we do wrong?" she whispers brokenly.

"We did everything we could," her mom assures, stroking her hair.

And it wasn't enough. Rachel's wails are proof of that.

There's the sound of running feet and Mac appears, then Gabby, Colt beside her, looking a little unsteady on his feet. Like a wave of despair, their shoulders drop one after the other as they register the scene before them.

Gabriel appears with two or three other angels. They glance around the room, then turn and leave, their faces a mixture of disappointment and disgust. Arielle's face flushes with shame. She let everyone down.

She closes her eyes, trying to stop the tears, only to be assaulted by images. A foretelling of what is to come. The obelisk explodes, shards of rock disintegrating as yellow light destroys it. She gasps, clamping her hand over her mouth to stop herself from screaming.

Reign falls to his knees in front of her, clasping her face with his hands. "You saw the obelisk again, didn't you?"

Arielle nods, biting her lip so hard it hurts. She focuses on her mother's arms around her. On the strength in the hands cupping her cheeks. On the anchor his green gaze has become.

"It's coming," she whispers.

It's only a matter of time before the next Gate of Hell is opened.

CHAPTER 42
REIGN

P aul's funeral is a big one. As people spill out of the dojo where Rachel insisted the wake be held, it's obvious he was loved by the community. Men and women of all ages clutch tissues and dab at their eyes. Children hiccup as fat tears run down their faces, their parents comforting them.

Rachel is a pale waif as she accepts their condolences, seeming almost unaware of her own tears staining her cheeks. Reign's not sure they've stopped from the moment Paul was murdered right in front of her.

Reign stands at the back, leaning against the brick wall, not really sure how he's attended two awful events in such a short period of time. Two deaths that have stolen the light of life from their family's lives.

And two Innocents who have been sacrificed to peel back another layer of Hell.

Reign jams his hands in his pockets, uncomfortable in the slacks and collared shirt. There's a lot that needs to be figured out. Which Sin has escaped? What will it mean for everyone? Who's the next Innocent? And how the hell do they kill this next super demon?

A hundred questions. Not one answer.

Arielle exits the small office near the front doors, placing another box of tissues on the table nearby. She moves toward Rachel, who shakes her head imperceptibly. Rachel's insisted on doing much of this on her own, as if she's proving she's strong enough to shoulder this. Arielle hesitates, but then changes direction, respecting Rachel's wishes. She glances up, her eyes unerringly finding Reign across the room.

He stills as his heart starts thudding, as if it's reminding him it only beats for her. She smiles a little as she walks toward him.

Reign's hands form fists in his pockets. She's so beautiful. So amazing. So strong.

And she deserves more than he can ever give her.

"Hey," she says softly, stopping a few feet away.

"Hey," he responds gruffly, then quickly clears his throat.

Arielle glances over her shoulder as if to make sure there's no one nearby. "We haven't had a chance to talk alone."

They really haven't. Although three days have passed since Reign yanked the sword out of Paul's chest, bile stinging the back of his throat, and Colt carried his body out of the flour mill, they've always had someone around them. There's been Rachel to hold together. Arielle's been connecting with her mom in a way that makes his soul smile. And he's been spending time with Mac, trying to put his finger on the changes in his best friend. She's stronger, surer, and yet somehow more lost than he's ever seen her.

Arielle shifts her weight and he feels the distance shrink between them. "I realized a few things in that factory, and one of them is to say what needs to be said, no matter what."

Reign pushes away from the wall before he's even realized what he's doing. Trying to get himself under control, he swallows. "Me, too."

Her wide eyes feel like they're swallowing him. "You did?"

"Ari..." His words instantly dry up. He hates that he has to do this here, now. But she needs to know. "What happened between us..." The blue fire in her eyes flares as if she's remembering every one of those moments. As if they touched her, too. "It wasn't what you thought it was."

The blue flames flicker as if they're in danger of being snuffed out. "What?"

Reign clenches his jaw, determinedly pulling up the defenses he should never have let drop. He stacked those walls around himself for a reason.

"Don't you see? It was Lust's doing." It's the only way someone like her could fall for someone like him. "She had us feeling all of that, just like everyone else."

None of it was real.

Arielle blinks. "That's exactly what she said."

The confirmation is a sledgehammer to his gut. The blow is so powerful he almost doubles over. A part of him was lying. The feelings he has for Arielle are the realest he's ever experienced. They resonate with truth. Sing with purity. And the other part of him was foolishly, stupidly hoping that maybe she felt the same, too.

He nods once, sharply and succinctly. "It was nothing but an illusion." He twists his lips into a smile. "She took advantage of our friendship and tried to complicate things."

Arielle's gaze tears away from his, staring at a point past his shoulder. "Friends? That's what you want?"

No, roars his soul.

"I think that would be best." And Arielle deserves the best.

She pulls up her own parody of a smile. "That bitch's legacy continues, huh?"

"She sure pulled a number on us," he jokes through gritted teeth.

Arielle takes a step back. Then another. "Anyway, I'm going to check on Rachel. She hasn't been drinking enough water."

She spins on her heel, her gossamer hair flying out as she turns away as quickly as she can. She walks away stiffly. Not looking back.

Reign sags back against the wall. He did the right thing, he tells himself.

It hurt. A fucking lot.

But it was the right thing.

GABBY

Gabby walks quickly to the far corner of the parking lot of the dojo, drawing in deep breaths. It can be overwhelming to be in a room filled with so much grief and loss.

Especially when you know more pain is coming.

She watches Colt walking toward her, not surprised that he went a little slower. He's giving her time to get her emotions under control, along with the ones she's absorbed through osmosis. It's one of the many reasons she loves Colt. He has faith she can do things on her own. And then he's there if she can't.

He slips his arms around her and she sinks into his chest, holding him tight. "Anything I can do to help?" he asks.

"You're already doing it," she murmurs, breathing in his scent.

He presses a lingering kiss onto her hair, then sighs. "There is much to be done."

She lets out her own breath on a long huff. "There really is."

She pulls back to look at his handsome face. "I can't stop thinking about the symbol."

He nods knowingly. "Your memory being wiped was a concern."

Gabby suppresses another sigh, wondering how many of those she'll be doing over the coming days. "Yeah, it was suspish. We need to find out who did it and why."

"Most definitely," says Colt, his lips twitching. He sobers again, dropping his forehead onto hers. "We will fight this," he promises her.

Gabby's arms tighten. "We will." With everything they have. "And we'll win."

They have to.

MAC

Mac watches Arielle walk toward Reign and she looks away, glad to give them a bit of privacy. Those two really need to tell each other how they feel. She hasn't seen two people more fated to be together in her life.

It's nice to think something good is happening amongst all this sadness.

She picks up another quiche from the table beside the office when Sierra appears out of the office, looking perplexed. "Have you seen Ari?"

Mac shifts a little so she's blocking the view of the back of the dojo. "I think I just saw her duck into the restrooms."

"Oh, okay." Sierra picks up a quiche too, then glances down at it as if she's not quite sure how it got into her hand. Frowning, she wraps it in a napkin and throws it in the trash can.

"Is everything okay?" asks Mac, wincing at the loss of the flaky morsel of deliciousness.

"I wanted to speak to Ari about something important." Sierra pulls in a breath. "I've made a decision."

"Sounds serious."

Sierra nods, her face most definitely serious. "I know how we can stop future Gates of Hell from opening."

That has Mac's attention. "How?"

"We need to find the Holy Grail."

Mac instantly deflates. Sierra may as well put in an order for a transgender unicorn while she's there. "Right."

"And I have a lead. I can't believe I didn't see it before."

Mac leaps right back on the rollercoaster this conversation is turning out to be. "You do?"

Sierra nods, then frowns. "But it means going away for a while. Blaise is coming with me."

"You're leaving?" Mac asks, not quite sure she heard that right. Sierra and Arielle had just become an awesome mother-daughter duo.

"I wish I didn't have to. But after what happened..." Sierra glances at Rachel, who's trying to smile as the last guests leave. "The Grail is the only thing that can stop all of this. And we need to find it before the angels and demons do."

Mac watches as Rachel's shoulders drop the moment she thinks no one's watching. Gabby lost Shell. Rachel lost Paul. Who will be next?

Sierra's right. The Grail is the key to all of this. Mac's gaze snaps back to Sierra. "I want to come with you."

She blinks in surprise. "You do?"

"Yes," she says, realizing this is exactly what she wants to do. This is how she plays her part in this fight. The note she never got to finish reading while she was under flashes in her mind. Find it, it said. "I want to help you find the Grail."

The note must've been talking about the Grail.

"But what about Reign?"

A pang stabs Mac's chest. Leaving him will be hard. "This is how I can help him, too. He's a Grail Keeper with no Grail."

And without it, Mac's not sure Reign will ever believe he truly is the Keeper of the Grail.

Sierra's eyes taking on an assessing glint. "You know, I was grooming you to become an Archivist."

"Wow," says Mac, a little taken aback. "That's cool."

"You have a thirst for the truth, Mac. And the courage to follow it. It's exactly what the Archivists are looking for."

"But, I'm a demon," she says, remembering the hatred the angel had thrown at her, even after she saved him.

Sierra smiles. "A being, whether it's angel, demon, witch, werewolf, vampire, is only evil by choice. Not by design."

The calm acceptance in Sierra's gaze reinforces this is the right decision to make. That Mac's finally finding where she fits in. "Then I'm most certainly, definitely, indubitably in."

Sierra beams. "That's wonderful. We're leaving this afternoon. There's no time to waste."

Mac blinks. So soon? "Good thing I don't have a lot to pack."

Sierra glances past Mac's shoulder. "Oh, there's Arielle." She frowns. "This is going to be a hard conversation to have. Losing Shell then Paul has really hit her hard."

"She's stronger than any of us realized." Apart from Reign. He's always believed in Arielle. "And she'd want the Grail found as much as any of us."

To save future Innocents. To save the senseless deaths of humans caught in the crossfire.

Sierra nods, although her frown doesn't dissolve. "You're right. Arielle's the one who retrieved Cain's essence, freed Mac, and killed Lust. We all underestimated her.."

Giving Mac's wrist a quick squeeze, she walks toward her daughter, looking like she's fortifying herself.

Mac understands how she feels. She glances at the back wall to find Reign's gone. Telling him is going to be hard. Leaving him will be even harder.

But at least he has Arielle now.

EPILOGUE

Arielle stands at the window of her room, knowing it's coming. She can feel it. It's only a matter of time before the next obelisk is destroyed, even though Cain is out of the picture. The sky is a jaundice yellow, a giant hazard sign warning everyone.

She thought she'd figured it out. That the key was working together. Going it alone was where she went wrong.

But they failed.

And she's never been more alone in her life. Her mother's gone, off on a quest to find the Grail, taking Blaise and Mac with her. Saying goodbye had cracked Arielle's heart.

A heart that was already bruised and wounded after the conversation with Reign. His feelings for her were nothing but a Lust-induced haze. Their kisses were fueled by an illusion. And apparently she can't trust what she feels for him.

So many things seemed so right. And they weren't.

Wiping her hand down her face, Arielle goes to the mirror, knowing she looks like crap but needing the confirmation. She gasps in horror at what she sees, and it has nothing to do with the disheveled hair or pale skin. Her eyes are orbs of black. She blinks and it's gone, leaving her wondering if she imagined it. Desperately hoping she did.

You're not alone, hisses the voice that now lives in her mind. *And you've never been stronger.*

She pulls the obsidian out of her pocket. She has it with her always, unable to bear being parted from it.

It glows with onyx fire in her palm.

XEVEN GLANCES at the vial in his hand, the soft glow illuminating his palm. With Cain mysteriously gone, he almost didn't come here. The part of him that doesn't want to do this almost won.

But then Azazel appeared in the mirror, the angel reminding him this needs to be done. That it's the only way.

Which is why he's now standing here, beside the monolith. Xeven runs his other hand down the cool stone of the obelisk, marveling at its centuries-old strength.

At how easy it is to destroy.

He doesn't give himself a chance to think this time. He acts quickly, lifting his arm and slamming the vial into it.

The impact is instantaneous. Cracks fracture through the black stone, golden this time, like the sun is exploding from within. Xeven stumbles backward, his arm raised to protect his eyes as it crumbles, almost dissolving under the pressure.

The demons escape swiftly, like rabid dogs that had been snapping and snarling on the other side of the Gate. Black wisps, they fly into the sky, progressively turning it dark and foreboding.

The last to exit is a golden figure. It shoots into the sky like a comet, vibrating with anticipation. This Sin is impatient to wreak its havoc. Hungry for what the humans on Earth can provide it.

Death. Devastation. Destruction.

Xeven walks away, his work done, but hating his part in it.

And knowing when the time comes, he'll do it again.

Ready for the next installment in Keepers of the Grail?
Dive into GATES OF GREED
http://mybook.to/GatesofGreed

GATES OF FURY

Another Gate. Another Sin. And time is running out.

Reign and Arielle know the next Innocent must be found, despite the overwhelming odds. Darkness is rising, threatening the world as they know it.

There's a new enemy—a demon manipulating humans' most basic desires. A mysterious organization with alliances as old as time. And evil is weaving its dark magic among their ranks. Magic powerful enough to rival the Grail itself.

And yet, the battle within is as powerful as those they face. Reign struggles to trust. Arielle's no longer sure what she's fighting for. And love is refusing to be denied.

The price of failure is unimaginable.

Because a plan has been put in motion that goes as far back

as Adam and Eve. And dark forces will do anything to open the next Gate of Hell, bringing Lucifer one step closer to freedom.

GRAB YOUR COPY HERE
mybook.to/GatesofGreed

THE KEEPERS-VERSE IS ALWAYS GROWING!

Exciting news! The Keeper Chronicles will continue to grow, with each new addition adding to its epicness. Each interlinked series will have you falling for unforgettable characters, being swept away by captivating romance and thrilling adventure, and re-visiting old friends (you'll discover all your favorites popping up when you least expect it!).

It's like your very own choose your own adventure! Where will you go next?

Keepers of the Chalice
A vampire. A huntress.
A cure that will change everything.
Check out Book 1, Vampire Unleashed, HERE.

Keepers of the Light
Angels and demons have battled for millennia. Their inevitable war has begun.
Check out Book 1, Hidden Angel, HERE.
http://mybook.to/HiddenAngel

HAVE YOU READ THE KEEPER CHRONICLES PREQUEL?

As an exclusive for my subscribers,
you can download it for free!!

When Sierra sneaks out, determined to escape her over-protective family, she stumbles across a young man covered in blood. His last words are a plea. *Find the Grail Keepers. Warn them.*

Ryder is the young cop who was last seen with the murdered victim. Sierra doesn't trust him, no matter how drawn she is to him. Except it turns out they're both looking for the same thing—the Holy Grail.

They're quickly drawn into a dangerous hunt involving cryptic clues, a mysterious stone, and a Grail that hasn't been seen for centuries. One that leads to more questions than answers. Can Sierra trust her impulsive emotions? Should she

339

believe Ryder's words or the truth she sees in his eyes? And ultimately, should she follow her heart?

Especially when every decision will decide the fate of countless lives.

CLICK HERE TO DOWNLOAD FOR FREE!

Also by Tamar Sloan

KEEPERS OF THE CHALICE

A vampire. A huntress.

A cure that will change everything.

Vampire Unleashed

Vampire Unveiled

Vampire Undone

Vampire Undefeated

Vampire United

KEEPERS OF THE LIGHT

Angels and demons have battled for millennia.

Their inevitable war has begun.

Hidden Angel

Chosen Angel

Marked Angel

Forbidden Angel

Fated Angel

PRIME PROPHECY SERIES

Their love will spark more than their hearts.

Prophecy Awakened

Prophecy Accepted

Prophecy Fulfilled

Legacy Awakened

Legacy Accepted

Legacy Fulfilled

THE SOVEREIGN CODE

Humans saved bees from extinction...and created the deadliest threat we've seen yet.

Harvest Day

Hive Mind

Queen Hunt

Venom Rising

Sting Wars

THE THAW CHRONICLES

Only the chosen shall breed.

Burning

Rising

KEEPER
CHRONICLES

ZODIAC GUARDIANS

Twelve teens. One task. Save the Universe.

Scorpio Sting

Cancer Sight

Gemini United

DESCENDANTS OF THE GODS

Demigods as you've never seen before.

Child of Crossroads

Daughter of Time

Secret of Fate

Son of Poseidon

Blood of Medusa

ABOUT THE AUTHOR

Tamar really struggled writing this bio, in part because it's in third person, but mostly because she hasn't decided whether she's primarily a psychologist who loves writing, or a writer with a lifelong fascination with psychology.

She must have been someone pretty awesome in a previous life (past life regression indicated a Care Bear), because she gets to do both. Beginning her career as a youth worker, then a secondary school teacher, before becoming a psychologist, Tamar helps children and teens to live and thrive despite life's hurdles like loss, relationship difficulties, mental health issues, and trauma.

As lover of reading, inspired by books that sparked beautiful movies in her head, Tamar loves to write young adult romance. To be honest, it was probably inevitable that her knowledge and love of literature would translate into writing emotion driven stories of finding life and love beyond our comfort zones. You can find out more about Tamar's books at www. tamarsloan.com

A lifetime consumer of knowledge, Tamar holds degrees in Applied Science, Education and Psychology. When not reading, writing or working with teens, she can be found with her husband and two children enjoying country life on their small slice of the Australian bush.

The driving force for all of Tamar's writing is sharing and

connecting. In truth, connecting with others is why she writes. She loves to hear from readers and fellow writers. Find her on all the usual social media channels or her website.